the DRAGON'S PRICE

the DRAGON'S PRICE

A TRANSFERENCE NOVEL

BETHANY WIGGINS

CROWN
New York

Text copyright © 2017 by Bethany Wiggins
Jacket art copyright © 2017 by iStock, (blue mist) © 2017 by Shutterstock

Visit us on the Web! randomhouseteens.com

Educators and librarians, for a variety of teaching tools, visit us at
RHTeachersLibrarians.com

Library of Congress Cataloging-in-Publication Data
Names: Wiggins, Bethany, author.
Title: The dragon's price: a Transference novel / Bethany Wiggins.
Description: First edition. | New York: Crown Books for Young Readers, [2017] |
Summary: "An action-packed fantasy adventure about one girl's choice to be
sacrificed to a dragon instead of marrying a future king—but when she's lowered
into the dragon's lair she can't even begin to imagine the consequences that
lie ahead"—Provided by publisher.
Identifiers: LCCN 2016008249 | ISBN 978-0-399-54981-6 (hardback) |
ISBN 978-0-399-55116-1 (glb) | ISBN 978-0-399-54982-3 (epub)
Subjects: | CYAC: Fantasy. | Dragons—Fiction.
Classification: LCC PZ7.W6382 Dr 2017 | DDC [Fic]—dc23

Printed in the United States of America
10 9 8 7 6 5 4 3 2 1
First Edition

This story is dedicated to my son, GRW,
for the gift of the dragon's scale.

Chapter 1

Today is my sixteenth birthday. I am wearing a gown I can barely walk in, my artfully styled hair is giving me a headache, and I feel like I am going to throw up.

"Hurry! Bend down!" Nona snaps, tugging on my shoulder with frigid fingers. "I can hear them marching down the hall!" I lean forward and she quickly fastens a gold tiara in my hair just as the chamber door swings open. I jump as four armed guards stride in.

"Princess Sorrowlynn, we are hereby ordered to escort you to the opening ceremony of the Mountain Binding," says the tallest guard, Ornald. It sounds like a death sentence, and my hands begin to tremble, so I clutch the delicate fabric of my skirt in them and square my shoulders.

The guards studiously do not look at me, staring instead at the gray stone wall behind me. I glance from them to Nona, who is slouching in the corner of my bedchamber and chewing on her thumbnail. She stops chewing long enough to nod and wave me toward the guards.

"I don't want to go." My voice quivers like I am on the verge of tears, and I take a tiny step backward.

Ornald scowls and stops studying the wall to look at me. "If you don't come by choice, my lady, I have been instructed to drag you to the courtyard. Please don't make me do that. That's no way for a Faodarian princess to make her grand entrance into society, is it?" he asks, his eyes pleading.

"Instructed by whom?" I ask.

Ornald frowns. "Beg pardon, my lady?"

"Who instructed you to drag me? My mother or my father?"

The guard clears his throat and puckers his mouth like he is about to spit, but then stops himself. He tugs on the collar of his red uniform and says, "Lord Damar, your father, instructed me to drag you if you don't comply. Let's show him you've grown into a lady and can follow orders." A small smile softens Ornald's square face. "You look like a lady today, my lady."

I glance into the mirror. My light brown hair is braided in a crown around my head, the golden tiara gleaming in front of it. The sapphire-blue dress I have been stuffed into is low-cut, and the corset gives me double the curves that I normally have. The eyes staring back at me are on the verge of panic. I do not know this woman I am looking at. I feel trapped in her body.

"Princess Sorrowlynn?" I blink and turn away from my reflection. Ornald holds his arm out to me even though it is forbidden for guards to touch royalty. It is a gesture that would get him demoted if he weren't already the lowest man in the guard despite his being one of the older men. But somehow that tiny gesture offering human contact sends a bit of courage through my trembling body.

I swallow, put my frigid hand on the red sleeve of his uniform, and nod. "Ready," I whisper, and together we walk into the shadowed passage.

The walk through the palace goes by too fast, even with me tripping on my skirts every three steps. My mother and father are waiting for me by the palace doors. Both of their gazes go directly to my hand, resting on the arm of a lowly guard, and my father's face turns crimson. My mother purses her lips and her blue eyes narrow. I quickly clasp my hands behind my back as Ornald steps away from me.

"Who dressed you?" my mother snaps, eyeing my gown. Her perfume is so strong that I can barely breathe.

"Nona," I say. She is the only person who has dressed me since the day I was born.

"Your corset is too loose. Has she forgotten how to string a corset?" Her eyes flash accusations at me.

Probably, considering this is the first time I have ever worn one in my life, I think, but hold my tongue. One does not talk back to the queen.

Outside, a horn blares, a clarion call announcing the looming arrival of our guests of honor, and the irritation disappears from my mother's face and is replaced with majestic indifference. She lifts her chin and grasps her silver-and-gray skirt in one hand, and lays her other hand on my father's proffered arm.

Two guards throw open the massive double doors leading out to the palace's courtyard, and my mother and father walk outside into evening sunlight. They are greeted by the cheering and applause of a massive crowd. Ornald gives me a small shove forward, and I stumble from the shadows into sunshine. Regaining my balance, I grasp my skirts in both my hands and climb a small staircase that leads to a raised dais.

The courtyard is filled with nobles and commoners, and like water and oil, they remain steadfastly separate of each other. The commoners, at the far edges of the courtyard, seem to suck the sunlight away with their drab and dreary clothing. At the base of the dais, the nobles reflect the light, making it difficult to look at the white, silver, and gold clothing they favor.

My gaze drifts over their eyes, which are devouring every visible inch of me from the tiara in my hair to the silver-embroidered hem of my dress. Everyone wants to see the youngest Faodarian princess, who has been hidden away in her rooms for most of her life. But they look at the young woman standing before them, in a dress she's never worn before, with her hair braided in a coil for the first time. They don't see me at all. They see only what my mother wants them to see.

The whispered words *offering* and *Suicide Sorrow* drift through the crowd like wind, and I grit my teeth, fighting the urge to plug my ears. Even whispered, their words seem to batter against me. And then I hear something else, hoofbeats, and my knees start to tremble.

The nobles turn and face the open gates leading from the courtyard to the rest of the world. The commoners quickly copy them. My heart starts thundering in my ears, louder than the horses' hooves, as the king of Anthar and his party gallop into the yard and part the crowd with their animals. They stop directly in front of the dais and the smells of leather, horse, and sweat compete against my mother's perfume for supremacy. The horse clan has arrived.

Their animals are sleek and beautiful: rippling muscles, glossy bodies, strong legs. Ribbons and beads and flowers have been braided into their manes, like something I would do to my dolls when I was a child. A smile forms on my lips as I look from the horses to their riders—and then it falters.

These dark-haired, strapping men and women are examining me from their saddles like I am for sale. At that thought, my face starts to burn, because I *am* for sale, in a manner of speaking.

I stare back at them, trying to guess which man I will be offered to, but they all look the same, with long black hair and skin as golden as toasted bread. More disturbing are their women, sitting astride their horses instead of sidesaddle, and dressed no differently from the men: brown leather pants and chain mail that has been shined until it looks like sparkling silver. Curved swords hang at their hips, and strung bows at their backs. Out of the whole group, only one person stands out. He is at the back of the party, and a cut on his cheek has bled trails of red all the way down to his jawline. I shudder at the thought of associating with these barbarians.

"For three centuries you and your sons have been our honored guests. That tradition still holds strong," my mother, the queen, bellows, practically in my ear. I try not to flinch and take a small step away from her. "I bid you and your family welcome, King Marrkul."

The biggest man, the one at the front of the group, nods to my mother. He has gray streaks in his dark hair, and a beard that looks like a bird's nest hangs halfway down his chest.

I shift my gaze from the king to the man on his right. He looks powerful and stern, and at least two decades older than me. When our eyes meet his jaw clenches and he glares, so I lift one eyebrow and look at the next man. He, too, looks powerful and stern and way too old for me to marry. He flashes his white teeth in a grin, and my father hisses into my ear, "Smile, Sorrow!" So I turn to my father and smile. "Not at me. At them." He rolls his eyes in the direction of the horse clan, and I can see how desperate he is for me to make a good impression. So I do as he wants and turn my practiced smile toward them, the smile that doesn't show my teeth, that makes me look soft and regal, like my mother.

"I thank you, Queen Felicitia," the Antharian king says, his accent thick. "May I present my oldest son and heir, Ingvar," he adds, holding his hand out to the man on his right. My three older sisters all were offered in marriage to this brute, but he turned them down. Now, standing in the exact same place they all stood, and meeting the Antharian heir for the first time, I realize how lucky my sisters are to be married to Faodarian noblemen.

Ingvar looks at me again, his eyes moving up my body, and the smile slowly fades from my face. I can't smile because a hollow ache has opened up in me, stealing every emotion I have been feeling, but one. For the first time since birth, my name fits. I fight to keep the tears at bay.

Chapter 2

This baby will die by her own hand. That is the fate Melchior, the royal wizard, glimpsed when I was born. It caused my mother such distress that she locked herself in her chambers and cried for days. She refused to touch me, look at me, or speak, even name me. I was given to Nona, a scullery maid who'd lost her own baby, and she was told to never take me out of the nursery. Finally, after I had been called *girl* for a year, my father named me Sorrowlynn on behalf of the heartache my existence caused, and I have been called Sorrow ever since.

My three older sisters fared much better with their fate blessings. Melchior glimpsed Diamanta, the future queen of Faodara, outliving three husbands, and at age twenty-one, she's already outlived one. Harmony was seen making peace wherever she went. The Antharians should have chosen her for their queen, as it is rumored they are always fighting among themselves when they are not fighting their neighbors to the west, the Trevonan. My third sister, Gloriana, would bring joy to all who met her, and it is true. I can think of nothing bad to say about her.

I, though, would die by my own hand. I stare at my soft,

narrow hands and wish the old wizard were still alive so I could slap him across the face for that fate blessing. And then I remember how kind he was, and take it back. Before he disappeared, Melchior would spend hours in my chambers with me and Nona. He always wore the same faded green tunic over tan hose and had his graying hair tied in a tail at the nape of his neck. When I asked him why he dressed like a peasant, he said, "When you are as old as me, clothing no longer holds much pleasure. It simply becomes a necessity." We would spend hours piecing puzzles together while he would tell stories of the eight dragons he'd seen with his own eyes. He always compared the fate of the dragons, or Faodara, or Anthar to the puzzles. Every single time we finished one, he would say, "It isn't until all the pieces come together that we see the whole picture, Sorrowlynn."

Diamanta yanks the laces of my corset hard, and I grab on to the bedpost to keep from toppling backward. I gasp as deep a breath of air as I can before she gets it any tighter.

"Sorrow," she snaps, "it is obvious you've never worn one of these the right way before. You're supposed to breathe *out* when I pull, not in." I grit my teeth and breathe in even deeper, making my ribs as big as possible. She huffs and slaps my butt, but it hardly hurts through the layers of petticoats. "Please, for the love of Faodara, let me at least give you the *semblance* of a womanly figure," she growls, putting a foot up onto the bedpost to get more leverage. "The horse king is going to be looking to see if you've got the body for grandchildren."

I shudder at the memory of Ingvar's eyes examining my body, at the thought of bearing his children. "That's the point," I say, keeping my ribs as wide as possible. "The worse

I look, the less likely I am to be picked for the heir's future bride. And besides, I think it is ridiculous that we still do this horrendous, ancient Mountain Binding ceremony. I do not see how my agreeing to marry a scruffy old brute will have the power to keep a fire-breathing dragon locked beneath a mountain. And if I don't agree to marry him, will I truly be fed to the dragon? That is savage, and inhumane, and crazy."

"Did you learn nothing from our history tutors?" Diamanta asks, glaring at me. "Three centuries ago, the Antharian king woke the dragon with the intent to have it destroy Faodara, but it didn't follow the king's orders. The beast nearly destroyed *both* of our countries before a wizard's binding spell was able to imprison the vile creature. Unfortunately, the spell requires an ongoing sacrifice to work, which—"

"Is dependent on me sacrificing myself to the Antharian heir in order to keep the dragon locked away," I blurt. "I listened to our tutors."

"You're not exactly *sacrificing* yourself, just offering yourself in marriage. It's only if you refuse to offer yourself in marriage that you are sacrificed to the fire dragon. But the Antharians haven't picked anyone from our line for three generations. I doubt they will change that for you, considering they turned down Gloriana two years ago. She's more pleasant and more pretty than you. And so are Harmony and I, and they didn't take any of us. If they didn't want us, they're definitely not going to pick you."

I glower at her, but she's right. My three older sisters have thick, golden blond hair, blue eyes, and gentle curves. I have unruly brown hair and green eyes, and not quite as many curves, not to mention I stand half a head taller than all three of them. If they didn't pick any of my sisters, what makes me think they will pick me? All the air swooshes out of my lungs. Diamanta uses the opportunity to cinch the corset into place before I can take another breath, and I can feel my ribs compacting.

"It's just a silly tradition. For all we know, the fire dragon is long dead," she says.

"If it is a silly tradition and nothing more, why do we still do it?"

"We do it for two reasons. To keep peace between Faodara and Anthar, and just to be safe; if the dragon is still down there, we don't want to risk setting him free." With nimble fingers, Diamanta ties the corset laces. She looks at my reflection in the mirror and grins as she runs her hands down both sides of my ribs. "Look how tiny your waist is now." Her grin turns to a frown and her hand pauses just above my hip. "What is this lump?"

I smile and say, "It is my dagger, dear sister." Diamanta's eyebrows creep up her forehead and for a moment fear darkens her eyes. I know she is thinking of my fate blessing, thinking something like, *Is Sorrow going to kill herself with her own hand to avoid an arranged marriage?* "I'm not going to kill myself!" I bellow, rolling my eyes.

"Then why are you wearing a dagger to dine with the horse king and his sons? To cut your food?"

"It is the dagger the wizard Melchior gave me when I turned eight. He told me to always wear a weapon for protection, so I do. If you think I should take it off, undo my corset and I will," I say, my voice taunting.

"Melchior gave that to you? After what he predicted at your birth, that's a pretty sadistic gift. Maybe he didn't *vanish*. Maybe Mother found out about that knife and had him secretly beheaded." Diamanta puts her hands on her hips and smirks. "You don't need to wear that dagger because you won't need to protect yourself. That is what the guards are for." A gleam flashes in her blue eyes. "And it's not like you're going to be able to use it without undressing first. I can see it now. *Please don't try to kill me yet! I have to strip so that I can get my dagger and defend myself!*" She puts a hand to her chest and starts giggling.

I shrug and try to sigh, but I can't get enough air into my lungs. "And if I die from lack of oxygen? Nona didn't get my corset nearly this tight yesterday."

Diamanta smiles her perfect, practiced smile. "Nona is too lenient with you. That is why Mother sent me to dress you. That is why I *volunteered* to dress you when Mother asked Gloriana and me for help." Her smile turns from perfect to devious as she examines me.

I look into the mirror and study myself. The dress beneath the corset is bright, sunset red, and goes up to my neck. The corset is a deep bloodred velvet with black stitching. If I look hard enough I can barely make out the bulge of the dagger above my hip. Diamanta steps up to me and places a tiny diamond tiara atop my head. It nearly disappears in the brown curls. "Well. You look surprisingly good for your first ball ever," she says. "And if you don't return to Anthar as a bride, you get to start looking for a Faodarian husband. Shall we go down to the dining hall and consort with the horse lords and the nobles?"

All three of my sisters were married to handsome young noblemen shortly after they turned sixteen and were refused by the horse clan. I have never even spoken to a boy close to my age.

We step out into the corridor. The air is slightly moist and heavy with the smells of roasted meat and fresh-baked bread. As we approach the great hall, Diamanta asks, "Are you ready for your big debut?" I shake my head and she laughs. "I was counting the days until I was old enough to be out in society. Once you get past your first-ball jitters, you'll love having a social life."

When we get to the great hall, my steps slow. Inside of the door, they stop altogether. Candles burn in the chandeliers, and garlands of flowers held together with ruby-red ribbons have been hung on the stark gray stone walls. I have never seen the hall look so beautiful. The leather-clad Antharians are easy to spot. They stand out like peasants among the flamboyantly dressed Faodarian nobles. The women, dressed in brown leather vests, with hunting knives belted above their bright skirts, look as barbaric as the men. And the way they laugh—mouths wide open and their heads thrown back, with no regard for manners or sophistication—has me gaping at them.

Someone steps up to me and holds out his arm. "Princess Sorrowlynn," he says, and I can feel his eyes on me. His voice is deep and has a slight accent. I stare at his glossy leather vest and the white shirt beneath it, which is unbuttoned enough to show a bit of golden chest, and my knees threaten to buckle. Is this my possible future husband Ingvar? My body freezes, and I cannot find the courage to look at his face.

"Don't be rude," Diamanta whispers into my ear, poking my ribs. "Take his arm!"

I nod and force myself to lift my hand and place it just above his wrist. Beneath his loose white shirt, his skin is firm and warm. Like a gentleman, he escorts me to the queen's table, centered on a raised dais at the farthest end of the room, and pulls out my chair before taking his place beside me.

"I guess they wanted the two babies of the family to keep each other company," my escort says. If I am by the baby of the horse clan, I am not sitting beside Ingvar. I try to sag with relief, but the corset digs into my armpits, forcing me to sit like there is a metal rod in my spine.

I look at the head of the table. King Marrkul sits on my mother's left, with his oldest son, the future king Ingvar, beside him. On Ingvar's left sits a woman. She is chugging wine like it is water. When she puts down her empty cup, she twines Ingvar's long hair around her fingers and pulls his face to hers, kissing him on the mouth. I gasp. To show affection like that in public is astonishing, especially for a *woman* to initiate it. All of my life I have been taught that men always initiate intimacy of any sort, and nobility *always* remains formal. When she's done kissing him, she looks right at me and winks.

"My brother's wife makes a spectacle of herself when she is in your castle," the horse lord beside me says with a chuckle. "She likes how shocked you all are."

I finally look at the face of my escort. He is young, and his skin is like caramel-colored silk, except for the long gash on his right cheek. "You mean he's already married? If I marry him, I will be his second wife?" I ask. Visions of being a second wife hit me like a physical blow, and I think I might be sick.

The horse lord grins. "If you marry Ingvar, you will definitely be his second wife, because there is no way Jayah will sit back and let you have him all to yourself. She's the jealous type. She will probably treat you more like a servant if you are her sister wife, and if she ever finds you in Ingvar's bed, she'll kill you."

I press my hand against the hidden dagger at my hip and for the first time in my life wonder if I *will* die at my own hand, because I will kill myself before I become a second wife.

"It has happened only once before," the horse lord says.

"She's only killed a sister wife once before?" I stare at Jayah. Her hands are like clubs, and her neck is as thick as a man's.

He laughs as if what I said is the funniest thing he has ever heard. "No, the heir to the throne has taken a second wife from your family only once before, and that was because his first wife died. My great-great-grandmother was a Faodarian princess, and she was a second wife. That is where I get my hazel eyes," he explains. "From your bloodline. See?"

I don't look at his eyes. I stare at the food on my plate and try not to hyperventilate at the utter disgust of being a sister wife.

"My name is Golmarr," he says. Even his name is harsh and savage. Still, I stare at my food. I have lost the will to speak, so Golmarr talks and talks while he eats, telling me of the skirmish they had on their way here with the ruffians who live in the Glass Forest, and the extensive combat training he has received since he was big enough to hold a sword. He tells me stories about how his eight older brothers used to beat him up until he got big enough to fight back, and now not a single one of them can best him at swords. When he finishes his plate of food, he eats mine without asking. As the night wears on, a string quartet takes its place beside the royal table and starts to play a waltz.

"Would you like to dance, Princess Sorrowlynn?" Golmarr asks, standing. I would *not* like to dance. I have never danced with anyone but my three older sisters and my elderly dance instructor. I don't want my first official dance to be with a barbarian. Before I can say no, he is pulling out my chair and taking my wrist in his big, callused hand, and leading me past my frowning father and disapproving mother. I can already hear the lecture I will receive: *You are too good for a mere barbarian prince, and the youngest, no less! He will amount to nothing. The heir to Anthar is the only man worthy of a Faodarian princess's attention!*

I dare a look at Ingvar. He folds his arms over his wide chest and glares at Golmarr and me. I really, *really* don't want to be his wife. I hurry ahead of Golmarr and drag him onto the dance floor, away from my mother and father, away from his brother. Putting one hand on his bicep, I grab his free hand in the other, and we start to waltz.

He studies me with narrowed eyes as we move around the dance floor, dodging the other lords and ladies who have started to waltz. "I don't know how they do it in your kingdom, Princess," he says, "but in mine, the man typically leads."

"Deal with it or find a different partner," I retort, guiding us as far away from the royal table as I can. He quietly chuckles and lets me keep leading. My lungs strain against the corset, but I don't slow down.

"I saw you studying our horses when we arrived yesterday. Do you ride?"

I look up into his eyes and flash him my practiced smile. "Ladies are only allowed to ride sidesaddle, so we are given slow, docile beasts."

"You don't sound too happy about that." He adjusts his hand against the small of my back, and I realize I have stopped leading and he's taken over.

I shrug. "No. It's boring and unfair."

"I agree." He spins me around twice and then pulls me back into his arms, and I am surprised to realize dancing with him is fun. He holds me firmer and closer than Roderick, my dance teacher, and he smells surprisingly nice, like soap and cedar and leather. Roderick smells like olives and cloves, and his breath stinks. I find myself leaning a little bit closer to Golmarr and inhaling. "Have you *ever* ridden astride?"

I glance at the dais, at my father, Lord Damar, in his customary seat of respect at the queen's right hand. "I rode my father's horse once."

"And?" Golmarr asks, a twinkle in his fierce eyes—as if he knows how the story ends. He thinks I am going to say how much I loved riding.

"I was thirteen. Lord Damar sent five guards after me, and when they brought me back, he beat my bare legs with a willow switch in front of them." I lift my skirt just enough to show him one pale scar that still streaks my ankle.

Golmarr stares at me with wide eyes and steps on my foot. "I'm sorry," he blurts, deftly spinning me away from him and then back into his arms. "Are you all right? Did I break your toes?" He looks down at our feet.

A smile touches my mouth—just a hint of one, and not the practiced smile. "It didn't hurt."

"In my land, women ride *horses*, not docile beasts. If you want . . ." He clears his throat, and his eyes grow uncertain as they look into mine. For some reason I can't comprehend, my smile widens and my cheeks grow warm. "That is to say . . ." He glances at the dais. "Do you think the queen would allow you to go riding with me tomorrow morning before the ceremony?"

At mention of the ceremony, my stomach ties in a knot. If

the horse clan takes me tomorrow, not only will I be forced to marry their heir, I will be a *sister wife*, which is one hundred times worse than just being a wife to an old, mean-looking barbarian.

"My family's horses are the fastest in the land," Golmarr says, snapping me back to the present. "They can outrun every other horse. We breed them for speed and endurance. You could ride astride."

His words echo in my head. *Fastest in the land. Outrun every other horse. Speed and endurance.* I swallow and look up into his face, forcing my expression to remain placid. He has just handed me a plan, and he doesn't even know it. My heart starts pounding, and my breathing accelerates. At least, my *need* for oxygen increases, but with the corset squeezing me so tight, I feel like I am about to pass out. "I can't breathe," I blurt, taking my hand from his bicep and tugging on the top edge of the stiff corset.

"Can I do anything to help?"

I almost laugh. "If you attempt to remove my corset, sir, my father might try to kill you."

His eyes narrow and he studies me. "Your father might try? Or you?"

I blink at him and try to step away, but his powerful hand is on my lower back, guiding me through the dance moves with tight, flawless precision. "What do you mean?"

He puts his free hand on my hip, right over the hidden dagger. "Is that why you wear this?" My heart starts thumping against my ribs, and I put both my hands against his chest and push away from him as my face begins to burn.

"I can't breathe, and I do not feel like dancing anymore. I will watch the ball from the dais," I say, and turn away, weaving through the dancing horse lords and nobles. *Suicide Sorrow*, they whisper as I pass, giving me a wide berth.

"Princess Sorrowlynn," someone calls. I turn and look at the young horse lord over my shoulder. His black eyebrows are drawn together in a frown, but there is a hint of a smile on his mouth. His gaze travels over my body and back up my face. "You are a surprisingly good dancer. I hope I have the pleasure of holding you in my arms another time," he calls, dipping me a respectful bow. I curtsy and retreat to the dais and spend the rest of the evening watching the ball rather than participating in it.

Chapter 3

I don't sleep. When the night sky starts to pale, I take off my nightdress and pull on a simple hand-me-down dress, followed by a soft pink cloak. I shove my feet into hardly used riding boots and quickly pull my hair into a bun without bothering to run a brush through it.

Shoving all the jewelry and coins I own into a bag, followed by a flask of water and a heel of bread I managed to steal from the ball the night before, I quietly leave my bedroom.

The castle is silent, except for the low chatter of two guards keeping watch in the passage. I walk past them and they nod good morning at me, neither of them asking what I am doing up so early without my customary escort.

The stables are connected to the castle, just beyond the kitchens. Two more guards are standing at the doors leading out to the stables. My palms start to sweat as I approach them. Before they can ask what I am doing, I open the door leading out and blurt, "At the queen's request, I am checking on the horses that will be pulling our carriage to the fire dragon's lair," and stride past them with my nose in the air.

"Isn't that what the grooms are for, my lady?" one of them asks.

"That's what I said to the queen. If one of you would like to bring it up with her . . ." I slam the door before I can finish my sentence.

As I had hoped, the grooms haven't risen yet, and no one is in the stables. I sprint to the tack room and get a bridle and bit, a blanket, and a man's saddle—no sidesaddle for me today—and carry them to the horses.

The horse lords' animals are stabled with the royal family's docile beasts. In the dim light, I pick the horse closest to the exit and quickly start saddling it. It stomps its foot and looks at me, its nostrils flaring. "It's okay," I quietly croon. "You're going to take me to freedom."

Everything I know about saddling a horse, I learned in a book when I was thirteen so I could steal a ride on my father's horse. That was three years ago. It takes an excruciatingly long time to remember where all the straps and belts and padding go, and as I cinch the saddle into place, I hope I have done it properly. When the horse is ready, I lead it out of the stable and into the dim light of predawn.

I have picked a stallion—a huge, muscular, glossy tan stallion who is studying me as warily as I am studying him. I guide him over to the mounting stump because there is no way I will be able to mount without a little help. He nods his head and nearly pulls the reins from me as I climb onto the stump. With trembling hands, I grab the pommel of the saddle and slither onto the horse, belly first, until I can get my leg over his hind end. My skirt crawls up to my knees. I grip the fabric and force it down to the tops of my riding boots. Slipping my feet into the stirrups, I lean forward to pat the creature on the neck, but before I can, he puts his head down and sprints, tearing through the courtyard, trampling the azaleas in my mother's prize flower bed, and past the guards keeping watch at the open front gates.

The momentum throws me backward. I grapple for the reins and wrap them around one hand, using them to pull myself upright again, and then give a firm backward yank to slow the stallion's pace. But he doesn't slow. He whips his head from side to side, nearly wrenching my shoulder out of socket, and runs faster. I squeeze my knees together hard and lean forward, pressing my cheek against the animal's neck. The wind catches my hair and unravels the bun. The horse's mane whips my face and sticks in my open mouth, so I shut it and pray I don't fall off.

We are tearing down the main thoroughfare through the city, the stallion's hooves echoing against the cobbles. There are vendors on the sides of the street, setting up their wares. When I pass, they stop and stare, some of them shaking their fists and yelling at me, but I can't hear what they're saying over the sound of the wind rushing past me and the ringing hoofbeats.

A slow smile spreads across my face. I am riding a horse lord's stallion, astride, careening toward the outskirts of the city. I am going to be free. I will not have to humbly submit to marrying King Marrkul's heir or risk being fed to the fire dragon. We thunder over the wide stone bridge spanning the Glacier River, and pass from cobblestone to a hard-packed dirt road, from stone buildings and houses to farms and fields. The very air seems to grow brighter, and my body lightens as the stress of my choices lifts from me.

Still crouching low against the horse's neck, I look south at the rolling hills and green fields that eventually turn into the massive, snowcapped mountains that separate Faodara from

Anthar. Southeast, the Glass Forest looks like a distant patch of dark clouds hugging the horizon. I peer over my shoulder for one last look at the castle, squeezed at the base of the dark gray Wolf Cliffs, and almost fall out of the saddle. A black horse is galloping full speed behind me, so close its nose is practically on my horse's flank. Golmarr glares at me from the animal's back, his long, dark hair streaming out behind him.

Within seconds he's beside me, maneuvering his steed so close to mine that our knees bump. He is riding without saddle or stirrups. "Your mother's men," he calls, nodding back toward the city. "They're probably five minutes behind us." My hands go cold and my legs sting with the memory of being whipped. Golmarr reaches over and pries the reins from my fingers. "Don't use those," he yells. "We train them to respond to our bodies instead of bits. The bit just makes him mad."

I wrap my hands in the horse's mane.

"You need to stop," Golmarr says.

Stopping is the last thing I want to do, so I lean forward and silently urge my horse to run faster, reveling in the wind speeding past my face and streaming through my loose hair, in my racing heart and pumping blood. If Golmarr wants me to stop, he's going to have to make me. Otherwise, I will ride this stallion as far as it will take me.

He calls out a word I have never heard before, and my horse stops galloping. I nearly fly over the animal's head as my momentum carries me forward. The stallion peers at me and then wanders over to the side of the road, to a patch of emerald-green grass, and starts eating. Golmarr turns his horse around and guides it over to me, and my eyes travel down his long, leather-clad legs and stop at his feet. They are bare.

"You are stealing my father's prize stallion," he growls. My face burns with shame, but I hold my chin high and scowl into his furious eyes. He studies me for a moment, taking in my wild hair, pink cloak, and skirt, which is bunched around the tops of my boots, and his eyes narrow. "For my entire life, I have been told that your noblewomen are soft, submissive, and meek. You are not, are you?"

"I certainly am," I insist, glaring and folding my arms across my chest.

Golmarr's eyes soften, and then his mouth curves up at the edges and he smiles. His teeth are straight and gleam against his tan skin, and for some reason, when he smiles, my lips want to return it. "Did you like riding him?"

"Yes," I whisper, sighing and running my hand over the horse's neck. "If I die today, I will be glad this is the last thing I did."

His smile fades. "Do you mean if you are offered to the fire dragon?" I nod. "They only feed you to the dragon if you refuse to offer yourself in marriage to my clan. Just say you'll marry into my family and your mother will sacrifice a lamb in your place."

I think of Ingvar and his wife and shudder. "I will not wed your brother. I would rather die!"

"What if I told you you could wed any of us?"

I recoil. "You are all violent barbarians."

"You would rather be sacrificed to a dragon than marry an Antharian prince? Is your opinion of us truly so low?" he asks, glowering at me.

I study him. Aside from the scabbed cut on his cheek, his skin is flawless, his eyebrows and eyelashes are as dark as his hair, and his fierce eyes are like a swirl of pale brown and gold and green. Looking at him makes my heart beat a little faster, and I want to smile again for no reason. Something stirs deep inside of my chest, and I cannot think of any words to answer him.

At my silence, his eyes darken with anger. "So the possibility of being a future queen, of having wealth and power, of riding our horses whenever you choose, in clothing more suited to the sport"—he gestures at my skirt—"doesn't make it all worth it? You would rather die a horrible death than marry a horse lord?"

"I just turned sixteen! Being forced to marry a forty-year-old man—"

"Ingvar is forty-two," Golmarr interjects.

"He's old enough to be your father!"

"Ingvar's mother died in battle. My father remarried a younger woman, and she gave him two more sons." He throws his hands up in the air. "What does his age matter, anyhow? He is the heir to the most prosperous kingdom in the world."

I shudder. "Being forced to marry a *forty-two*-year-old man who already has a *wife* is not worth *any* price! And they haven't actually *fed* any princesses to the fire dragon for more than one hundred years!" I yell, and grab the pommel of my saddle as the stallion shifts nervously beneath me.

"That's because for the last hundred years your women have all willingly submitted to be married to our future king!" he yells back, leaning so close to me that his horse bumps mine, and I can see little flecks of gold around his pupils. "Aren't you familiar with the terms of the Mountain Binding?"

"Of course I am!"

"The Mountain Binding," he says, disregarding me, "is the agreement our two kingdoms made three hundred and six years ago. The reason your family always has girls, and mine always has boys." He tilts his head to the side and studies me. "Do you know *any* of this? Don't they teach you this when you're a child learning to read? You *do* know how to read, right?"

"Of course I know how to read," I snap. "I told you, I am well acquainted with the terms of the Binding. I am well taught in all areas!"

His black eyebrows slowly rise. "But you've never been taught how to wield a dagger."

I put my hand over my hip and press on the concealed weapon. "I beg your pardon? Why would you say that?"

"Because if you knew how to use it, you wouldn't carry it beneath layers of clothing. You would carry it somewhere easily accessible. Like this." Out of nowhere he produces a wicked-looking dagger and twirls it around in his fingers a few times before slowly and deliberately putting it back up his sleeve.

I huff my breath out and put my nose in the air. "I know how to use it," I say, my voice haughty. In a flash, he is off his horse and pulling me down from mine. One of his arms cinches around my neck, the other pulls my body firmly against his, and I flail and thrash at him. I scream and scratch his arms, and try to pry myself from his grasp.

"See what I mean?" he says, releasing me. I stumble away, and he grabs my elbow to make sure I don't fall.

"Do not touch me, sir!" I yank my elbow out of his grasp. Stepping farther from him, I smooth the front of my dress.

"If you had been trained to use that dagger, you would have had it out the moment I grabbed you. Self-defense is the *first* thing a woman of your rank should be taught."

"My people aren't violent like yours. I don't *need* the dagger. That's what the guards are for," I say, mimicking Diamanta. I gather my long hair and start twisting it back up into a bun.

"And when you are alone?"

"I'm never alone when I'm in the castle, and I'm not allowed to leave the castle grounds." Once the words leave my mouth I wish I could take them back.

"You're running away. Alone. With no way to protect yourself. And you've never been *out there*." He waves his hand toward the Glass Forest. "Do you know why my family always arrives at your castle armed?"

"Because you are bloodthirsty barbarians," I snap.

His eyes narrow. "The Glass Forest is infested with Trevonan renegades, Satari migrants, and mercenaries. If that lawless place is where you were planning to run, I think your chances will be better with the fire dragon. At least that way, you will have a *quick* death."

I glance at the distant forest. I have always wanted to see it.

"When we are taught to read, we are also taught of the spell binding our two countries together. Do you know about the spell?" Golmarr asks.

"I know every single word of it, since it has been drilled into my head since I was old enough to speak! Three hundred years ago your ancestor tried to take over Faodara by waking the fire dragon that lives in the mountains that separate our countries. The dragon wreaked havoc, so our ancestors found a way to lock it in the mountain. My nurse used it as a bedtime story."

Golmarr laughs and shakes his head. He takes a step closer, and for the first time ever I am glad that I am not short, because even with my height, it feels as if he is looming over me. "No. My ancestor did not try to take your land. *Your* king attacked Anthar, so *my* king woke the fire dragon, and it is not a *bedtime story*. It is in all of our history books."

I roll my eyes. "Yes, I am familiar with the accounts of the fire dragon burning both of our countries, cooking our soldiers in their armor, destroying crops and herds, until *your* ancestor begged mine to stop the dragon's slaughter in exchange for ending the war and signing a peace treaty. They tried but the fire dragon wouldn't stop its rampage. It had taken a liking to cooked human flesh."

He nods his head, and as if we read the exact same history books, continues, "Both of our ancestors combined all the treasure they possessed and bought a powerful spell from a wizard. To bind the fire dragon back inside the mountain, our two countries had to swear peace. To give the spell enough power to work, the Antharian king agreed that he and his progeny would bear only sons from that day forward. Your queens would bear only daughters. And each virgin daughter would be offered to the Antharian heir to renew the strength of the spell, or be fed to the fire dragon if she refuses to offer herself."

I ball my hands into fists. "That is so unfair! Four of my great-grandmothers have been stolen away by your people in the past three hundred years. Two have chosen to be fed to the fire dragon. Why are the women—the *virgins*, no less— *always* the ones who have to be forced into a marriage?"

He shrugs, and I notice a piece of golden hay in his dark hair. "Your ancestor started the war, so you got the worse end of the deal. But *none* of your women were *stolen away* by my people. They came willingly and lived good, prosperous, fulfilling lives. Princess Sorrowlynn, if you do not offer yourself to my family, you *will* be fed to the fire dragon to renew the spell's strength. If you *do* offer yourself, but we refuse, a lamb is offered in your place and you get to return home to your normal life."

"And if I offer myself and am forced to marry your heir?"

"If you offer yourself and we accept, the dragon gets a lamb for dinner, and you get to come to the grasslands and learn to ride our horses. We're not as uncivilized and blood-thirsty as you seem to think we are." He steps even closer, and I can smell soap and cedar and leather. "Please," he whispers, "just offer yourself." I swallow and reach up to take the piece of hay out of his hair, but he grabs my hand and holds it against his chest. "I know we just met, and I know you were trying to steal my father's horse, but I like you." A slow smile warms his face, and I find myself staring at his mouth. "You make me want to smile for no reason. In my grandfather's day, if a woman was brave enough to ride a horse lord's stal-lion, he would drag her off and marry her. You are different from the other noblewomen of Faodara—fearless. I think you would like living in Anthar, and I think I would like having you live there."

He stares down into my eyes, and my heart starts to pound. Aside from dancing in a packed ballroom the night before, and the rare arm of support offered by a guard or a coach-man, I have never been touched by a man. Not the way he is touching me now, his warm fingers entwined in mine, our faces close. And then my heart starts pounding for a different reason. "Wait . . . since I stole your father's horse, are you say-ing I'm *more* likely to be taken as the wife of your heir?"

He nods, and his fingers tighten on mine. "I wouldn't mind stealing you away."

The quiet morning comes alive with the sound of horses.

"I told you not to touch me," I snap, and step away from him as five mounted guards circle us, their hands on their sheathed swords.

"Princess Sorrowlynn, we have orders from your father to return you home immediately," Ornald growls, glaring at the horse lord. His dark brown hair is standing straight up in the back, like he just rolled out of bed. "If you refuse, we have been ordered to return you by force."

I swallow and study my shoes. Ornald was there three years ago, the day I was whipped for riding astride. When my father drew blood, Ornald took the willow switch and broke it. He was the captain of the guard. My father demoted him to the lowest-ranking position with no possibility of advancement.

Golmarr steps up beside me, so close that our arms bump. "Is something wrong?" he asks. "Last night I invited the princess to go riding with me. I did not realize Lord Damar would be sending guards after us." I take a deep breath and look up. Ornald glances from the horse lord to me, his green eyes guarded. "I'm not familiar with your rules. If I broke some sort of conduct, I ask that you blame me, not her."

"You're out all alone with our virgin princess," Ornald snaps. "It didn't occur to you that that is unacceptable?"

"On my honor as a prince of Anthar, I swear to you that I have behaved with integrity and honor, and have had only the princess's best interest at heart. My family and her family have a long-standing relationship of mutual respect. I meant no harm by inviting her out for a ride." I glance at Golmarr from the corner of my eye. For a barbarian, he is well spoken.

Ornald's gaze moves down the horse lord and stops on his bare feet. "Where are your shoes, boy?" he asks.

Golmarr looks at me and grins, and his eyes fill with mischief. "Princess Sorrowlynn was in such a hurry to leave this morning that I didn't have time to put them on." The guards laugh, Golmarr laughs, and I look right into his eyes and smile. "It doesn't help that I slept in the stables, either," he adds, pulling the piece of hay from his hair. "I had a feeling that the princess might want to leave before sunrise." He winks.

My eyes grow round, and my cheeks start to burn. He knew. All along he knew I was going to run.

"Well, mount up, and let's get back to the castle," Ornald says, dismounting to help me mount the stallion. "Nona is hysterical. You are supposed to be getting ready for the ceremony, Princess."

Chapter 4

I am bathed and oiled and perfumed. My nails are filed down, and my hair is braided into a coil around my head again. I am dressed in white lace bloomers and a matching camisole, four white petticoats, a voluminous white skirt, and a baggy white shirt that is buttoned up to my neck. Nona wraps a white pearl-encrusted corset around the white shirt. I don't have the heart to fill my lungs as she laces it up, so by the time she is done, I can barely breathe, and the late breakfast I ate is being squished. When she is not looking, I tie a silk handkerchief around my wrist. Taking the dagger from my dressing table, I slide it beneath the handkerchief and let the baggy fabric of my sleeve fall over it.

Nona presses a pair of white velvet slippers into my hands. Her fingers are like ice. "Put these on, love."

I point to the corset. "There's no way I will be able to reach my feet when I am wearing this thing." Nona shakes her head and kneels at my feet, helping me with the slippers. "They're going to get ruined the moment I step out of the carriage."

"A major drawback to having the ceremony in the mountains," Nona replies, standing.

"White is so expensive. I don't see why I have to wear everything white when it will get dirty. And pearls?"

"The offering has to be a virgin, and white represents virginity. The fire dragon will know the difference. You also need to remember that if the Antharian heir takes you for his bride, tonight will be your wedding night. This may be your wedding dress." She runs her fingers over the pearls on my corset, and I imagine they are Ingvar's old, thick hands. This morning, Golmarr said that in his grandfather's day, if a woman rode a horse lord's horse, she would be taken for his wife. I rode a horse lord's horse. Golmarr seemed to think that because of my actions, Ingvar will be more likely to accept me.

"If I refuse them, will they truly feed me to the dragon?" I ask, my voice shaking.

Nona's plump cheeks pale. "Don't refuse them, and we won't have to find out." She starts chewing her thumbnail.

"What is it?" I ask.

She removes her thumb from her mouth and says, "You're looking at this all wrong, Sorrowlynn. By sacrificing your own desires and saying you will marry the Antharian heir, you are protecting your people and the Antharian people from the fire dragon. You are sparing hundreds of thousands of lives. Do you recall that a century ago, the kingdom of Satar was destroyed by the stone dragon and the Satari fled to the Glass Forest? And in Ilaad, the people are now confined to their cities. They can only travel by boat from port to port, because if they set foot in the desert, the sandworm eats them. Now bend down so I can put this in your hair." She holds up a pearl tiara. I lean forward, and she pins it into place. Before I can stand, she slips something over my head. An icy chain falls around my neck. "There. All done."

I look down. She has put a long gold necklace on me. It hangs as low as my belly button. I lift it and look at what is dangling at the bottom of the chain. It is an oval flask the size of my palm and almost matches the color of the pearls on my corset. I hold it up to the sunlight streaming through the window, and it glows orange.

"What is this?" I ask, my voice filled with wonder.

"Strickbane poison," Nona says as matter-of-factly as if she had said *water.*

"Strickbane?" I drop the flask. It pulls the gold chain taut against my neck and clinks against the pearls on my corset. Strickbane, even absorbed through the skin, is lethal.

"It's a family tradition," Nona says, her brow furrowed.

"Tradition? None of my sisters wore this to their ceremonies."

"You're right. It is a new family tradition saved just for you." She puts her soft, familiar hands on my cheeks like she did when I was a small child, and looks right into my eyes as she speaks. "If you're fed to the fire dragon, you drink the poison and die before you're eaten, because it's better to be eaten dead than eaten alive. Just be careful and don't open it unless you must. When Melchior gave it to me, he said it was a very important piece of a bigger puzzle. He told me that the poison contained in this flask is over one hundred years old, and you know Strickbane gets stronger with time. You will need only a single drop." She lowers her hands and blinks. "What am I saying? You won't need the Strickbane. You're not going to be dragon food."

"Melchior gave it to you?" I run my finger over the flask. It is slightly rough to the touch, like sandstone.

"Aye, the day before he left. He made me promise to give

it to you for the ceremony. That is a dragon's scale carved to hold the Strickbane. It is supposedly from the very dragon that resides in our mountains, if he still lives. Do you remember your line for the ceremony?"

"Yes."

"Let me hear it."

I drop the dragon scale and roll my eyes, and in a monotone voice say, "I humbly submit to give my life to the kingdom of Anthar, to be the wife of their future king, and unite our two kingdoms through the bearing of his sons." The words taste like Strickbane in my mouth.

Nona nods. "That's good. I *almost* believed you. Remember, you have to say it three times to bind yourself to the promise. Once you've said it three times, you are committed. Now give me a hug." She opens her arms and I step into them. Tears sting my eyes as she squeezes me hard against her. "You're like a daughter to me, Sorrow. I wish you the best of luck and look forward to your safe return. I love you." She kisses my cheek and then turns away from me as she wipes tears from her cheeks with the backs of her hands.

"I love you, too." I take as deep a breath as the corset will allow and walk out of my chamber to meet my fate.

⊰ ≣✦≣ ⊱

The carriage ride to the mountains takes more than an hour, and since I am the offering this year, I am given the honor of riding in the *royal* carriage, sitting across from the queen and my father. My mother won't look at me, and I can't decide if it is because she is upset by the ceremony we are traveling toward, or if she is mad about me being caught astride a horse this morning.

My father won't *stop* looking at me. Every so often he glances down at my white skirt and his hand twitches. If I am not fed to the fire dragon or given to the horse clan, I will be going back home to a life where I am never allowed to go anywhere alone, to parents who have never shown me love and rarely kindness, and to a whipping that will leave my legs cut and bleeding. I will be shut away again, and forced to watch the world from my bedchamber window—watch as my father dotes on my sisters and spoils them with gowns and ponies and feasts and outings to the market. I clench my teeth together and pull the curtains open to stare out the window and realize that before me are three completely different destinies and I want none of them. None!

"Shut the curtain," my mother orders without looking at me. "The breeze is ruining my hair." She pats her tall, powdered hair.

"Yes, my queen." I pull the curtain shut and close my eyes.

Within minutes the carriage slows and then stops altogether. I pull the curtain open again and peer out. We have traveled to the very end of the road and stopped at the edge of a cliff. I have been in the mountains three times before today, for my sisters' binding ceremonies. Each of those times I was deemed too young to be out in society, so was made to watch from a carriage. Today will be the first time I am allowed to get out. Before the coachman can help me down like a proper princess, I hop out of the carriage and hear my mother's outraged groan.

I squint against the early afternoon sun as I stretch my aching legs and fill my lungs with fresh mountain air. Everything looks strange here—the jagged rocks, the pine and aspen trees, the wildflowers growing alongside the road. Even the air is different, filled with the smell of dirt and trees and the unknown. Tied to an aspen tree is a small, perfect white lamb. It is struggling against the rope around its neck, and for a moment I feel sorry for it.

At the cliff's edge, facing us, stand King Marrkul and his nine sons. They are clad in leather breeches and leather vests over low-cut white shirts that expose half of their chests. On their hips hang their swords, and bows are slung over their backs. They look dressed for battle, not a formal ceremony. Standing in the middle of them, with five men on each side, is an ancient woman with a hunched back, withered hands, long white hair, and milky-white eyes. Despite her eyes, she seems to be staring directly at me, and all I can think is *crone*. Something pinches the back of my neck, hard, and I turn to see my mother. "What, my queen?" I ask, glaring and rubbing my neck.

"Curtsy," she hisses from the side of her mouth, all the while smiling her practiced smile at the horse lords. I grasp my skirt in my hands and do as she says. The Strickbane poison dangles in front of me, the dragon scale flask shimmering in the sunlight like a lit lamp. The horse lords nod their acknowledgment.

When all the carriages have arrived, my three older sisters and their husbands come to stand beside me. "You look beautiful," Harmony whispers, touching my hair. Gloriana grasps my fingers and kisses my cheek. Diamanta merely eyes my corset and nods her approval. I lean over to her and ask, "Who is that old crone?"

"She is King Marrkul's witch. She was in attendance at my ceremony, remember?" Diamanta says.

"No, she was at *my* ceremony," Gloriana insists. Looking at her handsome young husband, she asks, "Don't you remember, Hans?" He frowns and looks at the old lady.

Harmony shakes her head. "She was only at *mine*. I would have remembered if she was at any of yours." I study my sisters and their husbands as they continue to argue about whose ceremony the withered old woman attended. I don't remember the crone from any of their ceremonies, and the woman is utterly unforgettable.

Without a word, I am escorted by my father to stand before the horse lords and their crone. She stares at the dragon scale flask, and her foggy eyes light up. When her gaze meets mine, she smiles a toothless smile, and despite her empty eyes, I know without a doubt that this woman is not blind. She leans toward me and sniffs, and all the hair on my body stands on end.

"She is different from her sisters," the crone says to the horse king, without taking her eyes from me. She sniffs again and licks her gums. "She is . . . doughty." I'm *what*? I don't know what *doughty* means, but the way she is looking at me makes me think the word must mean *tasty*, and the crone is hungry. "It was for her that your wizard disappeared, no?" she asks my father. I blink at the crone. She spoke to my father without adding on the customary *my lord*. Men and women have been put in the stocks for a day for such an offense. I turn to him and see the familiar fury turning his face crimson.

"Unfortunately, yes," he says, his voice tight with anger.

"She scared him away," she adds.

Lord Damar looks at me. "She scares all of us at times."

The crone hoots with laughter, and then, quick as a coiled snake, her hand darts out and clutches mine. I freeze as the woman pries my fingers open and looks at my palm. "Our fates intertwine," she whispers, running a brittle yellow nail over my fingertips. "But I, unlike Melchior, am not scared of you." She drops my hand and I lean as far from her as I can without taking a step back. "I am ready to proceed with the ceremony when you are," the crone says, addressing my father and the Antharian king.

As she says those words, a flash of memory comes back, of this very woman presiding over *all three* of my older sisters' ceremonies, and I wonder how I could have forgotten.

King Marrkul steps up beside me so I am centered between him and my father, and the three of us turn to face the gathered crowd with the sun at our backs. My father smoothes his pale hair and adjusts the sword hanging at his side, and starts speaking, welcoming the nobles and thanking them for coming. I can hardly follow what he is saying; my head is spinning, and I can barely breathe.

After a few long minutes of formalities, I jump at the sound of hissing steel as King Marrkul unsheathes his sword. He holds it high over his head so it gleams in the sun. It is well worn, and so polished that half of the designs on the blade have been rubbed off. It is a sword that has seen many battles. "I, King Marrkul of Anthar," he says, "swear to uphold and respect the binding of my kingdom to Faodara. What say you, Lord Damar?"

My father unsheathes his sword, a weapon he has never used, and holds it up. "I, Lord Damar of Faodara, speaking as proxy for Queen Felicitia, swear to uphold and respect the binding of my kingdom to Anthar." He looks at me. "What say you, Princess Sorrowlynn of Faodara?"

I fight the urge to wipe my sweaty palms on my skirt and swallow. The air is heavy, and I feel like it is going to make me snap in two. "I, Princess Sorrowlynn of Faodara . . ." The words falter as I think of my three choices: marriage, home, dragon. Marriage, home, dragon. All the while, the air seems to be getting thicker and thicker.

The people gathered to witness the ceremony start whispering. My mother is staring at me, her sparkling blue eyes eager, as if she can make me speak by sheer force of will. My three sisters, standing beside their husbands, look at each other when I don't continue. Gloriana pales and grips her husband's arm. Harmony wrings her hands. Diamanta takes a tiny step forward and whispers loud enough so I can hear, "humbly submit to give my life . . . *humbly submit to give my life!*"

I clear my throat. "I, Princess Sorrowlynn of Faodara . . ." I look at my father, at the anger burning behind his pale blue eyes, then turn and look at the nine sons of King Marrkul. My eyes pause on Golmarr's worried face and then stop on Ingvar, and all I can think of are his massive hands touching me moments after they have been on his wife. With that thought, I know which fate I shall choose. "I, Princess Sorrowlynn of Faodara, humbly submit to give my life," I say, my voice strong, "to the fire dragon instead of giving it to the Antharian heir."

"What?" my father retorts, grabbing my upper arm so hard it hurts.

Somehow, looking into his furious eyes, all the strength leaves my voice. "I choose the dragon," I whisper. The air is pushing on me so hard I can barely stand.

"What are you doing?" he growls through gritted teeth. His hand tightens so his nails dig between my bones, and I cry out. "When we get home, I am going to whip you until you can't cry anymore," he whispers.

My blood starts to burn. I jerk my arm out of his grasp and match his stare with my own overwhelming anger. "I choose the fire dragon over going home with you," I say, and my voice is strong, pushing back on the stifling air.

He shakes his head. "I forbid you to—"

"You cannot forbid me! I choose the dragon over going home with you!" I yell. Adrenaline rushes through me, and I turn to Ingvar. "And I choose the fire dragon over going home with *you*!" I look at the gathered crowd. "I choose the fire dragon!" I shout, my hands balled into tight fists at my sides. My mother sighs a practiced, regal sigh and turns her back on me. Diamanta is shaking her head, Harmony has fainted into her husband's arms, and Gloriana is still as stone, her mouth gaping. Aside from a gentle breeze whistling through the trees, the cliff top has gone utterly silent as everyone stares at me. I have made my choice.

And then one voice quietly speaks above the wind. "I choose her."

I whip around, and my white skirts whirl out in a wide circle. Golmarr has stepped forward so he is standing in front of his eight brothers. "I choose you, Princess Sorrowlynn," he says. "To be the wife of the future king of Anthar."

I shake my head and fight a wave of panic as the air grows so dense I can scarcely exhale. "No, I can't marry your brother. I would rather die."

He steps up to me and looks right into my eyes. "I choose you to be *my* wife, not my brother's. I plight you *my* troth . . . I promise to be faithful and loyal to you. As your husband, Sorrowlynn."

The crowd explodes with questions. My father steps between Golmarr and me, shoving the young horse lord aside even though he is a head taller and broader in the chest. "What is he talking about, King Marrkul?" my father demands.

"It is written in our history books," King Marrkul explains, his voice loud enough to carry to the gathered crowd, "that the son who marries your daughter automatically becomes the heir. If . . ." He looks at the crone. "If the union is *not* one made out of greed for power."

"I don't understand," my father growls.

King Marrkul puts his hand on Golmarr's shoulder, and pride shines in the king's hazel eyes. "If my boy's motive in picking your daughter to wed is purely greed for the title of king, the match will not be approved. If his motivation is other, it will be approved."

My father frowns. "And how can you tell the difference?"

"My son is a good and honorable young man, but I am not the judge of his motives. Nayadi?" King Marrkul calls.

At the word *Nayadi*, the crone shuffles forward. "Take her hand, Golmarr," she instructs, pointing to me with a withered finger. Golmarr steps around my father and coils his fingers in mine. He pulls me out of my father's shadow and holds our intertwined hands up to the crone. She takes them and runs a thick nail over our joined knuckles. My hand fills with warmth, and I don't know if it is from the crone's touch, or from Golmarr's.

"Well?" my father demands, yanking my hand out of the horse lord's. "Is this a union of greed?" He sounds hopeful. My heart sinks when I realize he doesn't *want* me to marry the Antharian heir. He wants me to go home so he can whip me. The air presses harder, and all I want to do is melt into a puddle and be absorbed into the soil so that I don't have to feel this pressure anymore.

"Or is this a union of love?" Marrkul asks, equally hopeful.

The crone shakes her head. "Not greed, but not love, either. There is a surprising amount of affection there—on both sides—but it is too soon to be love. It is a union of, shall we say, *pity* for the girl. He does not want her fed to the fire dragon. His motives are not spawned by greed."

Anger fills me. *I am to be a pity bride now?* I look at Golmarr. His cheeks are flushed, his eyes dark with worry and something else. Maybe sorrow. Slowly, he lifts his hand and holds it out to me, and my anger melts away. By his actions, he has turned himself into an offering. He is willing to take me for a bride, to be stuck with me for the rest of his life, not because he loves me, but because he doesn't want me given to the dragon. I look from his outstretched hand, to my father, to the cliff, and then I slowly place my hand in his. *I can do this,* I think. *I can go back with him and be his wife.*

"Do you accept?" King Marrkul asks, his voice practically pleading.

"Yes," I say. "I accept." All the weight pressing me down seems to lift. The air is thin again. I fill my lungs and feel like I might float away. Golmarr squeezes my hand as one of his brothers unties the lamb from the aspen tree and leads it over to us. I pity the tiny creature, obviously removed from its mother and trembling with fear.

"There is a problem." The crone's voice rings out loud and grating, and Golmarr's hand turns frigid in mine. "The ceremony is already done. This princess has made her choice to be offered to the fire dragon. She has stated it three times, and three times is a number of binding. She has sealed her fate." The crone looks at me. Her wrinkled mouth twitches up at the corners, and her eyes fill with an emotion I can't quite put a name to. Need? Hunger? Anticipation? "Take the rope from the lamb and lower the princess down!"

Everyone freezes, staring at me with stricken faces. A moment later, Ingvar and King Marrkul step up beside me and pull me toward the cliff, tearing my hand out of Golmarr's. I struggle against them and look over my shoulder. The Faodarian nobles look frozen in place. The Antharian women are looking at me as if they are proud of my choice. All three of my sisters are crying, and their husbands are trying to console them. My mother stands still, silent, eternally majestic. My father's eyes meet mine. His mouth is a thin, hard line. It is how he looked when he whipped me. "So be it," he says. "You have chosen your fate. And so ends the life of Princess Sorrowlynn of Faodara."

He turns and walks away, and Diamanta throws herself at his feet. "Please, Father," she cries. "Don't let them put her down there!"

"She chose this for herself." He pulls his legs from her grasp and together my mother and father walk to their ornate carriage and get in, not once looking back. I am not sad to see them go. They have never loved me. They have never known me.

A rope is slipped over my head, and I am too shocked to cry, or fight, or even protest. I look up into King Marrkul's face. His tan skin has gone white, and unshed tears are glistening in his pale eyes. "I'm sorry, child," he whispers. "I thought all Faodarian princesses were cowards. I thought we would be putting a lamb down in your place." He swipes his eyes with the back of his hand and tightens the rope around my chest. The pearl-crusted corset acts as a shield against the rope, and I can barely feel it. I can barely feel *anything*. "Hold the rope as we lower you to take some of the pressure off your ribs. We'll get you down as quickly as possible." He pulls a long, sheathed hunting knife from his belt and hands it to me. Somehow I manage to take it from him. "I'm sorry," he says again.

Eight of his sons come to help him lower me down. Golmarr is standing apart, staring at me. The Antharian king walks me to the edge of the cliff and helps me wrap the massive layers of white petticoats and skirts around my ankles so they won't tangle with my feet. And then I am walking backward, and my sisters are wailing, and the sun is shining too brightly, and the ground under my feet is changing from flat to sloped, until I am leaning back and walking down the sheer side of a cliff, and I am still too numb to even feel fear. After five steps, the cliff wall disappears, and I start to plummet.

The rope jerks taut, stealing my breath. It slides up under my armpits, popping pearl buttons off my corset, and I drop King Marrkul's hunting knife. It clatters on the rock below. I gasp and cling to the rope with both hands and look at the opening in the cliff, and all at once, the numbness is torn from me and I start to scream. I am staring into a great, round mouth, filled with darkness and damp breath. I scream and scream, and squeeze my eyes shut. The more I scream, the more I begin to feel.

The rope stops being lowered and is yanked and shaken, making me swing back and forth. I suck in a breath of air and stop screaming, and crack my eyes open. Before me is a massive cave opening into the cliff face. *Not* a mouth.

Above, I hear raised voices. Men shouting. Arguing. Growling. The shouting increases, and the movement of the rope becomes jerky, pulsing to a tempo despite the fact that it still isn't being lowered. Dirt and pebbles rain down on my head, so I look up. Someone is inching down the rope, his booted feet wrapped around it. It is the motion of him lowering himself, hand over hand, that is making the rope pulse. When he gets just above me, he stops and yells, "All right! Get us down quick!"

The rope is being lowered again, faster this time, until at last a small outcropping of rock touches my feet and I stand at the entrance of a cave. I peer over the side of the cliff, and my heart misses a beat. Far, far below, so far it looks like a piece of white embroidery floss, is the Glacier River flowing between jagged rocks. It springs from a glacier-fed lake cradled in the center of the mountains. Across from us is another sheer cliff face that rises up and turns into a snow-capped mountain peak.

Golmarr alights beside me and without a word takes a knife from his sleeve and cuts the rope from my ribs. More pearl buttons fall from my corset, bouncing on the ground and toppling over the cliff. Golmarr tugs the rope three times and it is whisked away. His eyes meet mine.

"Are you crazy?" My entire body is trembling, even my voice. "What are you doing down here?"

He scowls and puts the knife back into his sleeve, then bends and picks up his father's hunting knife from the ledge, roughly pressing it into my limp hand. "I figured you didn't stand a chance of surviving alone. But with me, your odds will be a little better. I am armed, and I have fought in half a dozen battles."

My throat grows tight and I can't talk, so I throw my arms around him and hug him as hard as I can. "Thank you," I croak against his shoulder. Then I realize I am holding him and quickly push away.

"Don't thank me yet." He adjusts the bow on his back, loosens his sword in its scabbard, and strides into the cave.

"Wait!" I call. He turns around, a mere shadow in the darkness, and scowls at me. "Where are you going?"

"To find a way out before the dragon finds us." He tilts his head to the side. "You weren't going to just sit here and actually *wait* to be eaten, were you?"

Yes, that was my plan unless I could scale the cliff, but I don't tell him. "It's as black as pitch in there. How are we going to find our way through the cave if we can't see anything?"

Golmarr strides back out into the sunlight and stops in front of me. He lifts the dragon scale flask that is attached to my necklace. "Do you know what this is?"

"Of course I do. It's a dragon scale."

"And do you know what they do in the dark?"

I look at the flask dangling from his hand. "Glow?" I guess.

He nods. "Yes. They have eternal light. At least until the dragon it came from dies. So if it glows, we know the dragon is still alive. It came from the fire dragon that lives in these mountains, right? Not from one of the others?"

"That is what I was told."

"Well, then let's get going. We don't have any food or water, so we need to find a way out of the mountain fast."

He starts walking back into the cave, but again I blurt, "Wait!" I unsheathe the hunting knife and hand it to Golmarr. Turning my back to him, I put my chin down and say, "Please cut this stupid corset off of me. I would like to spend my last living minutes breathing freely." He takes the knife but pauses. I peer at him over my shoulder. "What?"

"This could have been our wedding night." His face is so close that I can feel his breath on my skin. His fingers brush the back of my neck, and my cheeks start to burn. Carefully, he pops the corset's laces with the knife, and it falls away from me, leaving a wrinkled, voluminous white shirt tucked into my skirt. I kick the corset over the side of the cliff and then pull the pearl tiara from my hair and throw it down, too. Taking a deep breath, I turn to the mouth of the cave.

"I am ready," I say, tucking the hunting knife into the back waistband of my skirt. Together we walk inside. When the cave entrance is far enough behind us that it gives off no light, the dragon scale starts to glow.

Golmarr puts his hand on his sword. "It looks like the fire dragon is still alive."

Chapter 5

To say the dragon scale glows is like saying the moon lights the night. The moon does light the night . . . sort of. But not well enough to go on a walk through rocks and gravel and boulders without stubbing your toes every other step.

The air is damp and cool, and it stinks like animals—like a chicken coop that has never been cleaned out. I am a mess, tripping over my skirts, crawling over boulders on my hands and knees, tearing my nails and scraping my arms and legs. Golmarr gets ahead every few minutes, and then pauses for me to catch up. I can see his patience waning in the way he taps his toe and keeps looking over his shoulder, leading us deeper into the blackness of the cave.

"You're not very strong, are you?" He says it like it is an accusation and frowns as I slide down a rock on my butt.

I glare at him. "I've never climbed on rocks before."

"Not even when you were a child?"

I brush my hands together, ridding them of lingering grit. "I have never been allowed to leave my chambers except to attend private family events, and for dancing and riding lessons."

"You're not *allowed* to leave your chambers?" he asks.

"Not without my father's permission. And he rarely gives it."

He shakes his head in disbelief. "Why?"

"Because the queen doesn't like to see me," I admit, my voice quiet.

"The queen, as in your own *mother*?"

"Yes. She doesn't like seeing me because I have brought her nothing but sorrow since I was born."

"I'm sorry," he says, looking into my eyes.

I shrug, pretending like it is not a big deal, pretending like talking about it doesn't make it hard to swallow. "Don't be sorry," I whisper, looking away from him. "I hardly know her."

We keep making our way deeper into the cave, and Golmarr isn't as impatient when he stops to wait for me.

"If this is a dragon's cave, then where are all the bones and treasure?" I ask, swinging down from a grime-covered boulder taller than me. I wipe my hands on my shirt, leaving two dark smudges down the front.

"If a dragon truly lives in *this* mountain, if this is one of its caves, it isn't going to keep its treasure here. It is going to hide it as deep as possible. Look." He points up. I crane my neck and squint. The ceiling seems to be moving. Squirming. I hold the dragon scale above my head and shudder. A dense canopy of bats covers the cave's roof, making it impossible to see the stone they are hanging from.

"I guess that explains the smell and the stuff all over the boulders," Golmarr adds, his voice amused.

I cringe and look at my filthy palms.

"The legends say the fire dragon is as tall as a two-story house. There is no way it could fit in this cave. The ceiling is too low."

I shudder, still intent on the brown smears on my hands,

and wipe them down the front of my shirt again. Where I've wiped, my shirt is brown and red.

Golmarr lifts one of my hands, uncurling my fingers to look at my palm. "You're bleeding." Without another word, he reaches behind me, takes the hunting knife from the back of my skirt, and unsheathes it. "I'm going to cut your skirt shorter so you don't have to crawl over the boulders," he explains, kneeling in front of me and lifting the fabric.

I gasp and pull away from him and shake my head. "No, please! That wouldn't be . . . proper," I blurt. My cheeks start to burn at the thought of having my legs exposed.

He groans and looks up at me. "We are about to be eaten by a dragon, you're crawling on bleeding hands through bat droppings, and you're worried about being proper?" I bite my lower lip and nod. I *really* don't want him to see my legs. He stands and presses the knife into my hand a little too roughly. "Suit yourself."

We keep moving deeper into the cave—Golmarr leaping over boulders and me crawling and stumbling after him. In the darkness there is no way to measure time, except by how thirsty I am. The longer we wander, the thirstier I become. I lick my dry lips and keep going.

The cave curves to the left, and Golmarr stops, pointing to something long and coiled, resting between two rocks. He picks it up. It is a piece of rope leading deeper into the cave. "This looks like the same rope they lowered us down with. The rope taken from the lamb."

After we have gone twenty steps, he pauses and frowns, rubbing the rope between his fingers. "This feels different," he says, and holds it close to the dragon scale. The rope is blackened and brittle. "I think . . ." He holds it up to his nose and sniffs. His eyes grow wide and he drops it. "This is burned!" he whispers. "The fire dragon must cook its food before it eats it."

My stomach turns. "How? With the low ceiling, you said it wouldn't fit."

"I don't know. Maybe it's smaller than the history books say it is. But it has been here." Beneath our feet, the ground rumbles. Overhead, the thousands of bats coating the ceiling start to screech and drop, catching themselves in midair a mere instant before they hit us. They surge around us and over us, flying in the direction of the cave's opening. Golmarr and I look at each other with wide eyes. He clutches my hand in his and starts pulling me deeper into the cave.

"Shouldn't we be following the bats? We need to get away!" I say, grasping layers of skirt and petticoats in my free hand in an attempt to keep up with him.

"We're not trying to get away. We're trying to find somewhere to hide!" He leaps over a rock, and my hand is torn from his. I stumble on my skirts and fall to my knees. Without a word, Golmarr leaps to my side and lifts me to my feet. I silently curse myself for not cutting off my ridiculous skirt earlier, because far, far ahead, an orange glow lights the darkness. And I can barely run.

Chapter 6

The entire tunnel is illuminated. It looks like a long orange worm, and the light is growing brighter and brighter. The air around us is being drawn toward the light, sucking my shirt against my back and pulling loose wisps of hair that have escaped my braid forward around my face.

"Fire," Golmarr yells. "We need to find shelter!" He is looking everywhere, his eyes scanning the ground, the walls, the ceiling. I'm too petrified to move, so I stare at him in a daze. "Sorrowlynn! I need your help! We need to find somewhere to hide before the fire reaches here." He puts his hands on my shoulders and gives me a firm shake. "You're destined to die by your own hand, right?" I blink at him and nod. "Well, if you are burned to death, you are not dying by your own hand. That means you're going to survive this, so help me!"

I look around the cave, at the rocks, the walls, the ceiling, but there is nowhere to go. And then Golmarr's hand wraps tight around my wrist, and he is pulling me to the side, toward a jagged crack in the wall. The wind is roaring now, the tunnel glowing like midday. The fire is almost upon us.

Golmarr practically throws me at the crack. I put my hands up to shield my face and fall forward, landing hard on the ground. Golmarr tumbles to the ground beside me, and then we are engulfed in heat. I dig my elbows into the ground and drag myself forward, away from the smoldering air and deeper into the crack in the side of the cave. The farther I go, the cooler the air becomes. I crawl until I come to solid rock and can go no farther. Together, Golmarr and I huddle against the rock and shield our faces from the heat. I peer through my fingers. The crack we fell through looks like a slash of orange lightning. And then, like a flock of birds flying past a window, the fire is gone and we are plunged into darkness.

The dragon scale hanging from my neck looks hardly brighter than an ember buried by ash. The air is hot and dry and seems to solidify and darken, and then the horse lord and I are coughing as smoke fills our lungs and stings our eyes. I put my sleeve over my mouth and nose and breathe through it, but it hardly helps.

"Get down," Golmarr says between coughs, pushing me toward the ground. I press my cheek against the stone floor and breathe, and the air is a little fresher. Golmarr slithers on his belly toward the wall's opening. I stop beside him, our shoulders barely fitting side by side in the narrow fissure, and look out into the cave. It is like trying to see with a thick blanket over my head, but the air is a little less smoky. I lay my cheek down on my arm. The horse lord shifts, and I feel him lay his head down beside mine. His hair spills over my hand, and I run my fingers through it.

"How did you know?" I ask.

"Know what?" His face is so close to mine that his breath tickles my skin when he talks.

I inhale and choke on smoke. "That I am supposed to die by my own hand," I gasp.

"I've known all my life, I suppose. Well, probably since I was two. That's how old I was when you were born. My brothers and I talked about you a lot when we were growing up." His voice is hoarse from the smoke.

"I hate that ridiculous prediction. I have been called *Suicide Sorrow* behind my back for my whole life because of it," I grumble.

Golmarr laughs a whispered laugh. "Do you want to know what my brothers and I would say about you, *Suicide Sorrow*?"

"Not really," I say, which makes him laugh again.

"We would say, 'I wish I had a birth prediction like that, because I would know without a doubt that no matter what I did, I wouldn't die . . . *unless it was by my own hand.*' I remember taming a stallion a few years ago, and the first time I rode him he tried and tried to buck me off. All I could think was, *If I had a prediction like that stupid, spoiled Faodarian princess, this would be a lot less scary, because if I'm not careful this horse is going to throw me and I'm going to break my neck.*" He laughs, and I laugh, too. "That is why, when I saw that fire coming, I knew you were going to survive. That fire was not your own hand, so it couldn't kill you."

I lay in silence and think about what he said. There is only one thing that can kill me. I open and close my hands, and for the first time in my life, the weight of my birth prediction is taken from me.

"Suicide Sorrow," Golmarr muses. It sounds more like a warrior's name when he says it.

"Do your people have birth predictions?" I ask.

"Yes. *My* family does, anyway, since we are the ruling

family. Nayadi gives them to us when we are born, but because she is an invisible witch, no one knows we get them. We don't make them public, like your family does."

"Invisible witch?" I ask. "What does that mean?"

He is silent for a long time. The smoke has thinned, so the dragon scale lights up his face. He is staring at the cave ceiling, one arm bent behind his head, his forehead creased. "We don't talk about it," he says. "Let me rephrase that. I swore an oath of secrecy to never speak of her outside of my family." His gaze shifts to my face. "I'm sorry." Our faces are so close that my nose is almost touching his. He is flawless in the dim light, and his closeness makes my breath come a little quicker.

"That's all right." I smile. "I'm just glad you're here with me. It's nice to have a . . . friend."

He returns the smile and brushes a strand of hair from my cheek. "It is an honor to be considered such." He touches a finger to his forehead, and then makes an X with his two pointer fingers.

"What is that?" I ask, touching my finger to my forehead and then making the X.

"It is a formal salute of respect given between two people," he explains. "It means *honored friend*."

"You speak with your hands?"

"Over a century ago, the king of Anthar created a language spoken strictly with hand gestures instead of words so that his warriors could remain silent in battle. We still teach it to all of our warriors." He climbs to his feet and holds a hand down to me. I pull against his hand to stand. "We need to keep going."

"Wait." I take the knife from my waistband and hand it to him.

He frowns. "You don't want the knife?"

I grip my skirt and pull it taut. "Will you please cut my skirt so I can move more freely?"

He nods, kneels at my feet, and begins the arduous process of cutting through the fabric of the skirt and the four petticoats, depositing a pile of hewn cloth beside my feet. When he is done, he looks at my bare legs and sucks his breath in through his teeth. "That's why you didn't want me to see your legs."

I glance down, and a wave of shame dampens my mood. Even in the dim light, the scars stand out against my skin like puckered white veins. I smooth what is left of my skirt, pressing it down over my knees as far as it will go.

"Please don't tell me all of those scars are from you riding astride," he says.

"No. Only this one." I bend down and touch a thin scar on my ankle. "The rest are from other times. My father whipped my legs whenever I was disobedient," I explain. "I was a headstrong, disobedient daughter." My face burns with humiliation, and I hug my arms over my chest.

"*How* disobedient?" he asks, voice skeptical.

"I was forbidden to call the queen *mother*, and when I forgot, she would get so upset that she would take to her rooms for days, so my father started whipping my legs to help me remember." His face is as still as stone, so I continue, "It only took two whippings for me to never do it again. And once I got whipped because I hugged her. I didn't know I wasn't supposed to touch her—I was only five. If I daydreamed during lessons and my tutor reported it, my father would whip me, so my tutor stopped reporting it, and if I left my rooms without permission, I got whipped." I trace my finger over the biggest, puffiest scars. "The worst whipping I got was when Melchior—our wizard—left. That's what these are from." I can't bear to look at him, so I stare at his hands. They are clenched so hard that they're trembling.

"Why did you get whipped when your wizard left?" he asks, his voice harsh.

"He said his fate was tied to mine, and there was something he had to do for me. No one has seen him since, and there aren't any other wizards or witches in our land—except Nayadi—so my family no longer has the guidance of a seer."

"How old were you when he left?"

"Eight. My father carved grooves in the willow switch that time, and it tore my skin." I can still remember the white-hot pain, and the fury in my father's eyes. But the worst part was the days following. The agony of my bleeding legs lingered much longer than the initial whipping. "I hate my father," I whisper, finally looking at Golmarr.

He nods and the muscles in his jaw pulse. "I do, too." His gaze shifts to my slippers. "How are your feet?"

I wiggle my toes and cringe. "Sore, but I'll manage."

He looks at my legs once more. "Come on, Princess. Let's find a way out of here."

Some smoke still fills the cave, but most of it is in thin tendrils curling over the uneven rock ceiling. Once more Golmarr leads the way through the cavern, but with my shortened skirt making it easier for me to move, he doesn't have to stop and wait as frequently. When he does stop, his gaze flashes to my legs, and I wish I could cover the scars.

"He whipped my legs because he said no one would ever see them," I explain. "They would always be covered by skirts. If he whipped my back, I couldn't wear dresses that showed my shoulders because everybody would know my father is a monster. No one was ever supposed to see my legs."

"What about your future husband?" Golmarr snaps, voice angry. "He would see your legs."

"He said no one would ever want to marry me. I would be an untouched virgin until I killed myself at a young age."

His jaw clenches and releases. "With the way you were treated, I'm surprised you *didn't* kill yourself."

"Only my father treated me that way." I leap over a jagged stone—something I wouldn't have been able to do wearing a long skirt. "Nona, the woman who raised me, loves me." My chest aches at the thought of Nona finding out I have been given to the fire dragon. It will break her heart. I climb up a massive boulder spanning the entire cave floor and gasp. "Golmarr," I whisper. He's already jumped down.

"What?" In one swift move he is standing beside me, head almost touching the ceiling, hand on his sword. I lift my arm and point.

In the distance are dozens of glowing orange dots, like stars on the horizon, only these pinpricks of light are *moving*. Golmarr removes his hand from his sword and lifts the bow from his back. He strums the bowstring twice with his thumb, and then slides an arrow from his quiver. Putting the arrow to the string, he pulls it back and holds it up to his eye, then lets it fly. The moment the arrow is out of our small circle of light, it disappears. Three seconds later, two orange dots jolt and then disappear, and something shrieks. The other glowing orbs freeze for a moment, and then start rushing toward us.

Golmarr grabs the dragon scale necklace and shoves it down the front of my shirt, plunging us into darkness. "Don't move," he whispers, and I can hear his bow groan a split second before the twang of a fired arrow echoes through the cave. Another set of orange pinpricks goes dark, and now I understand what is up ahead. Eyes. Glowing orange eyes. Lots of them.

Golmarr starts shooting arrows almost as fast as my heart is pounding. The orange eyes are becoming fewer and fewer as his arrows find their targets, but they are not being extinguished fast enough. The remaining eyes are getting close. Too close. So close that I can hear the breathing of whatever they belong to. Without warning, Golmarr presses his bow into my hands and the swish of steel rings out. "When I say your name, light the way for me," he says. The air stirs, and there is a quiet thud on the ground below the rock. I reach out for my new friend, but feel only air. An overpowering sense of isolation steals the breath from me.

"Sorrowlynn!" I pull the necklace from my shirt, holding it above my head and filling the cave with a gentle glow. Five creatures run toward us. They are the size of big dogs, but are covered with a skin of glossy, dark scales. Five little dragons.

"*Mayanchi*," Golmarr growls and swings his sword into the closest creature. The thing hisses and lashes out at him with curved black claws, but Golmarr dances out of the way and lifts his sword in an arc over his head, slicing down into the dragon's neck and killing it. Another beast leaps at him, growling, snapping its sharp teeth at Golmarr's thigh. The horse lord staggers to the side and plunges his sword into the creature's scaly hide; the scales screech against the metal. He tries to yank the weapon free, but it won't come loose.

Another dragon runs at him. I scream a warning just as Golmarr throws a knife, hitting it in the eye. He puts his foot on the beast with his sword stuck in it and pulls, but before he can slide it free, the last two dragons reach him, one closing its mouth over his sword arm, the other jumping onto his back. Everything seems to slow down. Golmarr opens his mouth and screams, and the pain of it turns my stomach. He is going to die, and it is because he took pity on me.

Without a thought, I drop the bow, pull the hunting knife from my waistband, and leap to the ground beside Golmarr. Holding the knife in my right hand, I hack at the creature on Golmarr's back. The weapon feels awkward, and my blows hardly damage the thick scales, but finally, after lots of hacking, the creature falls from Golmarr's back and lands at my feet, hissing. I hold the knife over my head and swing with all of my strength, slamming the gleaming blade into flesh, and the dragon stops moving.

Golmarr reaches his free hand over his shoulder and pulls an arrow from his quiver, stabbing it into the eye of the beast locked onto his wrist. The animal jolts and jerks and splatters him with blood, and then stops moving. I grab the thing by its scaly snout and pry its jaws open, watching as one long yellow fang lifts out of Golmarr's skin, leaving a round puncture that instantly turns into a fountain of blood.

Golmarr gasps and drops his sword. It clangs against the rocky ground. He wraps his hand around his wounded wrist, and blood pours out between his fingers. "Sorrowlynn, cut a piece of your skirt off and wrap it around my wrist. Quickly," he says. I do as he asks, tearing my tattered skirt and pulling the scrap tight around his wrist. The dingy fabric turns red with blood in a matter of seconds. "Again," he says. I tear off a longer strip and wrap it around his wrist three times, and then tie it into a tight knot. He groans, but holds still. When I am done tending his wound, he sits on the cave floor and leans his shoulders against the boulder. Holding his bleeding wrist to his chest, he closes his eyes. The breath moves rapidly in and out of him. A sheen of sweat shines on his skin, and his face is speckled with black blood. I tear another piece of fabric from my skirt. Without asking, I cradle the back of his head and wipe the blood from his skin.

He grimaces and pulls away. "Is my face cut?" he asks, blinking bleary eyes.

"No. It's covered with dragon blood."

"*Mayanchi* blood. The little dragons are called *Mayanchi*," he says. He lifts his uninjured hand and touches the skin. "It stings," he says, looking at his fingers. There is a bit of inky blood on them. He touches one fingertip to his tongue and frowns, spitting. Squatting, he picks up his sword and balances it across his knees. The blade is glossy with blood. Taking the scrap of fabric from me, he wipes the weapon. Everywhere the blood is removed, the metal is as bright and shiny as newly forged and polished steel and pocked with shallow holes. "It eats through metal," he whispers, wiping his face and neck with his sleeve. "Do you have any on you?" His eyes quickly scan me, and I shake my head. "Good. You need to clean that knife, quickly."

I tear another scrap from my skirt and wipe the hunting knife clean. The metal practically glows.

Golmarr eyes the knife. "When you use that to fight, don't do little chops. Either hold it with both of your hands and swing with all of your strength, or better yet, use the tip and stab, thrusting with all of your weight. Aim for an eye if you can. It is soft and vulnerable." He pulls the arrow out of the eye of the beast lying dead at his feet and grunts. Where the dragon's blood has touched it, the wood is corroded. "Nayadi once told me that dragons have acidic blood, but I never believed her, because how could a blind old woman know something like that?"

I am hardly listening. My feet are throbbing. Burning. I look down. My white velvet slippers are oily black, and tendrils of steam are rising from them. I am standing in a shallow pool of dragon blood, from the beast I killed. I yank the slippers off as fast as I can and throw them, then tear more of my skirt off and plop down on the cave floor. Without a thought for manners or modesty, I spit on each foot and scrub at the blood coating them. The fabric removes the surface blood, but the creases in the soles are lined with black. "I need water," I say, trying to keep the panic out of my voice. My feet are still burning.

"I know, but we don't have any." Golmarr stands and wobbles. "Let's keep going. There is bound to be water somewhere in this cave. Dragons have to drink, right?" He holds his hand out and I take it. "You saved my life." He pulls me close and looks right into my eyes. His hazel eyes, lit by the dim glow of the dragon scale, are beautiful. "Thank you." He puts a finger to his forehead and then crosses it with his other finger. *Honored friend.*

Chapter 7

For once, Golmarr is slower than me. Even with my feet bare and stinging, and a body that has never done anything more physical than dance lessons and riding docile horses, I am the one waiting for him as he slowly makes his way up and down boulders.

We pass the *Mayanchi* Golmarr shot. Some are still alive, so Golmarr holds his sword in his left hand and kills them, cleaning his blade each time. "I had hoped to salvage some of the arrows," he mumbles. I look at his quiver. Three arrows with red fletching poke out above the leather lip.

"You only have three left?" I ask, panic apparent in my voice.

He looks at me sidelong. "I wore my ceremonial clothing and weapons today. I only had three to begin with, but my brothers gave me their arrows before I came after you, so I had twenty-seven." A hint of a smile touches his face, and I realize his skin is covered with sweat. "If I'd known I was going to be fighting dragons with you, Princess Sorrowlynn of Faodara, I would have most definitely packed a full quiver." He stops walking. "Will you hold the dragon scale over my injury?" I do as he asks. The bandage is soaked through with blood. Around the crimson bandage, the skin is puffy. I touch his skin. It feels like meat fresh off the fire. Slowly, I pull my hand away.

"I have never been taught healing of any kind," I say, "but I don't think that amount of swelling and heat is normal for a fresh wound."

He shakes his head and grimaces. "I've had my fair share of injuries, and none of them have ever *hurt* like this. I think I've been poisoned. The *Mayanchi* must have some sort of venom."

"Are you going to die?" I blurt before I think.

"Possibly. I feel like I'm dying already." He turns away from me and starts vomiting. I grab his thick hair in a handful at the nape of his neck and hold it out of the way. When he is done, he wipes his mouth on the back of his sleeve and throws his arm over my shoulder. "That's a little better," he says, and we start walking.

I slide my arm behind Golmarr's back and hold him close. His body is firm beneath my hand, and every time he takes a step, I can feel his muscles move beneath his skin. He smells like leather and sweat and smoke and blood. His long hair falls over my shoulder, and his weight makes walking ten times more awkward. "So," I say, pretending that having my arm around the lean waist of a horse lord is a totally normal thing. "How many horses do you have?"

"Sorrowlynn?"

"Yes?" I look at Golmarr's ashen face.

"I'm sorry, but I don't feel good enough to talk."

"That's all right." I pat his back and adjust his weight a little more evenly.

The cave seems to go on for an eternity. My stomach feels

like it hasn't been filled in weeks, and my shoulder and back muscles burn with the burden of Golmarr. The ground starts to slope downward, and then we come to a dead end. My heart drops into my stomach. "What do we do now?" I look at Golmarr for the answer. His face is so close to mine that I could pucker my lips and they would be touching his cheek, and then I realize his eyes are closed. "Golmarr?" I jostle him a little bit.

His eyelids flicker, and he slowly focuses on my face. "Princess Sorrowlynn?" he asks, furrowing his brow. His head falls forward so our foreheads are touching, and a goofy smile quirks his lips. "From the first moment I saw you standing on that dais in the evening sun, I haven't been able to stop thinking about you. Your eyes are the most beautiful eyes I have ever seen," he says, his words slurred. "Even prettier than Evay's. Hers are brown. Yours are . . . green." Despite the fact that he's obviously delirious, pleasure fills me. He closes his eyes and sighs. "If I die will you do something for me?"

"If I don't die, too."

"If you don't die, tell Evay I'm sorry. Tell her if things wouldn't have turned out this way, I would have married her when I came home."

"Wait . . . who?" I lean away from him, and his head sags forward. His body turns boneless and the weight of him increases, tilting me sideways until I fall to the ground, and he lands on top of me. Our small sphere of light disappears as the dragon scale is sandwiched between us.

Carefully, I wiggle my way out from under him and turn him onto his side. His breathing is deep, his mouth hanging open. I brush his tangled black hair from his face and make sure there are no rocks under his head. And then I summon all the energy I possess and stand.

All I want to do is fall back down beside the horse lord and go to sleep. But I thrust my chin forward, tuck back the loose wisps of hair hanging out of my crown braid, and stand tall. Putting one burning foot in front of the other, I start following the cave wall, looking for a new passage. Maybe we already passed one. Maybe we already passed dozens. With the small space the scale lights up, we could have passed thousands and never known.

I shimmy over rocks and hold the scale up to the cave walls as I go back the way we have come. And then, not five steps ahead, the air in front of me fills with light, a perfect tube of orange going from the floor all the way to the top of the cave, leaving a bright circle on the ceiling high above.

My heart starts thumping and I wonder if the cave is going to fill with fire again. I limp over to the tube of light and get down onto my hands and knees. Crawling up to the very edge, I peer over a hole the circumference of a water well and shiver at the thought of walking right past it and not falling in. Far, far below, so far that I almost wonder if I am seeing things correctly, is something so shiny I have to squint to look at it, like looking at the sun after the clouds have parted. A gust of warm, dry air wafts up from the hole, followed by a shriek so loud and so terrible that the very ground I am lying on shudders.

The light goes dark as a great, moving shadow blocks it, and I hear the snap of fabric catching air. A moment later, the shadow is gone, and the light shines up again.

Too scared and too mesmerized to move, I lay with my body pressed against rock and pebbles, and stare down at the light shining deep below. It is golden, like sunlight on water. It is as bright as daylight. It might be the way out. Or it might be the fire dragon's fabled treasure.

My eyelids become heavy, and I imagine the rock below me is cradling my body and rocking it. I give in to my weighted eyelids and let them slip shut. The instant they close, I realize something is making a sound. I think of the clock in my bedchamber, which is always ticking, but I hear it only if I consciously listen for it. Somewhere in the cave there is a click, click, clicking. I keep my eyes closed and focus on it. The dark space around me slowly comes to life with noise, a myriad of clickings, some loud, some so quiet I almost wonder if I hear them at all.

I climb to my feet and brush the grit from my skin, and start hobbling toward the sound. With the light coming from the well, I can see the cave better than I've ever seen it before. The walls sparkle and glitter like the night sky. The floor is strewn with thousands of blackened bones and rusted bits of armor and weapons. Above and to my right, the ceiling has two white lumps sticking out of it. Directly below are two matching white lumps, like teeth that have been rounded with time, jutting up from the cave floor. I limp over to the closest lump. It is as tall as my waist, and milky smooth. I put my hand on it and pull back. The stone is covered with a slippery liquid. I peer up at the twin ceiling lump. A single drop of water falls from it and clicks onto the lump beside me, bursting into a thousand minuscule droplets.

If the clicking I am hearing is water dripping, and I can see only two lumps, that would mean only two clicks. But there are lots and lots of clicks echoing through the darkness, maybe even hundreds. Turning toward the sound, I step up to the cave wall. As far as I can see, it is a sheet of sleek black stone covered with sparkles. I run my fingers over the rough surface, and after I have gone three steps, my hand disappears. It looks like the rock has bitten it off at the wrist. I gasp and yank it toward my body, and it comes out of the wall completely normal.

For a long moment, I stare at the rock, and then, summoning all of my courage, I lift both of my hands and ease them forward. When they are even with the glimmering stone, I push them a little further and feel . . . nothing but air. I take a tiny step forward and my arms disappear into the rock all the way to my elbows. Another step and my nose is a hair away from the wall, and my arms are gone. I squeeze my eyes shut and take one more giant step, and the clicking becomes so loud that I almost scream from the shock.

Slowly, I open my eyes. I am standing in a room more beautiful than the cliffside palace I grew up in. Massive white columns are braced between the stone floor and ceiling. They look like giant, delicate icicles, and they seem to absorb the pearly light from the dragon scale and reflect it back twice as bright. Hundreds of smaller, half-formed columns hang from the ceiling, dripping water down onto their other halves, as if the two stones are alive and reaching out for each other. In the center of the room is a lake with white columns shooting up from its center.

I clap my hands and squeal. I, Princess Sorrowlynn, have walked through a dark cave, passed through a stone wall that isn't really there, and found the water needed to save my life and the horse lord's, and I have done it all on my own. Tears sting my eyes as I stand a little higher, and then I stumble to the water's edge and thrust my burning feet into it.

The water is as cold as fresh-melted snow, and seems to wrap around my wounded skin. The burning is sucked away, and my entire body sags with relief. I plop down onto my bottom and scoot into the lake until the water is up to my neck, then lean my head back. The icy water suctions around my braided hair and onto my scalp, and my skin absorbs the chill. It penetrates my body and starts to make my bones ache. I stand, and a slew of water pours from me, making giant ripples that spread from my shins all the way to the edge of the light as I back out of the water.

Bending, I cup my hands and scoop water to my parched lips, swallowing it down with loud, needy gulps. When I have filled my belly to bursting, and am shivering with cold, I go back the way I have come.

The rock wall I entered through does not look like a rock wall from this side. It is a massive, jagged rent in the stone leading from the lake room to the passage. I can see the bright, burning well of light, and beyond it, Golmarr.

I hurry back into the passage and kneel beside him. He doesn't appear to be breathing. Pressing my hand to his cheek, I lean my face so close to his that our noses bump. "Golmarr," I whisper. "I found water." He doesn't move a muscle. "Golmarr." I shake his shoulder. "Golmarr." I pat his cheek. "Golmarr!" I yell, and slap him hard across the face. His head rolls to the side and stops, and tears fill my eyes. "Golmarr?" I plead, and my voice catches on a sob. "Please wake up." I put both my hands on his face and turn it toward mine again. A drop of water trickles out of my soaked hair, down my forehead, along the bridge of my nose, and plops right onto his lips. He sucks his bottom lip in, and I laugh with relief, pressing my cheek to his. His skin is like fire against mine. Reluctant to give up his body heat, I stand over him and wring my skirt out onto his face.

The skin between his eyebrows creases and he flinches as the water rains down on him. His dark lashes flutter, and then he blinks his hazel eyes and peers at me, and they are the most beautiful eyes I have ever seen, even if they are a bit bleary.

"I found water," I say, and smile.

Without a word, his lips part. I kneel at his side and wring my shirt out into his mouth. His tongue darts out and licks his lips as the water drips onto them, and then he swallows. "That's good," he whispers. "How far is it? My arm . . ." He lifts his injured arm an inch off the floor, and then it falls back down.

"It's not far. It's just through that wall." I point.

He moves his eyes in the direction I am pointing and blinks. "Am I dreaming? What is that light?"

"There's a hole in the ground. Something at the bottom is shining up through it." I take his healthy arm in my hands and tug. "Come on. The water helps with the *Mayanchi* blood. It might help your arm."

His eyes meet mine. "I can barely move, Sorrowlynn. You're going to have to help me."

"I know." I put his arm down and crouch behind him, pushing his broad, muscular shoulders up until he is sitting. Next, I loop his good arm over my shoulders. "Ready?" I take his silence to mean *yes*. "Get up!" He grunts with effort, and I wobble and sway beneath his weight. After a minute, he is on his feet, his head is on my shoulder, and we are stumbling and weaving like a couple of drunks. The effort chases the chill from my bones, and after a minute, Golmarr is damp with sweat.

When we get to the wall, he stops and squints at it. "There's a stone wall there," he mumbles.

"I know it looks like there is, but there really isn't. We are going to walk through it. The lake is just on the other side."

"Whatever you say," he whispers, and sags a little heavier against me.

We step through what looks like solid rock and emerge in the columned room. Golmarr stops walking, and his eyes grow round. "I have dreamed of this place," he whispers, and then he falls to his knees and his eyes roll back in his head. His body seems to go boneless and teeters forward and back before tipping headlong onto the cave floor. I sigh and remove the bow and quiver from his back before using his ankle to drag him the last few steps to the lake. Trembling with exertion, I flip him from his belly onto his back and submerge his injured arm in the icy water, all the way to his shoulder.

Using the hunting knife, I cut off another layer of my skirt and soak it, then drip the water onto his parched lips and into his mouth. Next, I wash his face. All the fierceness has vanished from his expression. My heart swells with gratitude for this man who risked his life to follow me into a dragon's cave, and I trail my fingers over his stubbly jawline. "Thank you, Prince Golmarr," I whisper.

By the time I have tended to him, my damp clothes are clinging to my skin and I am shivering with cold again, so I curl my body up against his, lay my head on his shoulder, and fall asleep.

Chapter 8

I am cocooned in warmth. I sigh and scoot closer to the heat, pressing my forehead against it. Air stirs the skin behind my ear, and I open my eyes. Before me is soft brown leather. I try to move my legs and find them entangled with . . . another pair of legs. Arms are secured around my back, cradling me to the warmth, and my head is resting on a bicep. "Are you awake?" a deep, accented voice asks. My heart starts pounding and I look up into a pair of pale hazel eyes framed by black lashes.

We are lying on the side of the lake, facing each other, our limbs intertwined like two trees that have grown so close you can't tell their branches apart. "You were shivering in your sleep, so I kept you warm," he says, tightening his arms around me and pressing his cheek to the top of my head. I shiver again, but it has nothing to do with being cold. Golmarr pulls me even closer, wraps his legs tighter with mine, and runs a hand down my back. "I figure keeping you warm is the least I can do after you saved my life again."

I force myself not to shiver and ask, "How is your arm?"

"A lot better. The *Mayanchi* venom must only be temporary,

used to paralyze." As if to prove his point, he unwraps his legs from mine and sits up. "See?" He holds his arm out and wiggles his fingers. The swelling has gone down, and the puncture is simply a wound that needs a few days to heal. While I look at his arm, I can feel his eyes on me, and all of a sudden I wonder what I look like. My hair must be a mess. And my legs! My skirt is halfway up my thighs. I sit up and yank the skirt down almost to my knees, and Golmarr laughs. "Still worried about that?" he asks with a twinkle in his eyes.

He turns and uses his left hand to scoop water to his mouth, and I realize the cave isn't dark. The water is pale blue and so clear it looks like glass. Nothing is in the water: no bugs, no fish, nothing. On the water's surface is a shimmer of sunlight. High above, between two massive white columns, is a jagged crack in the ceiling, and sunlight is pouring through it.

"A way out?" I ask, sticking my feet into the cold water.

"Maybe if we were bats."

I pull my feet out and cringe. They are black and blue, and have cuts all over them. One of my toenails is torn half off, the broken half glued to the skin with dried blood. I lift the corner of the broken half and give it a swift yank, separating it from the bit of skin still holding it in place. With a shudder, I throw it into the water.

Golmarr sits down beside me and removes his brown leather vest. The inside is inlaid with bits of smooth, flat metal.

"What are those for?" I ask. "Usually ornamentation is worn on the outside."

"This is a jerkin. It is armor," he explains, touching the metal. "It covers my heart and ribs. That way, if I am shot with an arrow, it won't kill me."

My eyes grow round. "*Have* you ever been shot before?"

He presses his lips together and flips the vest over. "Look." He touches a spot in the middle of the vest where the leather has a small tear. "Someone tried to shoot me in the back when we were crossing the Glass Forest to your kingdom. We traded our light armor for chain mail after that. That is why we arrived at your palace armed and injured." My gaze automatically moves to the long cut on his cheek, a black scab now. "That is how I got this," he says, touching the healing wound. "We fought back, and I got slashed with a knife." He sets the vest down away from the edge of the water and untucks his dirty white shirt from his pants, pulling it over his head. My face flames, and I avert my eyes. Golmarr laughs again. "Haven't you ever seen a man without his shirt on?"

I shake my head. "Definitely not."

"My brothers and I never wear shirts if it is warm outside and we're working or practicing our fighting. It saves a lot of shirts from the laundry."

I peer at him from the corner of my eye. On his left wrist is a small belt-like contraption that holds his dagger. He removes the dagger and begins sawing at the seam where his sleeve attaches to the rest of his shirt. After he's gotten the sleeve off, he starts on the other. "What are you doing?" I ask, almost forgetting that he's half-naked.

"I need fabric, and I don't want to keep taking it from your skirt if we can help it." When he cuts, the muscles in his arm tighten beneath his warm golden skin. I study him, the way his body moves, the bulge of his bicep leading to angular shoulders, the dip of his collarbone, which slopes up to his neck and his mouth. I study his lips, and my blood grows warmer. They are framed by black stubble and naturally curve up at the corners. My gaze wanders to his nose, which is long and narrow, and quite nice, and then I look at his eyes. He's staring at me, his cheeks slightly pink. "Now you've seen a man without his shirt on." His pale eyes turn predatory as he leans toward me, and for a heartbeat, his gaze lowers to my lips. "Was it as scandalous as you imagined it would be?" he whispers. I do not know what to say to that, so I shrug and turn away from him and hope he can't tell that my face is so hot even my neck and scalp are burning. He chuckles.

Kneeling in front of me, he takes my foot out of the water and gently pats it dry with his sleeve. Next, he wraps the cut sleeve around it, covering my foot from my toes to my heel, and securely tucks the end of the fabric under one of the layers.

My chest fills with warmth. "You cut your shirtsleeves off for me?"

"If my boots would fit you, I'd give you my boots." He dries the other foot and wraps it. When he finishes, his fingers slide up my ankle and touch one of the big, thick scars on my calf. I hold my breath and watch as he brushes his thumb over the entire length of it. His eyes meet mine. "In Anthar, scars are a badge of honor. They prove that you have faced pain and overcome it."

I swallow against a lump in my throat and throw my arms around his neck, hugging him tight. "Thank you, Golmarr." His hands press against my back and I hug him tighter, pulling against his bare skin. My body stiffens. I am hugging a man who is not wearing a shirt. I quickly shove him away and clear my throat. He throws his head back and laughs again, and I realize that laughing out loud like that is not quite as barbaric as I once thought it was.

When he puts his shirt and vest back on, his arms are bare

all the way up to his shoulders. He retrieves his bow from where I left it the night before and slings it over his back. I stand and try walking with the shirtsleeves covering my feet. The sandy lakeshore barely penetrates through the fabric, but anything bigger than a pebble is excruciating. I try not to flinch with every step, try to hide the pain so he doesn't know I can barely walk. Before I have taken five steps, Golmarr is beside me, looping my arm over his shoulder and taking some of my weight.

"It looks like you're the one who needs a little help this time," he says, and I realize, barbarian warrior or not, that he is the kindest man I have ever met.

⋯ ✠ ⋯

The lake is long and narrow, and at the farthest end from the illusion wall, a narrow stream trickles out of it. We follow the stream as it winds around the bases of the white columns (stalagmites, Golmarr says) protruding from the cave floor. "If we follow the stream, we will still have a water source," he explains. "And maybe, if we're lucky, the water will eventually lead to a way out. If we are *really* lucky, we might not even see the fire dragon." My stomach turns at the thought of the fire dragon, and I realize how incredibly famished I am. Dragon or not, if we don't find our way out, we risk dying of starvation.

With Golmarr's shoulder to lean on, and the fabric on my feet, we make good time. The cave is eternally noisy from the dripping of the stalactites—Golmarr's word again—to the stalagmites on the floor below them. The dragon scale still shines, reflecting on the milky stalagmites and stalactites, making them look like giant, glowing white opals.

As we walk, we find more little streams, all flowing into the one we are following, so by the time we've walked long enough for me to be damp with sweat, the main stream is more like a small river rushing around the strange formations of the cave. The ground begins to slope downward, forcing the water to flow faster, and after a while, the sound of babbling turns to a deeper rumble.

I take a step forward and jerk to a stop, pulling Golmarr hard against my side. His hand darts to his sword hilt. "What's wrong?" he asks.

I peer down at our feet. The ground disappears into blackness. "I think we're on the edge of a cliff," I explain. I take the dragon scale from around my neck and wind it once around my hand, then hang it as far forward as I can reach.

The cave floor looks like lumps of snow, slowly descending down, like a creamy, icy staircase, and the little river is pouring down it. The walls close in around the staircase, giving it the appearance of a narrow, descending black tunnel.

Golmarr sticks the toe of his boot into the water and slides it back and forth against the rock. "How strange—it's not slippery," he muses, and looks at me. "What do you think? Should we see where it goes?"

I peer into the darkness. "Do we have any other choice?"

"No."

I quickly unwrap the sleeves protecting my feet and tuck them into the waistband of my skirt. "Then let us go, an Antharian prince and a Faodarian princess, about to meet their fate together."

He laughs under his breath. "An unlikely pair," he agrees. And then he gives me the hand signal for *honored friend*.

"Friend," I whisper.

Chapter 9

Down and down we walk, eternally encircled by the weak light of the dragon scale. The darkness pressed against the light until I feel at times like I might suffocate on it. Distance means nothing when you can't see anything. I am simply walking down a never-ending staircase, my cold, aching body weak with hunger, in perpetual darkness.

I stop walking and put my hand against the cave wall. "My feet hurt. I need to rest," I say, and my teeth chatter. The cold has crept up my legs and into my blood. "I need to sit for a minute."

Golmarr grabs my hand to keep me from sitting. "Hold on." He frowns and unfastens the leather strap that secures the bow and quiver to his back. "Turn around," he says. I do, but watch him over my shoulder. He lifts the leather strap over my head, with the bow and quiver still attached. The black leather stands out against my dirty white shirt, but fits perfectly in the hollow space between my breasts like it was made for me.

"What are you doing?" I ask, shrugging my shoulders up and down against the weight of the bow. I have never worn any type of weapon before, aside from the small dagger that is tied to my wrist. "I don't know how to shoot this."

"If we get out of this cave alive, I will teach you to shoot." Golmarr turns me to face him, then turns his back to me and crouches low. "Climb on."

"Onto your back?" I ask.

He laughs. "Yes. Onto my back."

"You're going to *carry* me?" I can't keep the surprise from my voice.

"Sorrowlynn, just climb on. I carry bales of hay out to the horses every day, and you probably don't weigh much more. So climb on."

"But it's not . . ."

"Proper, I know. But neither is being fed to a dragon, or hacking a *Mayanchi* to bits, or cutting off your skirt, or sleeping curled up in my arms. But when necessary and proper battle it out, necessary always wins."

I put my hands on his shoulders and he grabs my bare legs behind my knees, hefting me up onto his back, and everything goes dark. I throw my arms around his neck to keep from falling off backward. He loosens them a bit and bounces me higher. "If you put your legs around me, it will make you easier to carry," he says.

I hook my ankles in front of him, and then pull the dragon scale out from between us, and light fills the stairwell once more. With me on his back, Golmarr continues down the never-ending staircase. I ease into him, my cheek beside his left ear, and try to absorb his body heat.

"See?" he says, walking down the waterfall stairs just as fast as he did without me on his back. "I'm strong. This isn't any more difficult than a day's hard work."

"Why do you work if you're a prince?" I ask. "Don't you have servants to carry the hay to your horses?"

"I work because I like it. I love being with the horses. And I don't live in a palace like you. My father's house is big, and he has a cook and a housekeeper, but that is only since my mom died. Someone has to feed us and clean up after him."

"But he is the king, right?" I ask, confused.

"He is the horse lord. He governs the land. Some call him king, but he isn't a king the way your mother is a queen. He doesn't sit on a throne, or have to always be on a dais so that he can look down on his people. And he never goes anywhere with an armed escort . . . unless you count me and my brothers as armed escorts," he adds.

I think of his tall, strapping brothers and the way Golmarr fought the *Mayanchi*. I feel his muscular body against mine as he carries me down the stairs. "I would count you as an armed escort. No one would dare to touch your father with his sons by his side. Is your father not worried that one of his subjects will try to assassinate him?"

"No. My people honor him and love him because they respect him. They would never hurt him. When we leave our lands, though, he worries." He bounces me up a little higher on his hips and keeps steadily splashing his way downward.

"Does he have more than one wife?"

Golmarr stops walking and frowns at me over his shoulder. "He has no wife. She died in childbirth. We don't have multiple wives."

"But I thought you said if your brother—Ingvar—married me, I would be his second wife."

"I was teasing you, Sorrowlynn. He was never going to pick you, since he was *already* married. It was a joke." He shakes his head. "And that is why you picked the fire dragon in the first place, isn't it?"

"Partially," I admit. He starts walking again, splashing his way downward.

"I'm sorry. After I teased you about it, I told you that only one Antharian heir has taken a second wife from your family before, and that is because his first wife died. I thought you would understand I was only teasing about multiple wives when I explained that." He shakes his head and mumbles, "I guess I truly deserve to be down here with you."

"But the Mountain Binding. The histories say that for it to remain in place, all Faodarian princesses have to offer to wed the heir of Anthar. If he's already married, wouldn't that make the binding obsolete?"

"Nowhere does the binding state that our heir *has* to marry yours, or that he has to be unwed. As long as the Faodarian virgin princess is offered, and we acknowledge it at the ceremony, and feed the dragon a lamb, the Mountain Binding retains its power whether or not we choose to wed her. No one from my clan was planning on marrying anyone from your kingdom."

"Why?"

He shrugs, his shoulder muscles rolling beneath my arms. "Because we don't like marrying genteel women."

We walk in silence for a moment before I garner up the courage to ask, "So . . . who is Evay?"

Golmarr pauses for a heartbeat, and then continues walking. "Evay? How do you know about her?"

"You talked about her right before you passed out from the *Mayanchi* poison. You said that if you died, you wanted me to tell her that you would have married her if you made it back to Anthar."

"I don't remember that. Evay is—was—my sweetheart."

When he doesn't continue, I rest my chin on his shoulder. An uncomfortable surge of jealousy and hurt engulfs me, and I tighten my arms around Golmarr's shoulders and for a moment savor the thought that right now, he is mine.

"Sometimes our lives turn out in ways we never imagined they would," he says. "If we get out of here alive, I don't think I can marry Evay—for the past few months, I thought I loved her, but now I'm not so certain. What are you going to do if we get out?"

"I don't know," I whisper. "All I know is I don't want to go home." If I return home I will get a beating worse than I have ever gotten before. But if we survive the cave, I will be penniless and homeless and have not even a pair of shoes to my name.

Golmarr stops walking. "Stay with me," he says.

"What?"

"If we get out of here alive, stay with me. I will help you find a way to survive without returning to Faodara. I will protect you."

I tighten my arms around his shoulders and whisper, "Thank you."

After what feels like hours, Golmarr says, "I need you to get down now." He helps me back into the water, and I notice his arms are trembling. Taking the bow and quiver from my back, he puts them onto his own and leans against the wall. I crouch, and the bottom of my skirt floats on top of the water. Filling my hands, I drink, and then refill them and hold them up to Golmarr. He puts his hands beneath mine and brings them to his mouth, drinking. The touch of his lips on my fingertips makes my body jump awake, and I have to force myself not to yank my hands away. "Thank you," he says.

I stand on my toes and garner enough courage to quickly kiss him on the cheek. He presses on the spot where my lips touched his skin and asks, "What was that for?"

"You are a prince of Anthar. All of my life I have heard stories of how violent and aggressive your people are. But you . . ." He silently waits for me to continue. "You are kind and gentle."

"And I always heard how soft and submissive *your* people were. I will admit you're soft, but you are brave and strong-willed. There is a place and a time for violent and aggressive, and yes, my people are ferocious when they are fighting to protect their land and children and freedom. But there are also times to be gentle and kind." The sides of his mouth turn up, and he flashes his white teeth. "Just don't tell my brothers I said so. They'd beat me to a pulp."

Taking my hand in his, we start walking again. We haven't taken more than twenty steps when Golmarr pulls me to a stop. "Look," he says.

Below us and far ahead, the darkness has changed. Instead of solid black, there is a hazy circle of orange, barely brighter than the dark. "What do you think that is?" Golmarr asks, taking his bow from his back.

My heart starts hammering against my ribs. "The fire dragon? Does the fire dragon glow?"

"The dragon's scales glow, so the dragon itself must glow," he whispers, and starts creeping down the stairs, bow in hand. The farther we descend, the bigger and brighter the orange haze becomes, and I barely notice my aching feet and throbbing legs or my empty belly. As the light grows, the cavern becomes louder—a dull roar I feel deep in my bones. The air also changes, clinging to my face and skin like icy fog.

Soon, we no longer have to look down to see the orange haze. We are level with it. I open my mouth to ask Golmarr what he thinks it is, but he comes to such an abrupt halt that I jerk to a stop to keep from running into him.

"Look!" he whispers. The ground is flat, and the stream we have been sloshing down is fanning out over the cave floor and merging into a giant pool of water. At the other end of the pool are the orange glow and the rumbling.

Golmarr steps into the water and turns to me, black brows drawn down. "Do you know how to swim?"

I shake my head. "I had never even seen a lake before last night."

He takes my hand and guides me forward. "Hopefully, it won't be too deep." Together we splash through the water, and my teeth start to chatter as the cold that has been festering in my body takes full hold of me. The closer we get to the light, the louder the rumbling becomes and the wetter the air is. The pool laps around my thighs as I push my way through it. The jagged cave floor is agony on my feet. When we are more than halfway across the pool, I stop walking and stare, openmouthed, at the great glowing mass.

A giant waterfall is cascading down the sheer side of the cave and splashing into the very pool I am submerged in. White mist is surging up around it, and something on the other side of the waterfall is glowing, creating a half circle of orange light that is distorted by the falling water, and as tall as the castle I grew up in.

"Beautiful," Golmarr says, his voice barely louder than

the roaring water. He grips my hand more tightly and pulls me forward.

The closer we get to the waterfall, the softer the ground beneath my feet becomes; the uneven rock has been replaced with velvety mud. But the water is getting deeper and deeper, until it is up to Golmarr's shoulders and lapping at my chin, and I have to cling to him to keep from falling under. The air is so saturated with mist that I can barely see anymore, and breathing is more like drinking. And then I notice something else. The water around my ankles is *pulling* me forward, dragging me toward the waterfall. I dig my feet into the ground, but they slide on the lake bottom. Frantic, I claw at Golmarr, grabbing his leather vest in my fists, but he is being pulled, too, and then I am under the water, and his vest is ripped from my grasp, and I am moving so fast that I cannot tell which way is up.

The water holds me tight. Rocks scrape my arms and legs, my clothes are suctioned to my skin, and my lungs ache to expand. Before my blinking eyes, the water changes from black, to gray, to bright gold. Without meaning to, without understanding how to move in the water, I am thrust up into the air. It is warm on my face, and so bright I can barely open my eyes. Something solid crashes into me, and I cling to it to keep from going back under.

Holding on to a stalagmite, gasping for air, I watch hundreds of tiny bubbles wash past me, away from the waterfall I just plunged under. I am in the middle of a massive, round lake. At one end is the dark, arched opening I came through. The rest of the lake is surrounded by fire that burns taller than I stand. The air is so hot that it hurts to breathe, and it is brighter than noonday. A deep, constant rumble fills the chamber, and I can't tell if it is from the waterfall or from the raging fires.

Golmarr walks up to me, the lake sloshing around his ribs. His black hair is plastered to his scalp, and water is dripping down his face. He leans close and whispers, "Put your feet down. It isn't too deep over here. But look." He points to the farthest end of the lake, the direction all of the bubbles are moving, where the water is black. "Don't go over there. It looks deep. I think this is the fire dragon's lair," he adds, his wary eyes scanning the fire. "Those flames are burning on solid rock. There is nothing to feed them, and there is no smoke."

I examine the cave for any sign of the fire dragon and realize Golmarr is right. There is no smoke in the air. It is clean and crisp, and wavering from the heat. High above in the rock ceiling is a giant crack. On the other side of it, orange clouds are streaming across a purple sky. It is either sundown or sunrise, but I can't decide which. "If this is its lair, where is its treasure? The mountains of gold and jewels? Where are the piles of bones and rusting armor?"

"I don't know. But something lit the fire, and there's still air in the cave, even with the fires blazing, so it is possible for it to live in here. Look over there." He points to my left, and I follow the line of his finger. On the lakeshore there is only one place where fire isn't blazing: a wide, sandy path situated between two towering piles of burning rock—the perfect escape route out of the water.

"It's got to be a trap," Golmarr says. "I think it *wants* us to come out of the water."

"Why?"

"So it can kill us?" He says it like a question, and he looks at me. His hazel eyes are dark, his mouth pulled into a tight frown. "I really hoped we could have snuck out without meeting the fire dragon."

"You have three arrows left. Can't you shoot it?"

"My bowstring was ruined by the water." He reaches out and lifts the dragon scale flask. Pulling an arrow from his dripping quiver, he scrapes the metal tip across the scale. It doesn't leave so much as a scratch. "I don't think an arrow is going to pierce the dragon's scales . . . but I could shoot it in the eye. At least, if my bow hadn't lost its spring I could have tried." He reaches an arm around my waist, and my heart flurries against my ribs. His hand finds the small of my back, and my breath catches in my throat as I stare at his lips. And then he wiggles the hunting knife, still securely held in place by my waistband. "Do you remember what I said about wielding this?"

I nod. "Stab forward, or hold it with both hands and swing with all my might. No chopping."

A touch of a smile turns one corner of his mouth up. "Right. And go for the weak spots—eyes, throat, underbelly." He slides his sword from its sheath, and it dawns on me why he is reminding me how to fight.

I grip his water-stiffened leather vest in both my hands and stare right into his eyes. "You're going to fight the fire dragon now, aren't you?" He nods. Tears spring into my eyes. Pain cinches around my heart at the thought that this might be the last time I see him alive. "Please . . ." I have nothing to say. *Please don't die? Please kill it? Please don't leave me here alone because the thought of living without you hurts?* Instead, I throw my arms around his neck and, once more, hug him to me as tight as I can. His arms encircle me and hold me firmly against him. There is no *please*, so I say, "Thank you." He lets me go and before he can stride away to fight the dragon, I touch a finger to my forehead and then cross it with my other finger. A slow, sad smile graces his mouth, and he nods at me.

And then, with his sword still clutched in his hand, he silently drops beneath the water's surface, legs splayed out like a frog's, and glides away.

Chapter 10

When Golmarr reaches the lake's edge, only his dark head emerges from the water. He looks left and then right, and slowly, bit by bit, creeps out of the water, right in front of the sand pathway. His sword reflects firelight as he uncurls to his full height.

Behind me, I hear the snap of fabric catching the wind—the same sound I heard when I was looking down the well of light—and a gust of searing air pushes against my back, creating ripples on the lake's surface. I whip around and look over my shoulder and forget to breathe.

A massive dragon is soaring in the air behind me. Its body shimmers like glowing orange jewels catching the light from the fire. Giant feet are tucked up beneath it, tipped with curved gray claws. It flaps its wings of tattered gold, sending another burst of blistering wind through the cave that makes the fire sputter and dance. I gasp a breath of air to yell a warning, but it sears my lungs and silences me. I swallow and force my voice to scream, "Golmarr! Run!" Ducking behind the stalagmite nub I've been holding, I tremble as I watch the great beast soar over my head. The dragon glides on the air, its wings barely fitting between the stalagmite columns, and swoops toward Golmarr. "Run!" I shriek again.

Golmarr does not run. He turns toward the dragon and lifts his sword. His bare arms flex with muscle as he swings the sword around, slashing at the air with the grace of a warrior. "If you have any honor, you will land and fight me!" he yells. The dragon flies over Golmarr but turns in the air, circling back the way it came. "Fight me," he yells again.

The dragon turns to Golmarr once more and soars toward him. He raises his sword, ready to charge, but before the dragon is close enough for him to use his weapon, a deluge of white fire bursts forth from its mouth, engulfing the horse lord. The fire passes him, hits the cave wall, and goes out, but Golmarr is covered in flames. They lap at his skin, cling to his clothing, and curl around his hair. He screams, and the sword drops from his hand. He falls to his knees, his scream replaced with silence. "Get in the water," I cry. His body crumples to the ground, and he lies there, a smoldering pile of flesh and clothing.

I dig my feet into the ground and start pulling myself through the water, clawing against it, and finally slosh out of the lake. Stumbling onto shore, I throw my dripping body onto Golmarr's. His flesh sears my skin, and steam hisses out between us as the flames consuming him trickle to nothing and die. I roll him onto his back, and his vest burns my hands. I gasp and pull away. The vest's metal plating has burned the leather to white ash. I yank it open, and the metal squares fall out of the leather, sizzling against his chest. With hardly a thought for my fingers, I knock the plates off his body. Beneath them, his shirt is ash, and his skin is blistered. He smells much like a piece of meat that has been too long on the flames: burned to a crisp. I turn away and gag.

A gust of searing wind slaps me in the face. Sparks rain down from the nearest fire and singe my skin and burn tiny holes into my skirt. I look up, and then up some more, at a beast easily as tall as two houses stacked on top of each other. The fire dragon is perched atop the pile of rocks beside me, and the fire is blazing around it so it looks like a creature made of flame . . . yet it is immune to the fire.

I grab Golmarr's ankles and start dragging him down the sand path, to the only exit I can see, but an arm of fire slithers across it and fences me in.

You think I will simply let the two of you walk away? You are the first living human beings I have seen in half a century. Entertain me for a spell before I eat you. I drop Golmarr's legs and press on my forehead, wondering where that thought came from. Foolish girl. Surely you are not the one the wizard spoke of before I ate him.

Those words, spoken in my head, in my very voice, are not my words. Despite the heat making the air ripple, I shiver and look back up at the fire dragon, and then step between it and Golmarr's unconscious body.

The beast is studying me with eyes that gleam like polished copper. Pearly, pale orange scales cover its body, scales twin to the one hanging on my necklace, and for the first time I wonder how this dragon scale became separated from its owner.

It was taken by the only person who fought me and did not die. She got the trophy she sought, but she paid dearly, the dragon explains, its words becoming my thoughts. It shakes its head, and a pair of spiraled horns catch the firelight. I shall eat you without burning you first. You deserve a most painful death to pay for your ancestors' binding me under this mountain and cursing me to a life of boredom. I used to be magnificent, but look at my wings! The dragon opens its great wings, sending ripples of heat that burn my skin and sear my lungs when I breathe it in. They are shaped like a butterfly's delicate wings, and look like glowing gold stretched taut between bone, but they are not beautiful. They are tattered, torn on the edges, and have holes in them. Bedraggled.

Bedraggled? This is what your family has done to me! They are rent by the rocks when I fly through the stifling closeness of this cave! I can hardly fly anymore. I have been stripped of my freedom and my dignity. Feelings of anger and sorrow accompany its words. It pulls its wings against its body once more. And so I shall eat you piece by piece, saving your head for last so you see it all, and you shall get stuck in my teeth, and I will like it. And when I get bored in the years to come, I will remember this day and replay it in my head over and over.

Its words freeze me in place and fill me with such dread that I can't even draw breath. I hear its laughter buzzing in my head, and it lifts one massive clawed foot and steps down the side of the burning rock toward me.

I turn toward the lake and start running, but a wall of fire shoots up in front of me, blocking my way. The dragon lifts its other foot and boulders spill and topple, tumbling down onto the sand path and rolling to a stop at my feet. I leap out of the way to keep from getting burned, but the rocks aren't on fire. They are as pale and clean as if newly hewn from the cave wall.

With one final step the dragon is before me, its razor-sharp talons sinking into the sand. I crane my neck to look at it, and it opens its mouth, showing me rows of curved yellow teeth. Are you not going to run? it asks.

"You have blocked all the pathways," I say, amazed that I can speak at all. "I cannot run."

I hear the laughter in my head once more. Poor little princess, trapped with nowhere to go. Are you not going to lift a hand to fight me, at least?

I look at my hands, feel the pressure of the hunting knife at my back and the weight of the dagger in my sleeve. Slowly, I pull the hunting knife free and look from it to the towering dragon. It is so big, and my weapon is so small; it is like agreeing to fight a lion with a sewing needle for a weapon. My hand begins to shake so badly I can barely keep my fingers wrapped around the knife hilt.

You disgust me. You possess no courage, no ability to fight. If you were courageous, you would try to dive through my fire barriers and run. If you knew how to fight, you would attack me with that puny blade, even though you would die trying. You deserve to be eaten, so I shall eat you now, and I will savor every excruciating moment of your pain.

Anger drives my fear away, and I scream and lunge for the dragon's foot, stabbing the small scales just above the claw with every fiber of strength in my body. The blade jerks to a dead stop against the scales. I hear the laughter in my head again.

I guess you do possess one drop of courage in your weak, human body. I like the taste of courage. Show me your courage as I eat you!

Nona, my sweet Nona, pops into my head, and I can hear her voice as if she is standing beside me. It is better to be eaten dead than eaten alive. With that thought, I finally understand my birth prediction. The relief of it makes me weak in the knees. It is time to make the blessing come true. I throw the knife to the ground and take the flask of poison from where it hangs and clasp the lid between my thumb and finger. I am ready to die by my own hand.

By your own hand? No! The dragon's wings burst open, and it shrieks. Before I can unscrew the lid from the poison, the creature lowers its head and lunges for me. I fling my arms up to protect myself as its sharp teeth snap down. A fang slides through the back of my hand, and I scream as the skin opens and my bones separate. The tooth comes out through my palm and shatters the dragon scale still clutched in it, and I think the pain alone might kill me. Other teeth close around my elbow and tear through flesh and bone, and with an agonizing snap and the sound of tearing fabric, my arm is in the dragon's mouth, and the pain in my hand simply stops existing, being replaced by the agony in my elbow.

The dragon swallows my arm and sleeve—even the dagger still tied to my arm with the white handkerchief—without chewing, and I fall to my knees. Blood pours from the stump of my elbow, turning my shirt and skirt crimson. It drips onto the ground between my knees, and the sand soaks it up before it can spread. My mouth falls open, and I scream, not from the pain, or the fear, but from the shock, the *horror*, of not having an arm.

Princess, the dragon says, its voice battling with my scream. Hold up your wounded arm. I lift my stub of an arm to show the beast what it has done, and it spits a ball of flame at me. I stop screaming and turn my face away as fire hits the bleeding stump, sizzling my blood and searing my skin. There, little girl. My fire has cauterized your wound enough that you won't bleed out before I am done with you. I look at my arm. The bleeding has changed from a torrent to a persistent trickle.

I turn to run from the dragon and leap through the wall of fire separating me from the lake. The fire barely scalds my skin as I pass through it, but before my feet touch down on the other side, the dragon's tail slams into my ribs. The breath is wrenched from my lungs, and I am soaring through the hot, parched air. Icy water collides with my face and fills my nostrils, and I start sinking. My hair comes unbound and streams around my head. Firelight ripples in rings on the lake's surface, and as I watch, the water around me turns cloudy with my blood, making everything appear red. My back thumps the lake bottom, and two bubbles trickle out of my nostrils.

The frigid water is a relief to my skin, and I don't know how to get up to the surface, so I lie there, staring at the world through the wavering red lake, and wait to die. Two more bubbles escape my nose, and as they reach the surface, giant talons splash into the water. Claws close around my body and yank me up out of the lake, flinging me against the burning rocks, and the dragon—wings outspread—circles in the air above me.

I roll down the rocks and come to a stop on the sand path. I whimper, struggling to breathe. With gentle fingers, I push on my ribs. Instead of solid bone I feel a tangle of small shards. I look back at the dragon, still gliding through the air, but something is different. It appears too heavy for its own wings, with its body sagging beneath them. The creature tilts to the side, and its left wing collides with a white column. The wing collapses, and the beast falls sideways through the air before hitting the lake. Water explodes around it.

What was in your flask? the dragon asks, its voice weak and hollow. It lifts its head out of the lake, its copper eyes intent on me. And then it coughs. The fire consuming the rocks dims and splutters, and for a minute the cave becomes quieter.

"My flask was filled with Strickbane poison," I say. Every breath I take shoots fire into my lungs.

Strickbane?

A single tear slips out of the corner of my eye and drips

down my cheek, and I nod and answer with a thought: *You ate my poison.*

The dragon opens its terrible mouth and shrieks. Its wings unfurl and snap against the air, lifting the massive creature out of the water, but one wing has been torn and barely holds any air. The dragon careens sideways and collides with a colossal white column stretched from the lake floor to the cave ceiling. The stone bursts into hundreds of pieces and crumbles into the lake, taking the dragon with it. The burning rocks flicker again.

A scale-covered foot reaches out of the water, and then another, as the dragon digs its claws into the settling pile of rubble and drags itself out of the lake. I struggle to my feet and watch. When the creature has reached the top of the wreckage, it opens its mouth and thrusts its head toward me, just like it did when it spewed fire at Golmarr. A wave of tepid air gusts into me, whipping my wet hair away from my face and nearly knocking me over. Around me, the fire shudders and shrinks to half its size, making the cave go dim. The dragon pulls its head back and roars its breath at me again, and everywhere its breath touches the fire, it goes out, so I am standing on the plain sand path with no walls of fire penning me in.

The creature shrieks and lifts its foot, and swipes its talons at me, but they don't come close to where I am standing. Heaving its body forward, it drags itself out of the lake and crashes down on the rocks piled beside the sand path. I jump backward as the dragon snaps its massive jaws at my legs, but it is not close enough to reach me.

And then its head falls to the rocks, and its rib cage moves, rapidly expanding and deflating, but the rest of its body is motionless. I take another step back, and the dragon's eyes follow my movement. I take two more steps, and still the dragon lies unmoving. Doubled over my crushed ribs, my stub of an arm dangling at my side, I turn my back to the dragon, turn toward the exit, and find Golmarr at my feet. He hasn't moved, his eyes are closed, and his breathing is shallow. I look from him to my missing arm and wonder what to do. Even though my wound has been partially cauterized, it is still bleeding too much. Should I escape and leave him to die? I cannot move him—not in my state, and if I wait for him to wake up, I will probably bleed to death. If I run, I will probably bleed to death. If I do nothing, I will probably bleed to death. A wave of dizziness hits me, and I wobble from side to side. I can already feel the life draining out of me.

You are the greatest coward I have ever beheld, too scared even to run! Even in my head, spoken with my own thoughts, the dragon's voice is barely more than a whisper. It is still staring at me with its luminous eyes. I am not an it, it says. I am a he. My name is Zhun. Run while you can, for Strickbane is dragon venom. It will not kill me like it will kill you.

I look at Golmarr again, and a sob tears at my throat, jarring my ruined ribs. I cannot leave him here with the fire dragon.

Leave him and run, you fool! Zhun commands. He breathed in my fire. It is burning him from the inside out. You cannot save him, even if you remove him from my presence! No man can survive dragon fire in his lungs.

"Will you eat him?" I ask.

Of course. But he will not feel it. Look at him. He is battling death already.

Zhun is right. Even I can see imminent death in the rapid rise and fall of Golmarr's chest and the lack of color in his cheeks. Beside Golmarr lies his sword, the metal blackened by flame. For the first time I actually look at his weapon. The hilt is made of two intertwined dragons with emerald eyes. My heart starts hammering in my chest, and I take a small step toward it.

Come here, Princess! the fire dragon wails. For I can feel my blood clearing the poison as we speak! I am ready to eat you! His great copper-colored eyes dart from me to the sword. I hobble up to the weapon and wrap my left hand around the dragon hilt. The metal is warm against my palm. As I lift it from the ground, my ribs shoot agony into my lungs, and blackness threatens to overcome me. I wobble and wait for the dizziness to pass, and then, still hunched over, I walk to the rocks and look up at Zhun the fire dragon. Come here so I can eat you! I can already feel my body healing! Zhun shrieks, his voice filled with fury. I swallow and take a step up the rock pile. When Zhun doesn't move, I slowly climb the boulders, making my awkward way up to stand beside the massive beast.

He smells like rotting meat and charcoal that has been doused with water. His scales look like orange opals the size of my palm, and spikes of pale gold jut up from the creature's spine. I put my left elbow on the dragon's shoulder to keep from falling and feel the heat coming off his body. Swallowing down a surge of fear at being so close to such a magnificent and deadly creature, I stumble to his head and stop beside his eye. His lone eye studies me, the pupil a long, narrow slit framed with gold. I will eat you! he screams inside my head, but lies motionless. I lift the sword and place the sharp tip against the filmy skin of the dragon's eye. I will eat you! he shrieks again.

"Not if I kill you first," I answer, and then tighten my hand on the sword hilt and thrust the blade forward with all the weight and strength left in my ruined body. Searing, scalding dragon blood splashes against my skin and coats the raw stump of flesh where my arm has been severed, mixing fire into my blood. With every beat of my heart, I feel the fire spread through my veins until it is burning my heart and my pulse doubles, thundering against my shattered ribs. Zhun bursts into golden flames, an explosion of light that encircles me. The fire surges, billowing against my skirt and whipping my hair away from my face, and I flinch. My brain feels like it is growing, pressing against my skull so hard that I moan and then scream. Images fill my mind, flashing past so quickly I cannot tell what they are. I let go of the sword and wobble, and my knees buckle. Head over heels, I tumble down the side of the rocks until I land on the sand. The fires blazing around the cave surge and flare all the way to the ceiling and then simply stop existing. Blackness smothers the cave and swallows me, and everything stops hurting as I cling to the darkness.

Chapter 11

A man blinks at me, squeezing tears from his dark blue eyes. His crown tilts precariously atop his bald head, and his clothing is soiled and torn. "Please!" he begs, grabbing my arm. "Please! You have to stop the fire dragon!"

"So you finally realize that you are not the king who is destined to unite the six kingdoms, King Napier?" I ask, but my voice is not my own. I am speaking with the voice of a man.

"I would have ruled fairly!" he says.

Someone beside me curses, and I turn to him. His long black hair is matted with blood on the side of his head, and his left arm, covered with blistered and blackened skin, hangs limp at his side.

"You filthy son of a . . ." The black-haired man lunges at the bald king, swinging his good arm at the king's head and flinging his crown across the room. I recognize the room. It is the throne room of my mother's castle. "You started this war to satisfy your own greed, and now claim you would have ruled us fairly? We are a peaceful people! We farm and breed horses. Thousands upon thousands of my men have died because of you! When I return to Anthar, I will have a kingdom populated with widows and children and destroyed by dragon fire. Who will feed them? Who will take care of them? Who will protect them?

I will have to teach my women to fight if we want to keep our land from the hands of the Trevonans! We will have to arm our children!" he rails.

I hold my hand up—my thin-fingered, wrinkled hand. For a brief moment, I look at the mirror on the wall behind my mother's throne and see Melchior the wizard looking back at me. His hair is not as gray as I remember it, and his skin is smoother, but I recognize the twinkle in his eyes when they look into mine. I am seeing through his eyes, hearing through his ears, speaking through his mouth, and sharing his body. "Yes, King Dargull, go back to your grasslands and teach your women to fight. Arm your children if you must. And . . ." I sigh. "I know a way we can bind the fire dragon under the mountain, but for it to work, you must pay two very high prices. First, all the gold and jewels in your treasuries. Second, your children, and your children's children, will be bound by this pact for generations to come. Your two countries will have to live in peace." I turn to King Napier. "Because you are the one who woke the fire dragon, the heavier burden will fall upon your progeny. Every Faodarian princess born under the binding will have to forfeit her own desires, or her life, in order for this to work. Is this something you can both agree to?"

King Dargull of Anthar nods eagerly. For a long moment King Napier of Faodara studies me. Finally, he closes his eyes and nods his head.

"If this is the only way to bind the fire dragon under the mountain, then I agree," King Napier says.

"It is the only way," Melchior says. "But it is also a very important piece to a puzzle that will eventually shape itself into the death of the fire dragon."

The dream fades as consciousness slowly settles over me. My eyelids are red from the light shining on them, and I am warm.

I fill my lungs with air and stretch my body until my arms are over my head and my toes curl. I haven't felt this good in a long time. Except my stomach. Based on how hungry I am, I must have slept well past breakfast.

I crack one eye open and the sun is shining directly into it, so I squeeze it shut and call, "Nona?" She doesn't answer. The only things I hear are the ticking clock and birds chirping. I push myself to sitting and pause, closing my hands. Lifting my fists, I open them and watch as damp sand falls in clumps onto a short, bloodstained skirt.

I am sitting on sand, in a perfect, jagged slash of sunlight. I peer up and see a stone ceiling cracked to the sky, and birds flying in and out of the opening to land in the little mud nests they've built on the cave ceiling. Water drips from stalactites, ticking onto the cave floor. . . .

In a massive, gut-wrenching burst, my mind recalls the fire dragon, the cave, and Golmarr. I suck in a breath of air and realize it doesn't hurt to breathe. Pressing on my ribs—strong, whole ribs—I gasp again and hold my right hand up to my face. Sunlight gleams off of my perfect, clean skin, and my filthy shirt is torn off just above my elbow. I wiggle my fingers and then hold my left hand up beside my right. They are different. My left hand is filthy with dried blood and dirt. My right hand looks like it was just soaked in a tub and scrubbed with soap. It is clean and whole and . . . not bitten off at the elbow.

Something beside me gurgles and gasps, and I leap to my feet, expecting the dragon. Golmarr is lying in the sand, in the exact position I last saw him. He looks carved from stone, he is so still.

I rush to his side and fall to my knees. "Golmarr!" Blisters have formed on his chest where his vest burned it. His black hair and eyebrows are a stark contrast to his ashen face. He gasps a small, shallow breath of air, and I can hear it gurgle deep down behind his ribs. I know, with complete certainty, that he is mere moments from death. Tears sting my eyes and drip down my cheeks, splattering on the sand beside his head.

"I am so sorry," I whisper, and put my hand on his cold cheek. As I stare down at him, my thoughts begin to swirl out of control, and the sunlight seems to grow brighter. I sway and close my eyes, and a scrap of knowledge surfaces in my mind like a bubble working its way to the lake's surface. My eyes fly open, and I stare at Golmarr in silent, breathless shock. I know how to help him.

I put my other hand on his other cheek so I am holding his face, then use my thumbs to gently pull his chin down so his mouth is wide open. Moving my face directly above his, I summon all the good things I am made of—love, innocence, agency, joy, and a thousand other things—and then exhale them into his open mouth. They float out of me as a trickle of light, brighter even than the sunlight warming my shoulders, and pool at the back of Golmarr's throat. I have to force myself not to recoil from the shock of seeing a part of me enter him. A moment later, when he inhales a tiny sip of air into his lungs, the light moves into him with his breath. As it slips down his airway, I shiver and pull away. My hands lose all their warmth and begin to tremble. Cold sweat beads on my brow as I stare at him, waiting to see what happens.

Golmarr gasps a massive breath of air and rolls onto his side, coughing out a big puff of orange smoke that smells like wet charcoal and blood. His eyes flicker open and focus on me, and he leaps to his feet, hand reaching for the sword that always hangs at his hip. But the sword is gone. He spins around searching for it, and then his eyes grow wide as he stares at something over my shoulder.

I turn and see *him*—the fire dragon, Zhun—where he lies dead atop the pile of rocks. His body looks like rusted stone, and his wings have been burned off so only the bones remain. My heart aches at the sight of him, and it takes me a moment to realize I am feeling sorrow for the great beast.

"Did I kill it?" Golmarr asks, scratching his head. Handfuls of hair break off in his fingers. He shakes the hair from his hand and strides up the rock mound. I gape at him, at his perfect golden skin, at the missing burns. Only his brittle hair and blackened, ruined clothing show the memory of fire. "Look at this thing!" he says, running his hands along the dragon's dim scales. At the creature's head, he pauses and scratches his head again. Where there should be an eyeball there is a dried, bloody mess with a dragon-and-emerald-decorated sword hilt sticking out of it. He pulls the weapon free. "My sword? But I don't remember . . ." He turns and looks at me, his brow furrowed. His eyes take me in for the first time, studying my long hair, my bloodstained shirt and skirt, and stop on my legs. He lifts his sword between the two of us and snarls, "Who are you, and what did you do with Princess Sorrowlynn?"

My mouth falls open and shut, and then open and shut again. Finally, I turn and look over my shoulder to see if he is speaking to someone else, but we are alone. "What are you talking about, Golmarr?" I ask, thinking my hair might be confusing him, since it has been braided and piled on my head. I run my fingers through my waist-length hair and frown. It feels strange, so I hold a strand of it up and gasp. My hair has changed from kinky curls to glossy waves of brown. I lift my fingers to my face and try not to panic as I press on my skin and bones, wondering if my face has also changed.

Without lowering his sword, Golmarr leaps and hops down the rocks and stops in front of me, his eyes wary. I ask, "Do I look *different?*"

He examines my face for a moment and then stares intently into my eyes. "No, you look the same. But ..." His gaze travels down my clothing and stops on my legs. Looking down, I almost choke.

I plop my butt onto the sand, with my legs stretched in front of me, and run my fingers over smooth, unscarred skin. Tears sting my eyes. I throw my head back and laugh. "Look at my legs, Golmarr!" I cry. "They're perfect!"

Golmarr puts a hand on his right cheek, rubbing his skin. "My cut cheek is healed," he says. I bite my bottom lip and nod. His cheek isn't the only thing that has been healed. Holding his hands out, he examines his fingers. "Look, Sorrowlynn." He steps up beside me so I can see his hands. They are wide, with long, narrow fingers that are the same golden tan as the rest of him, except for several small white scars on his knuckles. "Those are old scars from fighting," he explains. "They didn't go away like your scars." He looks at his sword and then at the fire dragon, and back at me. "What happened?"

My vision glazes over as I remember. "He was hiding up there." I point to the cave wall.

"*He?*" Golmarr asks, glancing around the dragon's lair.

"The fire dragon was a he. His name was Zhun. When he came out of hiding, he blasted you with fire." I look up to see if he remembers.

He runs a hand through his long hair, and it rains down

around him like pieces of black straw. Next, he examines his stiff, blackened leather vest, the holes scorched into it, the missing metal armor plates, and below, the disintegrating once-white shirt. He lifts his shirt and inspects his suntanned chest. "Where are the burns?" he muses, looking at me. "Did you get burned?"

"Only a little. He ate my arm," I whisper. Golmarr's eyes take in my torn sleeve. "And the poison I was holding . . . and the knife from Melchior." Pressing against my firm, hard ribs, I add, "He hurt me." My body shudders with the remembered pain, and I pull my knees against my chest, glad that I am still sitting.

"And?" Golmarr prompts, kneeling in the sand in front of me.

"And the poison paralyzed him. He was helpless. You and I could have run, but you were unconscious, and I was too injured. I didn't know what to do, so I took your sword and . . ." I swallow, remembering the glossy coating on the dragon's eye. "I put it through his eye. He would have eaten you if I didn't." I lay my head down on my knees and shiver with cold.

Golmarr stands and walks to the lake, thrusting his sword into the water. He pulls it out and rubs it on his fire-stiffened leather pants. Holding it up to the light, he frowns, and a wave of regret makes my stomach hurt. Because of the dragon's acid blood, by leaving his sword in Zhun's eye, I have ruined it.

"Did his blood destroy it?" I ask. Golmarr is so intent on examining the weapon that he doesn't hear me. I climb to my feet and sway back and forth, and then make my way to his side. "Did his blood destroy it?" I ask again.

He shakes his head and lays the blade across both his

palms, holding it out for me to see. "Look at this!" The sword is so shiny it looks more like silver than steel. The emerald eyes of the dragon hilt catch the sunlight, making green orbs flicker on Golmarr's bare chest where his vest and shirt are burned away.

"When a dragon dies," I say, "its remaining energy and magic die with it in the form of fire. It is called death fire. Zhun's death fire reforged your sword, changing the steel into something stronger than a human can make. This is a dragon death fire sword. A reforged sword." I throw my fingers up over my mouth. "How do I know that?"

"Death fire, hey?" Golmarr asks. There is laughter in his voice, as if having me spew a history lesson on a subject I don't even know is incredibly amusing. I look up and he leans forward, pressing a quick kiss to my forehead. For a minute the cold shivering through me is chased away by warmth. "Thank you!" He looks around. "I wonder if there is any type of food in here."

"The dark end of the lake has fish," I blurt, and press my fingers to my forehead. "I don't know how I know that, either. But a person can survive for weeks without food, as long as she has a source of water."

Golmarr's brow furrows, and he presses a hand to his stomach. "I know this sounds crazy, but I'm not hungry. I feel . . ." He studies me a minute. "I feel like I just consumed a feast, only without the bellyache. I feel *full*. I feel like there is energy overflowing from me." He shrugs his shoulders up and down a few times. "I feel better than I have ever felt in my life." He looks right into my eyes and smiles. Dimples form in his cheeks, and I wonder how I never noticed them before. My gaze darts to his mouth, to his white teeth, to his lips, and I feel the overwhelming urge to grab his face in my hands and press my mouth to his. He might feed a hunger I never knew I had. The thought makes my head spin, and the ground seems to quiver beneath me, so I step away from him.

"So, Sorrowlynn," Golmarr says, casually peering around the cave. "How did the fire dragon—Zhun—get in and out of here?"

Images of water flood my mind, of gliding through it, bubbles surging around me as the deep end of the lake presses upon my body. The water changes, growing brighter and brighter, and then I burst up out of it, and I am beneath blue sky, and my wings stretch wide as they catch the air in them. I soar up over snowcapped peaks. How I long for the open air!

I blink away the vision of sky and ice and wind and point to the far end of the lake. "He got out through the dark water. It connects to another lake surrounded by snowcapped peaks." I stare at the water and whisper, "I know how to swim, Golmarr. How do I know how to swim?"

"Can we get out that way?" he asks, ignoring my question.

I shake my head. "It is too far for a person to swim."

He peers up at the crack in the ceiling, but already I know we will not be able to get out that way. "Zhun melted the rock around the fissure until it was slippery smooth, making it impossible to escape." I grab my head in my hands and moan. "I shouldn't know that! What is wrong with me?"

"I am going to ask you one more thing," Golmarr says, his voice gentle. He puts his arm over my shoulders and pulls me against his chest. I lean into his body and try to absorb the heat from it, try to fill my hunger for warmth. "Where," he asks, "does the dragon keep its treasure?"

The answer to his question is in my head before I have time to think about it. "Zhun had two treasures. First, his knowledge. Second, his freedom. But our ancestors took his freedom from him." I whimper. Pain and sorrow tear at my chest, so powerful that I can barely breathe. Tears flood my eyes, and I start shaking with sobs for the imprisonment my ancestors caused the fire dragon. Golmarr's other arm comes around me and he holds me tight. The heat from his body radiates outward and clings to my skin, and after a short while, I stop crying. "What is wrong with me?" I ask, my voice hoarse.

He rubs his hands over my back. "According to Nayadi, my family's witch, when someone kills a dragon, a transference occurs. Its treasure automatically transfers to the slayer. You, Princess Sorrowlynn, slayed the fire dragon. Therefore, you inherited its treasure."

I inherited the fire dragon's treasure. My brain fills with sparks of light and bursts of color with that realization, and everything around me seems to solidify and bind together more perfectly than it ever has before. My feet connect more firmly with the earth, and the earth connects with my feet, like I have grown roots. I know this cave, every rock, every column, and I love it. I pull away from Golmarr's embrace and run to the lake, diving headfirst into the water. My arms cut through liquid, pulling me down. I trail my fingers over the sandy lake bottom and smile. When my lungs ache with need of air, I burst forth from the lake's surface and lie on my back, staring at the cave ceiling as I float atop the surface.

Within moments, my body begins to shiver, my teeth knocking together, and I swim to the shore and climb out. "I can swim," I say, grinning at Golmarr as water drips down my face and body.

He returns the smile, and wonder fills his eyes. "You're beautiful," he says.

My grin falters, and my heart pounds against my healed ribs. "So are you," I admit.

Golmarr tilts his head to the side, and his eyes turn fierce. "I'm beautiful? I thought only women were beautiful."

I shrug and shiver and laugh all at once. "Come on. I might know a way out of here." I bend and pick up the hunting knife from the sand path, securing it against my back.

"But we don't have a light."

"I don't need a light. I can find my way in the dark," I whisper, and take his hand in mine.

Chapter 12

We leave the dragon's chamber by way of the sand path. It leads to a narrow tunnel barely wide enough for Golmarr and me to stand abreast. When we have gotten far enough away from the sunlight streaming through the dragon lair ceiling that the cave is almost pitch-black, I stop walking and close my eyes. Somewhere, deep in my mind, is the knowledge of how to get out of this cave. I can *feel* it in there. My thoughts grasp on to a memory, and a face flashes in my mind's eye.

His blue eyes are what I remember, always twinkling and always far away, as if he lived somewhere else in his head—somewhere wonderful and bright, not the confining walls of my mother's castle. But they are not twinkling now. No, Melchior the wizard's eyes are flashing with determination as he hurries through the very tunnel I am standing in, a ball of brown light held in his outstretched hand. The ground beneath his feet rumbles, and he lengthens his stride. "Do not torch me yet, Zhun," he hollers. "I wish to see you face to face first, you vile worm. I have a message that needs to be passed on to someone."

Melchior? The word is spoken in the wizard's head, and I know it is the fire dragon. Come to me, slayer, and speak. And then I shall eat you alive for killing my mate and locking me under this mountain!

"*Yes, you shall,*" *Melchior whispers, and I feel the wave of apprehension that makes his old bones quiver.*

"Sorrowlynn?" Golmarr grips my upper arm and gives it a shake, pulling me away from the memory of my old friend.

"Wait," I say, focusing on Melchior. Finally, I know why he disappeared. He was eaten by the fire dragon.

"Sorrowlynn! We are not alone," Golmarr hisses, and I hear the familiar swish of steel sliding against a scabbard. Melchior vanishes as my eyes open, and without so much as a thought, I pull the hunting knife from my waistband and center my weight over my feet. The weapon feels perfect in my hand, like it has always been there. I slash the air with it, swinging it from side to side to test the balance, and smile. The horse king gave me a very well-made weapon.

Ahead, in the black depths of the tunnel, orange orbs are moving toward us: hundreds of them, a river of them flowing along the curve of the narrow passage. "*Mayanchi,*" I whisper. "If you thrust your weapon into their hide, their scales close around it, holding it in like barbs. That is why your sword got stuck in one," I explain. "Strike the underbelly. It is soft, with no scales."

Golmarr coughs. "All right," he says, voice unbelieving. He assumes a fighter's stance and waits for the *Mayanchi* to come to him, where there is just enough light by which to fight them. I do not wait. I charge the glowing eyes, blade grasped in my hand, my bare feet pounding the sandy ground, and for a split second I wonder what in the world I am doing. I don't know how to fight! Yet I do not slow.

I reach the nearest creature and my weapon blurs through the air as I roll to the ground, slicing the *Mayanchi*'s underbelly. One slice with enough force will kill it instantly. I know this like I have killed a hundred of these creatures. But this one does not die. I lift my arm to swing again, confused, and my muscles shudder and fail to do what I want. What I *need* them to do. I am weak.

Golmarr slides to a stop at my side, his blade dancing through the near-black tunnel as he battles the little *Mayanchi*. His muscles and body, unlike mine, are doing just what they should: fighting with strength and precision. For a heartbeat I watch him, silhouetted against the distant entrance to the dragon's lair, and reverence settles over me. He is well taught, his movements those of a disciplined warrior.

I roll to my knees and thrust my dagger into the *Mayanchi*'s underbelly. For a split second, I feel a blade pierce my belly, and a surge of desperate fear chokes me. My mind expands as the *Mayanchi*'s intelligence fills my brain, and all of a sudden, I *know* this small creature that I have just killed. Tears prick my eyes, and I drop my blade.

"Stop!" I wail, grabbing Golmarr's arm midswing to prevent him from killing again. "They mean us no harm!" Golmarr shoves me behind him to protect me, but I shove back, thrusting myself between him and the mass of glowing-eyed *Mayanchi*. "Stop it, Golmarr! I know what I'm doing!" The *Mayanchi* gather at my feet and hiss at Golmarr. "They mean us no harm," I say again, pressing my hands against Golmarr's chest to hold him back. "They mean *me* no harm," I add, turning my back to him—a human shield to keep him safe. "They served Zhun. Now I am ... the one they serve," I whisper, and shudder at the thought. I crouch down so my eyes are level with the little dragons' eyes and hope they can understand me. "I know I can't speak to your thoughts like the fire dragon did, but I forbid you to hurt him. Hurting him would be like hurting me. Go from here and be at peace." The mass of *Mayanchi* back away from us and then turn and disappear into the dark tunnel.

Warm fingers trail over my arm, and Golmarr turns me to face him. He stares at me with wide eyes, and his hand comes up to my face, his palm warm against my cheek. "Look at you," he whispers. He lifts my hair away from my neck and leans close, so his warm breath touches the skin below my ear. "You are glowing, Sorrowlynn. Your skin ..." His thumb brushes my collarbone, and my blood tingles in my veins. As he looks into my eyes, his hands trail down my arms and find my hands, and our fingers intertwine. When he lifts them between us, my fingers glow a pale gold between his shadowed fingers.

The light from my skin illuminates his face. He squeezes my hands and moistens his lips with his tongue, and I want to grab him and press my mouth against his, hard. I tear one hand from his and wrap it around the back of his warm neck, and pull his face toward mine, so close that I can feel the heat of his skin on my lips. He stares right into my eyes, and I can feel his breath quicken. And then I think of what is proper and what is not, and shrink away, pulling my hand from his.

I gasp, utterly mortified. "I don't know what came over me."

Golmarr clears his throat and brings his hand up to the back of his neck, and then a smile stretches his mouth wide. He shakes his head in obvious disbelief and lets out a big breath of air. Picking up the hunting knife from the ground, he presses the hilt into my hand, and his fingers linger on mine. "You need to clean that," he says. "Before the blood ruins it."

I nod and cut two pieces of bloodstained fabric from my skirt, handing one to Golmarr. As I run the material over my blade, I say, "If we follow this tunnel, we will come out on the side of a mountain overlooking the Glass Forest."

From the corner of my eye, I see Golmarr stand a little bit taller. "Really?" he asks, voice filled with wonder. "We *are* going to get out of here?"

I think of the blue sky and snowcapped peaks I saw through the dragon's eyes. "Really," I whisper, yearning for the freedom of open spaces, for the chance to see colors again.

His brow furrows. "How far is the exit? We don't have a food or water source."

The entire tunnel system takes shape in my head. It reaches as far north as the Wolf Cliffs, where my mother's castle is, and as far south as the mountains that create the northwest border of the Anthar grasslands. "It takes the *Mayanchi* two days. I know where water is along the way."

"What do the *Mayanchi* eat?" Golmarr asks, sheathing his sword.

"Little critters. Rodents, mostly, that live close to the cave's exits. For three centuries they have been bringing the fire dragon deer and elk, and anything else they could kill in the mountains. Sometimes they would eat part of that, but if Zhun got mad or too hungry, he ate them, so they brought the best food to him." I cover my eyes with my hand. "This is so weird to know so much."

"Here is what I don't understand. How do you know so much about the *Mayanchi*?"

"When I killed her—the *Mayanchi*—her knowledge merged

into my mind like the dragon's. I know everything she knew." The soiled cloth I've been cleaning my blade with drops from my hand. "Not only did I inherit Zhun's treasured knowledge, I also inherited the means to gather it the same way he did. Every time Zhun killed something, he stole its knowledge. Now I have that ability." With that understanding comes the feeling of being filthy. I cringe and wish I could take a bath.

"You took the *Mayanchi*'s knowledge? That's . . . interesting, for lack of a better word," Golmarr says. "And what about the fighting? How do you know how to fight all of a sudden? Fight like a *human*? If you got the fire dragon's knowledge, wouldn't you try to bite the *Mayanchi* to death, or gouge it with your fingernails, like a dragon would?"

Before I can answer, Golmarr grabs me from behind, one arm cinching around my throat, the other around my waist. Without conscious thought, I break his hold on my neck and ram my elbow into his ribs. I spin away from him and draw my blade, placing the tip at his chest.

"Whoa!" He jumps away from me and stumbles backward until he comes up against the cave wall.

My hand trembles as I slowly lower the hunting knife. "I didn't think about what I was doing," I say, shocked at my response to being restrained.

He grins and rubs his ribs. "That was intense. Do you remember what you did when I unhorsed you the day you tried to steal my father's stallion?" He doesn't wait for my answer. "You squirmed and tried to scratch me! That, what you just did, is not how a dragon would fight. It is how a human would fight. How a soldier would fight. A warrior. That is not how a dragon fights. So how . . ."

I know the answer to his question, and he hasn't even asked it. "I know how to fight like a human because Zhun stole the knowledge of every single person he ever killed—that was how he gathered his treasure: by killing. Every person he killed increased his treasure of knowledge. And it has all been transferred to me."

"So your head is filled with the knowledge of every single warrior that fought Zhun and died by his fire?"

"Yes," I say, and look at Golmarr with wide, shocked eyes. "I think I know everything there is to know."

He steps up beside me. "You need to add this to your knowledge. I promise I will never hurt you. Just don't accidentally kill me, all right?" He smiles, and it makes me feel soft and light and warm inside—a welcome change to how I *was* feeling.

I return his smile. "All right."

<hr>

We walk until we are too weary to take another step, and then sleep sitting up, side by side, with our backs against the cave wall and my head resting on Golmarr's shoulder, or his head resting on mine. We do it a second time, walking until we can go no farther, then sleeping side by side again. When we wake, we discover that the tunnel veers up and the air turns from damp and musty to scented with plants. My bare feet, battered and bruised once more, slip against the steep ground, and I fall more than once, scraping my knees each time.

Up and up we walk, and even though I start sweating with the effort, my fingers are like ice, and my teeth start to chatter. My muscles tremble with weakness from lack of food, and when I stand up too fast, blackness fills my eyes, and I fall back down. Golmarr isn't much better. I can see how his legs stumble beneath him, how his breathing is labored.

"Surely we will see light up ahead soon," Golmarr pants as we continue our climb.

Our steps become slower and slower, and I start walking with my eyes narrowed to mere slits, so when we walk around a giant boulder, it isn't until my feet step on plants, and drops of water splash against my face, that I realize, with a surge of pure joy, that we are out, and it is night, and the sky is merely concealed behind rain clouds. I fall to my bottom and run my hands over rain-soaked vegetation.

Golmarr plops down beside me and laughs a hoarse, weak laugh. "If I weren't so exhausted, I would kiss you right now, I'm so happy to be out of there," he says. "But I don't even have the energy to kiss a pretty girl."

"That's good," I say. "Because I am too tired to be kissed."

He lifts my hand. "You don't glow out here."

"I only glow if I'm underground," I blurt. Not caring that I am being rained on, I curl up on my side and close my eyes. Every time I start to drift to sleep, though, I shiver with cold and jerk awake, only to find Golmarr studying me with a frown on his face. Silently, he kneels beside me and lifts me into his arms. Cradling me against his chest, he walks back into the cave, leans against the stone wall, and sinks down to sitting. Holding me tight, with the warmth from his body easing my chills, I finally sleep.

Chapter 13

I wake and the first things I see are my scabbed knees looped over Golmarr's arm. And then I see my skirt, piled at the tops of my thighs, with my lacy bloomers hanging out, and have to fight the urge to jump out of his arms and yank it down. Carefully, I lift my head from his shoulder and peer at him. He is sleeping sitting up, his head tilted back against the cave wall, and he is snoring. Dark stubble that matches his eyebrows has grown on his face, giving him a very short beard that makes him look older than he is.

I ease my body out of his lap and he doesn't stir, so I creep out of the cave into radiant, stunning sunlight. I close my eyes and turn my face up to the sky and pull fresh air into my lungs. My arms come away from my sides, and I hold them out wide. I know how it feels to fly, how it feels to open my wings and have the wind snap into them. My heart aches with the knowledge that I will never fly. With a start, I force the thought out of my head and lower my arms. "Please get out of my head," I whisper. There is no response.

I am standing in a thick copse of dark green pines growing halfway up the side of a steep mountain. They are still wet from last night's rain, and every drop of water that is touched by sunlight glows like a diamond. I walk to the trunk of one of the pines and squat down, picking up a prickly cone it has shed. Tapping the cone against my hand, three nuts come out. I put one pitch-covered seed into my mouth and break the shell with my teeth. Inside is a soft, sweet nut. I smile as I chew it and start humming.

Holding out the voluminous fabric of my shirt, I begin filling it with pine nuts until I have gathered enough for a meager meal. Next, I crouch and run my hands over the wet vegetation and wildflowers. A small green plant catches my eye, and I know it is edible. I pick several handfuls and take them to the cave.

While Golmarr sleeps, I sit in the cave's entrance and shell the nuts. When I have nearly finished, I hear Golmarr stir. He steps behind me and rests his hand on my shoulder. I reach up to touch him and he gently squeezes my fingers. "What's this?" he asks, voice deep and rumbly with sleep. I peer up at him and can't help but smile. He can barely open his eyes to the sunlight, his sleeveless, burned clothing is a disgrace, and his dark hair is messier than a bird's nest.

"This is breakfast, lunch, and dinner," I say. He sits down beside me, and we eat our paltry meal in silence.

"Being an Anthar prince, I have eaten the best steak that my kingdom has to offer," Golmarr says, popping a green plant into his mouth. "No steak has ever tasted this good. Is this"—he motions to the remainder of our food—"something you were taught growing up in your cliffside castle, or is it part of the fire dragon's treasure?"

"I was taught only *important* things," I say with sarcasm in my voice, "like how to dance, how to walk with my shoulders squared, and how to smile without showing my teeth. When I wasn't being taught, I would read a lot—sometimes two books a day, but those were books about knights and silly princesses who could never save themselves. Nothing about how to survive in the wild. This food, and the knowledge of how to get it, is part of the fire dragon's treasure."

"Just think. If his treasure had been gold or jewels, we would still be starving right now. I know how to forage and hunt for food in the grasslands, but I have never learned how to do it in the mountainous terrain of your lands." Golmarr runs his hands through his hair, but they get stuck halfway. He winces. "Do you know anything about cutting hair?"

"I don't think so, but I can try to cut yours." I stand and pull my knife from its sheath, and Golmarr gets to his knees. I slide my hand between his neck and his hair, and he shudders.

"Why are you so cold?" he asks, clutching my icy fingers in his.

"I don't know," I say, and lift the fragile, burned strands of his hair. Placing my knife at the nape of his neck, I slice. Strands of hair fall over his bare shoulders and arms, and Golmarr groans.

I pause. "Does that hurt?"

"In Anthar, a man's strength is said to be tied to his hair. Faodarian men and Trevonan men have short hair. If I return home with short hair, I will be the laughingstock of the family. It hurts my pride to have it cut."

I stand in front of him and run my fingers through his hair. "If it makes you feel any better, I think you look nice like this."

"Nice?" he asks. "Not handsome? Or dashing? Or—didn't you call me *beautiful* once? But now I just look *nice*?"

I roll my eyes. "Cutting your hair does not change who you are in your heart. And, yes, you are very *beautiful*. No need to worry about that, but it is still brittle around your face," I add, hoping he can't tell that admitting he is beautiful brings heat to my cheeks. "Do you want me to cut it shorter?"

He cringes but nods, and I take my knife to it, carefully trimming the worst of the burned parts off. "What baffles me," Golmarr says, peering up at me as I work, "is how my hair is so burned if the rest of me isn't." He pats his chest. "And my clothes. How am I not charred nearly to . . . death?" Reaching up, he wraps his hand around my wrist, stopping the knife, and stands. "Sorrowlynn?"

I gulp. "Yes?"

With his hand still around my wrist, he narrows his eyes. "You said that before you killed the fire dragon, I was too injured to get out of the cave. Even with help. *How* injured was I? What exactly did the fire dragon do to me?"

"He flew at you. Do you remember that?"

Golmarr nods. "You screamed a warning. When I turned, the beast was nearly upon me."

"Do you recall anything after that?"

His brow furrows. "I remember a burst of light, and then I woke up and the fire dragon was dead."

"Did the burst of light hurt?"

Golmarr shakes his head, and his short hair swishes around his ears. "I don't remember it hurting. What was the light?"

"He blew fire on you, and you started burning. I put it out before it killed you."

"You put it out? How?"

"By lying on top of you," I admit, even though it sounds horribly scandalous. "I was wet from the lake. It was the fastest way to smother the flames."

His hand tightens on my wrist. "That was really brave. So, how injured was I? I have heard if you inhale dragon fire, you cook from the inside out."

"Your chest was covered with blisters, and you could hardly breathe."

He studies me with narrowed eyes and takes a deep breath of air. "If I was burned with dragon fire so badly that I can't remember it, then how was I healed? How did I wake up without a single burn? How am I able to breathe so well?" He touches his cheek. "And how did this go away?" I don't answer. "I assumed the dragon healed me like he healed you, but he didn't, did he?"

I shrug and stare at the ground between our feet, and try to pull my wrist from his hand, but he won't let go.

"*You* healed me." It is a stated fact. When I don't deny it, he puts his free hand beneath my chin and tips my head up, forcing me to look at him. "Did you truly heal me?" he whispers.

"Yes," I admit.

"Thank you." He pulls me against him and holds my head to his shoulder. "Thank you." The sun shines down on us and warms my hair, and I slowly sink into Golmarr and press my hands against his back. My eyes slip shut, and the thump of his heart matches mine, and I imagine our blood is pumping in perfect unison. He puts his palm over my ear, so his fingers are splayed in my hair, and I feel his lips on my forehead, and the sun seems to shine so bright against my eyelids I wonder if I am on fire. He leaves his lips there, and every time he exhales, his breath washes over my face and I breathe it in.

Memories of hundreds of other people's kisses fill my mind, and it is almost like I have experienced every single one of them. But I haven't. The urge to grab Golmarr's face, to tangle my hands in his chin-length hair and kiss him, makes my mouth water. I grip my hands tight behind his back and force them to stay still. I am a Faodarian princess. For me to initiate a kiss would be shameful—men are the ones who are supposed to do that. I think of the lace bloomers meant for my wedding night, which now hang below the level of my skirt, and giggle. I am shameful and scandalous and immodest and everything else I have been taught my whole life *not* to be. And I wish Golmarr would angle my face up and kiss me.

Golmarr releases me, and my hopes for a kiss are dashed. "Why are you laughing?" he asks, a touch of a smile on his mouth.

I look down at my clothing: the bloomers, the skirt that is more than halfway up my thighs—even my voluminous once-white shirt is missing the top two buttons. "I was just thinking how improper it would be for me to kiss you, but I think I have already crossed the line from improper to disgraceful."

One of Golmarr's eyebrows slowly rises, and he takes a long, slow look at my legs before meeting my eyes. "You were thinking about kissing me?"

I swallow and nod.

He leans in to me, so close that I feel his every exhaled breath on my face. "One of these days, you should give it a try," he whispers. "Probably sooner than later." He freezes there, his lips so close to mine that all I would have to do to kiss him is pucker. His lips thin and quiver, like he is fighting the urge to smile, and then he throws his head back and laughs. "I swear, Sorrowlynn of Faodara, you have more self-control than any woman I have ever known, and you are teaching me things I never knew I didn't know."

"Like what?" I ask.

"Like I really don't know as much as I thought I did. Especially when it comes to women." He cups the side of my face and says, "You make me feel things I've never felt before, and you make me want things I never thought I would want."

"Like what?" I ask again, mesmerized by his imperfections— the scruffy black beard that frames his lips, his tangled hair, the dirt smudged down the bridge of his nose.

"Like the kiss of a Faodarian princess. I think I want that more than I've ever wanted anything before." He smiles a crooked smile, and I catch my bottom lip in my teeth. "I'm looking forward to the moment you finally give in to that carnal nature of yours and get up the nerve to kiss me. Because in Anthar, the woman always kisses the man first." He winks, drops his hand, and turns away from me.

I press a trembling hand to my heart and force myself to take a deep, slow breath.

"We need to find water and shelter, and we need to get off this mountain. With the season starting to change, the nights will be cold at this elevation, as we discovered last night." He shrugs his quiver and unstrung bow onto his back. "How are your feet? Can you handle an afternoon of hard travel?"

"They are tougher than they used to be."

"Good." Without another word, he intertwines his fingers in mine, and we start down the mountain.

Chapter 14

My progress down the mountain is painfully slow. No matter how carefully I pick my way through strewn pine needles and lush undergrowth, something sharp or jagged always manages to find the soft arch of my foot.

Golmarr doesn't say anything about our pace. He stops every time we come to a stream and lets me rest as long as I want while we drink water and eat the watercress that grows along the streambed. Twice, he finds a snake sunning itself close to the water. He kills them both and guts them, then loops them over his belt.

The farther down the mountain we go, the steeper the path becomes, and the pine trees grow farther apart. And then, without warning, the trees end, and I am balancing on the edge of a cliff with Golmarr standing silent at my side.

The sky opens up—a spectacular blue dotted with patches of clouds—and seems to go on forever, stretching over the deep, uneven green of a forest far below: the Glass Forest. My heart seems to double in size as I stare at a sight more captivating than the costliest paintings hanging in my mother's castle, more breathtaking than the finest jewelry I have ever seen. I want to reach out and grab the scene in front of me, and hold it to my heart so that I never forget it. I yearn for wings so that I can fall forward from this cliff and glide on the air above the forest. I shake my head. That is what Zhun wanted, not me. Even so, tears of yearning fill my eyes and coat my lashes, blurring the scene below. I wipe them away and study the endless green. Something dark is circling above the forest, something that makes my nerves shiver a warning. From where I stand, I cannot tell what I am looking at, but my mind keeps whispering one word: *dragon*. My instincts tell me to hide or run. I grip Golmarr's shoulder and pull him into the shelter of the pines.

"Did you see that?" I whisper, too on edge to raise my voice.

Golmarr frowns. "See what?"

"There is something down there." I point to the Glass Forest. Golmarr lowers himself to his belly and crawls to the edge of the cliff. He stays there a long time while I hide in the shadows and watch. Finally, he creeps back.

"I didn't see anything," he says. "But we need to hurry and find shelter. There are tales of creatures living in the mountains above the Glass Forest. No one enters these mountains unless they have to."

"I have an idea," I say, and start searching the underbrush. After a few minutes, I find a pine bough as thick as my wrist and a little taller than my head lying on the ground. Taking the knife from my waist, I whittle away a patch of the spiky, sappy bark, just big enough for a handhold, and then use it as a walking staff.

"Brilliant," Golmarr says. "Now, let's hurry on and see if we can find some shelter for the night."

Shortly before sunset, the trail loops beneath the base of a steep gray cliff. Two giant rock slabs rest balanced against the cliff, their tops tipped against each other, making a triangular shelter that is closed on three sides. Already there is a shallow hole dug out of the shelter floor, with a few blackened sticks inside of it. I remember seeing a fire there before . . . except that is impossible, since I have lived my entire life behind castle walls.

"Let's spend the night here," Golmarr says. "You sit and rest your feet. I will gather wood and make a fire, and then we can cook these." He touches the snakes dangling from his belt. I do not know what my face looks like upon hearing we are eating snake for dinner, but Golmarr starts laughing. "Don't you eat snake for dinner in Faodara?"

"No! Do you eat it in your kingdom?"

He smiles and shakes his head no. "But I guarantee you, it is going to taste incredible. Fresh meat on an empty stomach is always a pleasure."

He hurries off, leaving me alone in the shelter.

A while later, he returns with his arms laden with wood, several different-sized strips of leather tucked into his belt, and his leather pants cut off above his knees, leaving his boots covering the lower half of his calves and the rest of his calves bare. Seeing a grown man's legs is almost as scandalous as seeing a man without his shirt on, and despite the fact that my legs have been bare for days, I blush and look away.

"Here." Golmarr holds two thin, sharpened sticks and the two snake carcasses out to me. "Thread the snakes onto the sticks like you're sewing stitches into cloth," he instructs.

I take the snakes and sticks, and before I have time to become squeamish, my mind and body know exactly what to do. Without even thinking about it, my nimble hands stab the stick through the snake flesh, loop beneath it, and pull it back out again, just like I am sewing. In less than a minute, the entire length of the snake is skewered. I do it with the other snake, and when I look up, Golmarr is staring at me.

"You've obviously done that before," he says.

I shake my head. "No, I have never touched raw meat before." I look at my hands in awe. "It is as if my fingers knew exactly what to do."

Golmarr studies me for a drawn-out minute. Finally, he says, "Like when you fought the *Mayanchi* in the cave."

"Yes, like that."

"I wonder what else you can do." He takes his unstrung bow from his back and a long string of leather from his belt, and then measures the leather where the bowstring should go, leaving a lot of slack. He ties a knot into each end of the leather and strings the bow with it. Next, he puts a dry, flat piece of pine bark on the ground and uses his foot to hold it in place. Last, he loops a stick through the loose leather bowstring and places the end of it on the bark. Holding the stick loosely in place, he starts sawing back and forth with his bow, making the stick spin quickly on top of the bark. Back and forth, back and forth he pulls the bow. The faster he does it, the hotter the spinning stick grows where it is pressed to the bark. After a few short minutes, smoke rises from the point where stick and bark meet. A moment later, a small orange flame jumps to life.

Golmarr sets the bow aside and deftly places a stack of brittle brown pine needles on the flame. For a minute, I think the fire has gone out. And then the needles burst with warm light as the fire devours them.

Golmarr lays the smallest sticks he's gathered onto the fire, and after they've been taken with flame, he places big, thick boughs atop it. When it has burned down a bit, I hold the skewered snakes close to the coals, and the mouthwatering aroma of cooking meat fills the shelter. When the snakes are browned and sizzling, I pass the bigger one to Golmarr, but he shakes his head and takes the smaller one for himself.

I hesitate for only a moment before biting into the bigger snake. Sinking my teeth into the hot meat, I pull the flesh from the bones and swallow without chewing more than twice.

"Good?" Golmarr asks.

"Yes. Very. Snake is my new favorite food." When nothing more than a long, narrow trail of vertebrae remains attached to the stick, I toss it into the fire.

Outside the shelter, full dark has settled over the land, and with it the air has grown uncomfortably cold. Golmarr steps out into the darkness and comes back with an armful of pine boughs, which he uses to block the triangular entrance to our small shelter.

He sits down beside me and we both stare at the fire. "I would like to ask you something," he says.

I hug my legs to my chest and rest my head on my knees so I am looking at him. "What do you want to ask me?"

His brows pull together, and his face loses all of its mischief. "This morning, you told me that the thought of kissing me is improper and disgraceful. Is it because I am Antharian? A *barbarian*?"

I open my mouth to tell him no, but he presses his fingers over my lips.

"I was not raised in a grand palace like you, and have never had servants wait on me hand and foot, but I am honorable and courageous and smart and strong—and as you yourself said, kind. I am a worthy match for any woman, no matter her rank. Even you." His voice trembles with passion and stirs my heart until it is beating so hard, I can feel it through my whole body.

His fingers drop away from my lips, and I hug my knees tighter and let the warmth from the fire heat my shins as the weight of his words settles over me. "When I said the thought of kissing you was disgraceful, it was because I have been taught that when a princess is being courted, she plays the role of the shy, naïve woman, and the suitor is in charge of initiating all intimate interactions. It is a role we are taught to play until we are betrothed. After she is married, she can take more liberties with her husband, but any other behavior would bring shame down on her family. Because I wanted to initiate the kiss, *I* was a disgrace. *Me.* Not you."

Golmarr nods and runs a hand through his hair. I watch the way the firelight moves over his face and think it is possibly my favorite face in the whole world. It is a face I could never get tired of looking at. "Is that why you jump away whenever we touch?" he asks. "Because you are scared of disgracing your family?"

"Jump away?" I ask.

"Yes, you jump away. If I touch you, you jump away. If I hug you, you push me away. If I look into your eyes, you look back for a long time, and then suddenly look away without any explanation. Is it because I am Antharian?"

I smile. "No."

"Then why do you?"

"I've never been around a boy my own age before," I answer.

"Look at this beard, Sorrowlynn," he says with a laugh, running his hand over the short growth darkening his chin. "I'm not a boy; I'm a man who—"

I reach forward and press my fingers over his lips, silencing him. His eyebrows slowly rise and his mouth curves up into a smile beneath my touch. The feel of his soft lips makes my head spin.

"If you want me to explain, be quiet," I say. His smile grows, but he nods, and I slowly remove my fingers. "When you look into my eyes, I want to act in ways that I have been told are improper and disgraceful, so I look away. And when you hug me, all of these emotions fill me and overwhelm me, and I can't breathe, so I step away to clear my head."

He studies me, his face uncommonly serious. "So in essence, the reason you look away or push away from me is because my mere presence makes you want to act in scandalous, shameful ways. In other words, you are fighting an internal battle to keep your filthy little hands off me."

I sit up tall and smack him hard on the shoulder. He leans away and starts laughing. "I didn't I realize I, an Antharian warrior, was so irresistible to you."

"You are a fiend, Golmarr!"

He stops laughing. "I'm just teasing you." He raises his hand and lets it hover over my shoulder. "Can I put my arm around you without you shoving me away?" he asks, his voice full of mischief.

"Yes," I say, and lay my head back down on my knees. He drapes his arm across my shoulders and his hand comes down on my arm. Gently, he runs his fingers over my shirt and I can feel the warmth from his fingertips through the fabric. He raises his hand to my neck and lifts my hair. I feel his warm breath on my skin, and then his lips as he places a kiss at the curve where my neck and shoulder meet. I can hardly breathe as excitement, fear, pleasure, joy, uncertainty—too many emotions to name—overpower me.

"That wasn't a hug, and I wasn't looking into your eyes," he murmurs against my ear, his voice a deep rumble. "Did that overwhelm you with emotions?"

I sit up and look at him with wide eyes. A smile spreads across his face, and I smack him on the shoulder again. "Stop teasing me, sir." He laughs and puts his arm around my waist, pulling me against him. I tilt my head onto his shoulder and turn my face toward him so my cold nose is on his neck. "I'm not pulling away," I whisper, and my lips touch his warm skin. He shivers and holds me tighter against him, pressing his chin to the top of my head.

I close my eyes and immediately feel the weight of sleep weighing on me. And then I see Ornald, my former guard, sitting in this very shelter, looking into my eyes, speaking to me, and I know what I am seeing is a memory passed on to the fire dragon by one of his victims.

"Is that why he forbids her to attend family functions?" Ornald asks, his eyes tight with anger.

"Did you suspect?" I am the one who says this, but it is not my voice. I look at my hands—large, thin, wrinkled hands—and a wave of shock ripples through me.

"I have suspected from the day she was born. She has my eyes and my height, and my darker hair. And she is not treated like a young princess should be treated." His nostrils flare with anger. "He is awful to her, Melchior. Every chance I get, I pass my pay on to

Nona and ask her to buy the child something nice so she doesn't feel the pain of living like a wretch when her sisters are given every indulgence their hearts desire." He runs his hand over his short beard. "Is he doing it to punish her, or to punish me?"

I think of the young Princess Sorrowlynn, always confined to her rooms, dressed in the worn castoffs of her sisters, eyes always shining with happiness and innocence despite her secluded life. "The child has known no other life, and Nona showers her with the sincere love of a mother. She is happy. Lord Damar treats her that way to punish you and her mother."

Ornald growls and jumps to his feet, pacing back and forth across the small shelter, his hand on his sword hilt. "Her mother? She is the queen! That child is her daughter no matter who the father is! Why doesn't she divorce her husband? She is miserable with him."

"Because her husband will kill the child if she takes any type of action against him, and she knows it. I have seen all paths concerning your daughter, and the queen has picked the path that will afford the child the longest life possible. It is a tangled web, Ornald, a puzzle that does not yet have enough pieces fitted together to reveal the whole picture. That is why I am going to see the fire dragon."

"What does a dragon have to do with any of this, Melchior?"

"He will give her the means to change the world. But she must know two things if she is to succeed."

Ornald crouches across the fire from me, green eyes intent. "What?"

"Once Sorrowlynn has obtained the fire dragon's treasure, the seven remaining dragons will hunt her down until they kill her, or she kills them. The reforged sword can cut through a dragon's scales, and the man who wields it will give his life to her, no matter what trials of his own he faces. And the first dragon is very close!"

Ornald stands and draws his sword.

"Wake up, child!" the wizard hisses.

Chapter 15

I gasp and lurch awake, pushing myself to sitting. Red coals are all that remain of the fire, and through the branches blocking the shelter's entrance, the sky is one shade lighter than pitch-black.

Golmarr sits up beside me. "What's wrong?" he whispers.

"The dragons are going to hunt me," I say.

Golmarr stands. "I know." He pulls his sword from its sheath, and it reflects the minuscule light from the embers.

"Your reforged sword. It can—"

"Cut through a dragon's scales," he says, finishing my sentence. Walking to the cave entrance, he peers out between the branches.

"How do you know that?" I ask. "Were you dreaming about Melchior, too?"

"Melchior?"

"My family's old wizard," I explain.

"No. Nayadi taught me everything she knows about dragons." He sits down beside me and lays his sword across his knees. "When I was born, she gave me a birth blessing unlike any ever given to my brothers or ancestors. She said, *This child shall be known as the first dragon slayer in a thousand years, and he shall wield a reforged sword.*" He turns the sword over in his hands, studying it in the dim light. "That is why my father gifted me a sword with a dragon hilt when I turned thirteen—because I have been told my whole life that it will be reforged by dragon fire one day." He laughs. "I think you can imagine my surprise to wake up and discover that you, Sorrowlynn, are the true dragon slayer. Suicide Sorrow, Dragon Slayer."

I don't laugh. "I wish I were not."

"Me too," Golmarr whispers. "Because now you are the one who will be hunted, not I."

He sheathes the sword and throws a log onto the fire, and I replay my dream in my head. I am not Lord Damar's daughter. I am the daughter of Ornald, the former captain of the guard, who got permanently demoted for intervening when Lord Damar whipped me. I always wondered why he stopped Lord Damar when no other man dared stand up to him. Now I know he was protecting his own child, and he paid a mighty high price.

I look at Golmarr and the reforged sword hanging at his hip. Melchior said the wielder of the reforged sword would give his life to me. Does that mean Golmarr will die protecting me? The thought makes my stomach feel emptier than ever, like the core of me has been carved out, but nothing is being put back in. How I wish I did not kill the fire dragon.

When the wood has caught the flame, lighting the shelter, Golmarr pulls the remaining scraps of leather from his belt. He sets them beside me and kneels at my feet. Placing his hand behind my bare calf, he looks up at me with a question in his eyes. "You're not going to turn into a warrior and hold me at knifepoint for touching you, right?" he asks.

"Not this time." I smile and he grins, flashing his white teeth. Carefully, he places my foot on an oval of leather. "Your pants?" I ask.

He nods. "I made holes around the edges and cut some long strips of leather into laces last night while you were sleeping." He starts lacing the leather shut, so when he is done, my foot is completely protected. "I found a better use for them," he says, moving to the other foot. When I am wearing makeshift shoes, I stand and try them out.

"They are perfect," I say, and have the urge to kiss him. Shoving aside everything I have been taught, I grab his shoulder and push up onto my toes, pressing my lips to his scruffy cheek.

Golmarr touches the spot where my lips touched. "Better," he says, "but my lips are a little bit farther to the left. You know, for the next time that urge overtakes you."

"I'll keep that in mind." I pick up my staff from the shelter floor and knock the branches out of the entrance.

A thin, fragile layer of frost has coated the foliage, and the morning is still. The western horizon is threaded with golden orange, the color of the fire dragon I slayed. With Golmarr in the lead, we start wending our way down the mountain, but after fifteen steps, I tug him to a gentle stop. "Not that way," I say when he turns to take what looks like the easier path. "This way." I point down a steep, rocky fissure littered with debris and dead wood, and can remember Melchior picking his way through it. "Trust me," I say. "I've been this way before . . . sort of."

Golmarr steps aside. "I trust you. You lead."

Down and down we go, and though my makeshift shoes slip and slide against my feet, creating friction, my skin is protected from the worst of the rocks and sticks, and we make good time. If we pass plants I recognize as edible, we sit for a minute and eat. It is at one of these resting stops that I notice Golmarr studying my hands. I look down at them, centered on the staff and about shoulder-width apart.

"You are holding that pine branch like it is a weapon," Golmarr says. "Were you given *any* type of defense training in Faodara?"

"None at all."

He grabs a long stick from the ground and a wicked grin lights up his face. Slowly, he gets to his feet, not once taking his fierce eyes from me, and positions himself in what I now recognize as a fighter's stance. Even dressed in rags, with dirt-smeared skin, he looks dangerous. His bare arms are corded with long, lean muscle, and without sleeves to mask it, I can see the width of his square shoulders.

"Try to hit my knuckles," he taunts, slashing the stick through the air like it is a sword. I stare at him, speechless, and he adds, "I bet you can't."

A smile tugs at my lips, and I stand, quickly surveying the ground for any obstacles. I lift my staff and realize Golmarr is right: I am holding it like it is a weapon. We stare at each other for a drawn-out moment, and I can't help but notice the green and brown of his eyes. Keeping my eyes locked on his, I swipe my staff at his knuckles. He grunts and leaps out of the way, bringing his stick in a wide arc toward my face. Without a thought, I lift my staff and block him. He uses his height and strength and bears down on my staff, and my weak arms start to tremble. Before they have a chance to give out, I twist toward Golmarr, making my short skirt twirl around my thighs, and press my back against the front of his body. With a sound thwack, I bring my weapon down onto his knuckles, just as his free arm circles my neck.

"You know how to fight with a staff," Golmarr says, though he is winded. I sag against him, barely able to stand on legs that feel like mush, and feel his body trembling against mine. "If we weren't both on the verge of starving, we'd be a lot better at that. We need to start building up your strength so your fighting skills will be more effective." He lowers his arm from my neck so it is braced across the front of my shoulders, and buries his face in my hair while he catches his breath. Golmarr lifts his head. "I think we will be in the Glass Forest before nightfall. I can fashion a snare and catch a rabbit or squirrel. And there are Satari in the forest. They might trade food for my knife." He holds his arm up, showing me the knife attached to it. His eyes wander to my bare legs. "Or maybe they'll give us food for free, if you do a little dance for them. They do have a reputation for liking pretty ladies."

I smack his arm with my staff and glare. "Absolutely not! That would be—"

"Scandalous, I know. That's the point," he says, slowly running his gaze over my legs. He bows low, a graceful bow that causes my heart to flutter, and holds his hand out in the direction of the Glass Forest. "After you, Princess Sorrowlynn."

Taking the edges of my ragged skirt in hand, I curtsy to him as deeply as I would curtsy to my queen mother. "Thank you, my lord Golmarr." When I stand, he is staring at me with wide eyes, and his cheeks are a shade pinker than normal. I laugh and he swallows, then shakes his head and blinks.

"Just don't curtsy for the Satari in that skirt . . . unless you want them getting a glimpse of your bloomers. Those are lace, aren't they?" He eyes the bit of material that hangs below my skirt with renewed interest.

It is my cheeks, now, that are glowing. "Yes, lace. They were for in case I married you. My wedding-night bloomers."

Golmarr clears his throat and rolls his shoulders. "I missed out on some scandalous bloomers," he says. I gasp and swing my staff at him again, but he jumps out of the way with a laugh. With me still in the lead, we continue down.

⊷ ⊱⊰ ⊶

The Glass Forest, we discover, climbs partway up the side of the mountain, choking the native pines until they are nothing more than skeletons shooting up into dense, wide leaves that hide the sky. The sunlight shining through the leaves is filtered to a murky, thick green. The air becomes damp with moisture, which curls along the ground in gray wisps, and Golmarr has to use his sword to cut our way forward through ferns and vines and wildflowers.

"Welcome to the Glass Forest," Golmarr mutters, hacking through a particularly thick vine. "Home of soldiers who deserted the Trevonan army; the Satari, who were chased out of their stone cities a century ago by the stone dragon; and all manner of foul bandits and ruffians who prefer living in a lawless land."

"It's beautiful," I whisper, touching the thick, moss-covered tree trunks as we pass them. "I have never seen anything like this." I stoop down and pluck a handful of tiny purple flowers from the ground, bringing them to my nose. They smell like peaches and vanilla. I start humming as I walk, and pick every new flower I see until I am holding a rainbow bouquet. "I have always wanted to see the Glass Forest, but I never imagined it to be this breathtaking." I press the flowers to my nose and sniff. Golmarr stops walking and looks me up and down. His dark brows furrow.

"What?" I ask, lowering the flowers and examining myself. My clothes look like a pile of rags draped over my body, and to think that they were once white almost makes me laugh. Now they are mottled gray, and the deep brown of old blood, like the very dirt beneath my feet. My left sleeve has a jagged tear in it, and my right sleeve is a torn, fraying mess that hangs above my elbow.

Golmarr sheaths his sword and untucks my baggy shirt, covering the knife at my waistband. Next, he crouches down and stands back up with a handful of damp soil. He studies my face for a moment and then wipes a streak of dirt down the bridge of my nose. I drop the flowers and force his hand away from me. "What are you doing?" I ask. "Am I not already filthy enough?"

He shakes his head and smears his hand over my chin and down my throat, covering my skin as far down as the two missing buttons expose it, all the way to the top edge of my camisole. I gasp and pull my shirt closed, and his eyes twinkle with amusement. "Sorry," he says. "But you're too beautiful. We need to make you as unattractive as possible."

"Beautiful?" I ask, thinking of my sisters, the true beauties of my family.

"Very beautiful." He examines me like an artist examining his painting, and then cradles the back of my head with one hand. Cupping my cheek in his other hand, he slowly wipes his thumb under my eye. "Almost perfect," he says. "But there's one more spot that I need to make far less tempting."

His thumb gently traces a smudge of gritty dirt over my lower lip, and I freeze. The hand cradling my head tightens in my hair. Golmarr stares at me and licks his lips, and I turn my mouth up toward his. I place my hands flat against his chest, and my thumbs extend past the edge of his vest and rest on his smooth skin. I can feel the crazy pounding of his heart, faster than my own. "It didn't work," Golmarr whispers, resting his thumb against both my lips. "Those lips are still begging to be kissed." He shakes himself and backs a step away from me. "You can't call me Golmarr while we are in the forest," he blurts, wiping a streak of dirt over his eyebrow.

With my heart still pounding from him smudging me with dirt, I nod. "I will call you Ornald."

"And you will be Jayah." I cringe at the name of Golmarr's sister-in-law—the woman who I thought would be my sister wife. "Jayah isn't so bad," Golmarr says, slashing a trail through the forest once more. "And speaking of Jayah, do you want to meet her?"

"No, not really."

"Are you sure? She is a great cook, and my brother, her husband, has some of the best cattle in my land. When I come home, they will throw me a feast."

"I don't care to meet her," I snap as I gingerly step over a rotting log with the aid of my staff.

He turns to face me. "Sorrowlynn, I am asking you if you want to come home with me," Golmarr says. He studies my face, watching for a reaction.

My mouth dances upward into a smile, and I bite my bottom lip, accidentally getting pieces of dirt in my front teeth. "Yes," I say, and the worry of where to go and what to do is lifted from me. "Yes!" I throw my arms around his neck and squeeze, and he hugs me so hard that my feet leave the ground. I stay in his embrace for a drawn-out moment, until he sets me down and steps away.

Once more, Golmarr starts whacking the bushes with his sword, and I stare at his shoulder, how it tightens and flexes with every slash. I want to press my fingers to his skin and feel the way it moves, feel the strength beneath it. I want any excuse to touch him.

The deeper into the forest we travel, the gloomier it becomes, until the air is so murky and dank, I almost feel as if I am beneath Zhun's lake again. The smell turns from damp to the cloying scent of wet clothes left in a heap too long. Mist rises from the ground, curls around the brown tree trunks, weaves between the ferns and flowers, and attaches itself to my bare legs.

A flash of the forest flickers in my mind, of trees coated with layer upon layer of mist that has frozen, until all the green is encased in ice, like glass. "So that's why they call it the Glass Forest," I muse, trailing my fingers over the damp, feathery leaves of a fern as tall as I am.

"Why?" Golmarr asks, peering at me over his shoulder.

"Because in the winter the mist freezes on the plants and they look like glass."

Golmarr shakes his head. "No, Jayah. The forest will freeze any time of year, even in the heat of summer."

I frown at Golmarr. "But how can that be? When it is warm . . ." I remember the creature I saw flying above the forest the day before, and think of *The History of Dragons*, a book too heavy to lift, which I was forced to read in the royal library when I was ten. "A dragon lives here," I whisper. "And it has breath of ice. The glass dragon."

"So say the legends, but no one knows that for sure. No one has *seen* a dragon in this forest and lived to tell about it for years, and no rumors of freezing glass have reached the grasslands since I was thirteen."

I shake my head. "No, the legend is right—the history books are right—and—" Golmarr presses a finger to his mouth for silence and waits for me to catch up to him.

"We are being watched by several Satari men, *Jayah*," he whispers. "Play along with whatever I say."

"Whatever you say, Ornald," I reply, gripping my staff a little more tightly. I whisper, "Will they try to kill us?"

"Not if we are lucky. The Satari are incredibly hospitable to anyone they do not consider threatening. If we'd been discovered by Trevonan renegades, we would have had to fight to survive." We keep walking, but Golmarr doesn't take the lead, opting instead to stay beside me. I scan the forest, looking for whoever is watching us, and see a tree trunk up ahead shift and move as brown-clad man steps away from it and then ducks into the thick green undergrowth.

"Ornald," I whisper. Golmarr nods his head so I know he also saw the man, and then he sheaths his sword and stops walking.

Chapter 16

"Come here," he whispers. I walk to his side. He puts his arm around my shoulders and presses his lips to my ear. "Stop holding that confounded walking stick like it is a weapon," he whispers. And then he looks into my eyes, and his eyes are narrowed, but he smiles so brightly that I can't help but smile back. "When your father finds out that we *aren't* married, he's going to kill me." Golmarr taps my nose with his finger and I blink at him. "At least we have a good excuse. Those bandits who stole everything—"

The hiss of steel being unsheathed fills the forest, and it comes from all directions. Golmarr's arm tenses on my shoulders, but he doesn't make a move for his sword. "Hello?" he calls, feigning surprise. Six brown-clad men step out from behind trees, and all of them have drawn swords.

"Satari," Golmarr whispers.

I force myself to keep only one hand on my staff and try my best to look like a helpless, weaponless girl who is lost in the forest.

"What have we found wandering our forest?" one of the men asks. Three gold loops hang from each of his ears, framed by thick, dark sideburns. He scratches his black-and-gray goatee with the hand not pointing a sword at Golmarr and studies us. We make quite a pair, Golmarr and me, with our torn and filthy clothes. The longer the man studies us, the more perplexed he looks, until finally he asks, "Who are you, and what has happened to you?"

"I am Ornald, from Carttown," Golmarr says, dipping his head in a quick bow, "and this is my true love, Jayah." He tries to press me forward as he introduces me, but I shove back against his hand. Golmarr chuckles, and the men surrounding us let their sword arms relax, though they do not lower their weapons. "Jayah and I were on our way to be married several days ago." He turns to me. "How many days do you think have passed since we should have been wed?"

I shrug, clueless as to how much time we spent in Zhun's cave, and the men laugh.

"Anyhow, we were sneaking off to elope—a union of the heart, not an arranged marriage—but somehow Jayah's father found out and hired a gang of thugs to stop it. They cut Jayah's skirt half off for the pearls sewn to the fabric and stripped us of all our belongings but my sword and this knife, which was hidden beneath my sleeve before I tore the sleeve off." He lifts his arm up, and the man with the goatee snaps and holds his hand out. Golmarr removes his knife and places it on the man's palm. "After that, they dumped us in the forest to starve or die at the hands of the forest dwellers." The armed men stand a little taller and nod, pleased with the conclusion of Golmarr's story. "We have had little to eat for days and are wondering if you might spare a morsel for my true love and me before we continue on our way."

The Satari leader's eyes narrow. "Why, pray tell, would the thugs leave a strong lad like you with your sword?"

Golmarr cringes. "Because I was conned into buying a piece of junk," he says, sounding pained. "The blacksmith said I was buying a sword that was the exact replica of the Anthar prince's famed dragon sword. But alas, when I tried to sharpen and polish it, I discovered the blade is not even made of real steel." Golmarr lifts his sword out of the scabbard just enough to show the base of the silver blade. "See? If I so much as cross blades with a well-made weapon, my sword will shatter." He lets the blade fall back into the scabbard.

The Satari laugh and return their swords to their sheaths. The one with the goatee grins, making his green eyes dance with mischief. "I am Edemond, patriarch of the Satari band called the Black Blades. It just so happens that we are having a feast tonight and you may join us, if you'd like."

"We would be honored to feast with your Black Blades, but we have nothing with which to pay for our food," Golmarr says cautiously.

Edemond shrugs and tests the balance of Golmarr's dagger. "I will keep your blade as payment. Tonight you shall feast with us, for we have reason to celebrate."

"Celebrate? What day is it that there is something to celebrate?" Golmarr asks, while at the same time I am struggling to figure out what holidays are close to my birthday. There are none.

"We celebrate the beautiful Princess Sorrowlynn and strapping Prince Golmarr." Edemond waits for us to react. I force my face to remain placid, something I learned by watching my mother.

"What about them?" Golmarr asks, tightening his hold on my shoulders.

"So you haven't heard? Not three days past, the horse clan rode through our forest, but they were short one son. The youngest, whose sword you purchased a replica of, was fed to the fire dragon along with the Faodarian princess. We heard that she chose death over being wed to a barbarian prince, and he chose to try and save her anyway." He frowns and mutters, "Young fools. Brave, but fools nonetheless. And so we feast in their honor! Come, my young lovers. A meal waits."

With three men in front of us, and three behind, we are escorted through the forest, along barely visible trails that wind between the trees. I use my staff as a walking stick even though my hands are itching to hold it like a weapon, and try to keep up with the Satari, but my body is so ravished with hunger that I can barely put one foot in front of the other. I take a step and stumble. Before I fall to the ground, Golmarr scoops me up into his arms. Gratitude warms my exhausted body, and I look into his eyes. They are so close that I can see the little flecks of gold around his pupils. "Are you all right?" he quietly asks.

"Just tired," I say.

"Let me carry you for now." I loop my arms around his neck, and he tightens his hold on me. I lay my head on his shoulder, and the Satari hoot and holler and make kissing noises as we walk.

"Carrying her over the threshold before you're married?" Edemond says, wiggling his eyebrows as he studies my bare legs. "You know, as patriarch of the Black Blades, I have the authority to marry you. It could be part of our evening festivities. A night you would *never* forget."

I choke on my own air and peer up at Golmarr's face. His cheeks are flushed, but he is smiling down at me so intently that my heart starts thumping against my chest. "What do you think?" he asks me. "Should we give getting married a second try? I don't think it could possibly end as badly this time around." I study Golmarr for any hint of how I am supposed to answer that.

"We will give you your own wagon for the night, too. A honeymoon wagon," Edemond says, stepping up to Golmarr and slapping him on the back.

"In that case, yes. Please marry us," Golmarr answers. "The sooner the better."

The Satari throw their heads back and laugh, and their joy rings through the misty woods. I stare at Golmarr, and he winks at me. Then he brushes a quick kiss on my forehead.

As the sun sets and the forest turns from green to an eerie, misty gray, I spot a caravan of brightly painted wagons positioned to form a giant ring around an area not quite so densely wooded as the rest of the forest. As we approach the wagon ring, Golmarr stumbles and nearly drops me, so I swing down from his arms. He leans forward, resting his hands on his knees. His whole body is shaking with exhaustion.

"We're almost there," I say, and lift his arm over my shoulders to take some of his weight. Edemond takes his other arm, and we pass between two wagons and enter the Black Blades' camp.

The air is filled with the smell of onions, meat, and smoke, and nothing has ever smelled better. Children are running about the camp, waving long, colorful ribbons tied to sticks, or they are play-sword-fighting by the light of the cook fires. Men and women are gathered around the fires, turning spits with whole boar attached, and stirring pans filled with browning onions. I stare at the pigs' crisping skin and want to gag. They look just like Golmarr did after he'd been cooked by the fire dragon.

"Are you well, lass?" Edemond asks.

"Well enough," I lie. "I'm . . . just surprised that your men cook." I peer across Golmarr to Edemond.

He raises one thick, arched eyebrow. "In Satar, the men cooked the food. It is a tradition we brought from our former stone city to the forest. Do the men in Carttown cook?" I shake my head, but I honestly have no idea. "Melisande," he calls, and waves his hand. A tall, striking woman dressed in a bright orange skirt and a pale green shirt steps away from a cook fire and walks over to us. Two giant loop earrings hang from her earlobes, and her dark hair is twisted into a bun over each ear. Her pale blue eyes take in the sight of Golmarr and me, and her steps slow.

"Who did you bring home with you this time, husband?" she asks Edemond. She purses her lips when her gaze finds my skirt.

"Two lovers who were wandering the forest and in need of food," Edemond says with a chuckle. "They want to be married tonight."

"You trust them?" she asks, eyeing Golmarr's sword.

"Enough to bring them to our camp."

Melisande nods and cups her hands around her mouth. "Mama, we need you!" she calls. A hunched, smiling woman starts walking toward us. Her hair is like white gossamer that is braided over her ears.

"Mama, my husband found a couple of ragamuffins wandering the woods." She glances at me sidelong. "He offered to marry them at our feast tonight. Can you help the lass get cleaned up a bit for the ceremony while I get the stone lanterns?"

The woman's wrinkled cheeks crease with a wide smile,

and she clasps her hands to her chest. "Young lovers!" she says. "A wedding! I will take care of her." She takes my hand in hers and leads me through the smoky clearing toward a small wagon. As we pass a cook fire, she calls for another woman to help us, asking her to fetch a lamp.

The wagon is dark inside compared to the firelit clearing. It smells like tea leaves and spices, and the wooden floor groans and creaks beneath our feet. After a moment, another woman enters carrying an oil lamp, and light fills the small wagon. Dried herbs and plants hang from the wagon's walls. There is a single, intricately carved stone chair in one corner of the wagon, and a very small bed beside it.

"Sit here, child," the old woman says, tapping the chair. She dips a cloth in a basin of water and hands it to me. "For your hands and face," she explains. I scrub my skin, and when the cloth comes away, it is filthy. She rinses it and hands it to me again, and I wash a second time.

Next, she takes a brush to my hair and starts humming as she quickly, but painfully, brushes the tangles from it. When that is done, she gathers the hair around my forehead and above my ears and pulls it back, braiding it behind my head so most of my hair still falls long and thick to my waist. "A traditional Satari wedding braid," she says. "You have nice, thick hair."

The woman who brought the lamp steps in front of me and wrinkles her nose. "Take that shirt off so we can dress you in something a little bit . . . less smoky," she says. My cold, weak fingers fiddle with the buttons on my shirt. When it is off and I am wearing only my stained camisole, the woman says, "Lift your arms." I do, and a soft, pale yellow dress is pulled over my arms and head. It has very short sleeves, so my shoulders are mostly bare, and it is too short, reaching just below the middle of my shins. "Slip that ruined skirt off," the woman says, and I let my skirt and petticoats fall around my ankles.

Finally, the old woman places a crown of dried yellow flowers around my head, so it rests just above my eyebrows. "Beautiful. Now you look like a proper Satari bride," she says, standing on her toes to kiss my cheek. "You don't even look like the same girl you did when you wandered into camp."

I smile. "Thank you . . ." I do not know their names.

"Call me *Mama,*" the elderly lady says with a smile. "I am the only living person left from the first generation of children born in the forest after Grinndoar, the stone dragon, forced my people to leave the kingdom of Satar. That makes me the oldest woman in this camp, so I am everyone's designated grandmamma."

"And I am Vivienne," the other woman says, and she kisses my cheek.

Mama leads me from the wagon to the side of a fire encircled by wide, flat logs for chairs. Golmarr is already sitting. His hair is wet and has been brushed away from his clean face, and he is wearing a fresh gray shirt and pair of brown pants. As I approach, his eyes slowly travel from my makeshift leather shoes to the flowers in my hair. When his eyes meet mine, a hint of a smile softens his mouth, and I find myself blushing, so I press my hands to my cheeks.

"Food for these lovers!" Edemond bellows, walking over to us, and a moment later a child holds a carved stone plate heaped with meat, onions, and singed flatbread out to me. The plate is warm on my fingers, which have never warmed up from the caves. "We are short on plates and seats," Edemond says when Golmarr isn't given anything to eat. "So sit on Ornald's lap, lass, and share that food with him."

Before I can inform Edemond that sitting on Golmarr's lap would most definitely *not* be proper, Golmarr's hands dart up and grasp my hips, pulling me down onto his lap. I open my mouth to ask for utensils just as Golmarr's freshly scrubbed fingers grab a slice of meat. He puts it into his mouth and his head falls forward so he is leaning against my arm and chewing as if he is so exhausted he can't even hold his head up anymore. Licking my lips, I grab a piece of flatbread and put it into my mouth.

Tears flood my eyes as I chew the hot, salty bread, and before I can swallow, they stream down my cheeks. Using a torn piece of flatbread like a spoon, I scoop up a mound of onions and cram them and the bread into my mouth. I do not touch the fire-crisped pork. Golmarr eats silently, devouring the food so fast I wonder if he chews before he swallows it. By the time I have taken four bites, my stomach feels like it is going to burst, and I force myself to stop eating.

"Are you done?" Golmarr asks. I nod and he devours the rest of the food so quickly, with such apparent need, I wonder how he's survived as long as he has on what little we've eaten. When the plate is empty, he wraps his arms around my waist and leans his head against my shoulder.

Three men sit beside the biggest fire and start playing flutes carved from pale stone. I sit in the firelit glade and listen to the music, and blush every time anyone looks at me, for it is beyond scandalous to sit on a young man's lap.

By the time full darkness has settled over the forest, Edemond wanders over to us. He has changed into a crimson shirt and matching trousers, and has a braided cloth belt woven with gold thread at his waist. "I am ready to perform your wedding. Are you finished eating?" he asks, a knowing smile on his face. Golmarr and I both nod. "Then let us marry you!" Edemond hollers so everyone in the camp can hear. The musicians stop playing, and men start moving log seats away from the biggest fire, clearing an open space in front of it. Women bring stone oil lamps to the cleared space and place them around its edges, making a circle of light.

"Golmarr!" I whisper. "We aren't truly going to be married, are we?"

He looks at me with heavy eyes. "Don't you want to marry me?" he asks. When I do not answer, a slow smile spreads over his sleepy face. "He won't be using our real names, so it won't be binding." This information sends an unexpected pang of regret through me, and I frown. Golmarr's smile grows wider. "Although I'm pretty sure you're finally going to have to give in to that carnal nature you've been fighting and kiss me."

I look around and swallow down a surge of panic. "In front of all of these people?"

He laughs and nods. "Yes. So make it convincing, or they might kill us yet."

I glance at his upturned mouth and feel woozy at the thought of finally putting my lips to it. If the price for kissing him is a fake wedding and Satari witnesses, then I am ready to get married. I take his hand in mine, pull him to his feet, and practically drag him to the space the Satari have cleared for us. When we are inside of the glowing ring of lamps, the forest grows quiet as the Satari settle down to watch a wedding.

I face Golmarr, with the Satari to my left, and the fire and Edemond to my right. The orange firelight glows on half of Golmarr's face, shading and highlighting his square chin and cheekbones and lips. He reaches forward and takes my hands in his, and stares at me, eyes intense. His hands are like ice in my chilled hands.

"As the direct descendant and heir of King Haggoth, the final ruler of the kingdom of Satar before Grinndoar the dragon forced us from it, I have the authority to marry these two people, by their own free will, in front of these witnesses." He clears his throat. "Ornald, repeat after me," Edemond says to Golmarr. "I, Ornald, vow to love, protect, and care for you, Jayah, until the day I die."

"I, Ornald," Golmarr says, "vow to love, protect, and care for you, Jayah, until the day I die." His hands tighten on mine, and he smiles a hint of a smile.

"Jayah, repeat after me," Edemond says. "I, Jayah, vow to love, protect, and care for you, Ornald, until the day I die."

"I, Jayah, vow to love—" My voice catches on the word *love*, and tears fill my eyes and stream down my cheeks for the second time that night, even though the words I am repeating are not truly binding. I clear my throat and say, "I vow to love, protect, and care for you, Ornald, until the day I die."

Sniffles fill the quiet forest. The women are dabbing their eyes with bright, multicolored handkerchiefs.

"Very good," Edemond says. "I, Edemond ap Haggoth, rightful king of Satar and patriarch of the Black Blades, pronounce you husband and wife. Now kiss three times to bind it."

I stop breathing and stare at Golmarr. He tightens his grip on my hands and pulls me closer, and his eyes narrow. And then he waits. Reaching up, I put my trembling hands on his shoulders. I stand on my toes, tilt my chin up, and lean into him. Our lips barely touch, and as I breathe in, I inhale his breath. After a moment, he pulls away and raises his eyebrows.

More convincing, I think, and all the kisses that were passed to me when I inherited the fire dragon's treasure come flooding into my mind. I slide one hand behind Golmarr's neck and pull him toward me a second time. When his lips touch mine, I press my mouth more firmly to his, and my blood seems to fill with fire. I close my eyes and slide my hand into his hair, and then I slowly move my lips against his.

He gasps and breaks the seal of our lips and leans his forehead against mine, staring into my eyes. Grabbing my face in both his hands, he pulls me possessively to him, and his mouth finds mine. His lips part and coax mine open, and he kisses me with the same urgent hunger with which he just ate his meal. I twine my hands in his hair and get lost in the taste of him, in the feel of his body against mine, in the way—

"All right! To the wagon with you lovebirds, before we have to cover the children's eyes!" Edemond calls, and Golmarr gently pushes me away. He stares at me, eyes filled with wonder and want, and I know my eyes look the same. "Unless you'd care to join us in some dancing?"

Golmarr wraps his arm around my shoulders and presses his mouth to my ear. "As much as I would love to dance with you again," he whispers, "I don't think I have the energy."

I shake my head. "I don't, either."

"The wagon, please," Golmarr says, and the spectators start to hoot and holler as the musicians begin playing their flutes once more.

"This way," Edemond says, and starts walking to the wagon ring that encircles the camp. Golmarr grabs my hand in his, palm to palm, weaving our fingers together, and we follow the man who should be a king to a sunset-pink wagon. "I wish you a good night," Edemond says with a wink, leaving us at the door.

Next to the door hangs a copper bell that has turned turquoise with tarnish. Inside, a stone oil lamp is burning, and someone has brought my staff to the wagon. A beautifully carved stone basin with water and soap is at one end of the wagon, a small table is in the middle, and at the other end, a narrow bed barely big enough for two people. Golmarr shuts the door and sinks into a chair at the table and starts unlacing his boots.

"When I said to make the kiss convincing, I meant for the Satari. Not for me," he says, eyes guarded. I blush and thrust my hands into the basin. The water is hot!

"What did I convince you of?" I ask with my back to him.

He stands. "You convinced me that . . ." I lift my hands from the water and turn to him. He steps up to me and puts his hands on either side of my face and runs his thumbs down my cheeks. "Even though that ceremony wasn't real, your crying was real when you spoke your vows," he whispers, and then he kisses both of my cheeks. My eyes flutter shut at the feel of his soft lips on my skin, and I lay my hands flat against his chest. He kisses my forehead, letting his lips linger there for a moment, and then turns from me. "I will sit with my back to you while you get clean."

Quickly, I soap and splash my face and neck, then wet one of the rags beside the basin and rub it in the soap. I scrub and rinse my body as much as I can without taking my clothes off.

When I am done, my damp skin is covered with goose bumps, and Golmarr is snoring in the chair, his long arms dangling limp at his sides. I gently shake him awake, and he stumbles to the basin as I slide the hunting knife from my waistband and put it on the table. Barely able to keep my eyes open, I crawl into the bed, curl up beneath the smoke-scented blankets, and listen to the music and laughter ringing through the forest.

As I am drifting to sleep, I feel Golmarr climb onto the bed beside me. I turn to face him and rest my head on his bare shoulder. He's not wearing his shirt, and for a heartbeat I consider sleeping on the floor. But he is warm, and I am too weary to worry about following rules of etiquette. . . . I *want* to sleep curled up against him—want to sleep nestled in his arms. I lift my cold hands to his chest and press them to his skin, and he shudders. "Your hands are like ice," he whispers, and wraps his arms tightly around me. I sigh with contentment. Before I can tell him he smells nice, I am asleep.

Chapter 17

I jolt awake and find myself in darkness, and for a heartbeat I think I am back in the caves until I realize I can see the first hint of dawn shining through two small windows. Holding my breath, I listen for what woke me. The wagon is still and quiet. Outside, the faint sounds of frogs and crickets fill the night, but nothing more. I settle back down against the warmth of Golmarr and stare into the darkness as I wait for my pounding heart to slow.

"What's wrong?" Golmarr asks, voice deep with sleep.

"I don't know," I whisper.

Golmarr runs his warm fingers across my bare arm, and my skin prickles with goose bumps. He pulls the covers up over my shoulder and tucks them under my chin. "I know you are from a much cooler climate than I, but are you always this cold?" he asks.

I burrow closer to him and put my freezing nose against his neck. "I didn't used to be. It started in the cave. Wading in the water made me cold. And when I healed you, it was like all the warmth went out of me and never came back."

Golmarr's body stiffens and he lifts his head. "That

doesn't sound good. How, exactly, did you heal me? Maybe if we can figure that out, we can figure out how to warm you up again."

"I don't know how I did it, exactly. I think healing is part of the dragon's treasure."

"Tell me how it happened," Golmarr says, clasping my hand in his and holding it over his heart.

"Every time you took a breath, I could hear fluid bubbling in your lungs. Your chest looked like the wild boar that the Satari were roasting." I cringe at the memory. "You were moments from death, but when I touched your face, I knew how to heal you. I felt all the things inside of me that were good, and then they came out of my mouth and went into yours. When you breathed them in, your body healed."

"I took part of your life," Golmarr whispers. Beneath my hand, I feel his heart speed up. "Sorrowlynn, what if healing me kills you? What if you slowly get colder and colder until you die?" Golmarr curses under his breath and runs his hand through his hair. "How can you restore your life?" he asks.

An answer surfaces in my thoughts, and I frown, for it seems too simple. "I need to warm up with fire."

"That's it?" Golmarr asks.

I shrug. "I don't know. We stood by the bonfire last night, and it didn't help."

He puts his finger under my chin and turns my face up to his. "Do you realize you are now magical? You are a witch, like Nayadi. A seer. A healer. A sorcerer. The ability to do magic is so rare and so coveted, if anyone finds out, kings will wage wars to own you."

"I don't feel magical." I close my eyes. "All I want is to be warm again, and to never worry about where I am going to live, or what I am going to eat. I don't *want* to be a witch. I do not want wars waged over me."

"Let's keep it secret. I swear I will never tell anyone. If no one finds out, you will be safe. Was magic part of the fire dragon's treasure?"

As he asks the question, I immediately know the answer. "No. When he ate my arm, my elbow was a bloody stump, and when I stabbed his eye, his blood mixed with mine. Zhun's blood contained his magic, and the magic he stole from Melchior." I still remember the burning of his blood on my wound, and the heat that spread from my arm to my heart, until it was pulsing through my entire body. "A dragon's magic is in its blood. If it mixes with human blood, that person becomes a magical being," I whisper as the realization takes hold of my thoughts.

Yes, a soft, lilting voice says in my head. And it is a truth that must be silenced.

I gasp and sit up. That voice echoing in my head is what woke me. It is the way a dragon communicates. "The glass dragon is coming!"

"How close?" Golmarr snaps.

"I don't know."

Golmarr throws off the covers and leaps for the wagon door, slamming it open. Reaching out, he rings the copper bell. "Dragon!" he yells. "The glass dragon is coming!" I sit up and hang my legs over the side of the bed. Golmarr grabs my staff and my knife and presses them into my hands. Sitting on the chair, he fumbles in the dark for his shirt and boots.

Outside, other bells start ringing, filling the dawn with clanging. Men are yelling, women are barking orders, and children start crying. Our wagon door opens, and a barefoot

Edemond steps inside holding a smoking lantern. "You sounded the alarm?" he asks, his eyes bleary with sleep.

Golmarr nods. "The glass dragon is coming. How do we survive its breath?" he asks.

"Stay indoors. Shut all the wagon windows. Don't let it breathe its icy breath on you. If you have shelter, the ice won't suffocate you. But"—he looks out the door at the lightening forest and rubs his goatee—"there hasn't been a sighting of the glass dragon in more than five years, since the last time it froze the forest."

I shake my head. "No, that's not true. I saw the glass dragon flying over the forest yesterday."

Edemond scoffs. "The good thing about the forest is it is so dense, you can hide anywhere. The bad thing is you can't see the glass dragon when it is flying because the trees are too thick. The forest keeps it hidden. So how, pray tell, did you see the glass dragon yesterday?" He is giving me a condescending look, as if I am a child caught in a lie.

"I was on the side of the mountain," I snap.

"You were on the side of the mountain? But that is Gol Mountain—the fire dragon's mountain. Anyone who sets foot on that mountain is killed by little black dragons and dragged belowground." Edemond looks from me to Golmarr, and then his eyes rest on Golmarr's sword hilt. His forehead creases, and he holds up his lamp and looks at Golmarr again, leaning toward him and scrutinizing his face. "How do you know the glass dragon is coming?"

"If Jayah and I run, there is a good chance the glass dragon will follow us and your camp will be safe," Golmarr says, ignoring Edemond's last question. "But how do we survive its breath if we have no shelter?" He stands, and his head almost brushes the wagon's ceiling.

Edemond looks up at him and swallows. "You can't survive," he says. "But the dragon never touches down in the forest. You will be safe here."

"No, we won't," I say, standing and putting the hunting knife securely in my waistband. "The glass dragon is going to touch down because it is coming for *me*."

"Hurry, man!" Golmarr shouts. "We need to get out before the glass dragon kills your people! How can we survive out there?" He turns to me. "Do you know?"

"If we were dragons, we would just have to breathe fire," I blurt.

"That won't work for us."

"It is said that a thick cloak will protect your skin and lungs if you have no other choice," Edemond says. He pushes past me and pulls open a drawer beneath the bed and starts pulling out clothing. At the bottom are several cloaks. He fingers through them and hands me two deep green cloaks, the same color as the forest roof. "Those are the thickest."

I put the smaller cloak on and hand the other to Golmarr, but before he can put it on, a splitting crack reverberates through the morning, like lightning striking so close that no thunder follows. Women start screaming and dogs start barking. Something thumps down on top of the wagon, and outside, leaves are floating through the air like green snow. Golmarr throws the cloak on and pulls the hood over his head, and runs out of the wagon. Holding my staff like a weapon, I follow.

Chapter 18

Pale blue mist as smooth as water glides along the forest floor. Every time Golmarr takes a step, the mist twists and swirls around his knees and follows him. People are running through the clearing, some carrying babies, some holding bedding, some wielding weapons. "Get inside now," Golmarr bellows in a voice stern with authority. It carries with it a twinge of familiarity, and I realize I am hearing the voice of a future king.

Something cracks again, and the top half of an enormous tree splits and plummets to the ground. Branches thicker than my waist snap from the trunk, and splinters of wood sail through the air. I throw my arm up and shield myself with the cloak. When I lower the cloak, a foot with moss-colored talons steps into the clearing, followed by another as a green dragon settles onto the misty ground.

The sound of muffled screams resonates through the clearing, and faces are pressed against wagon windows, watching.

The glass dragon's black wings fold against its dark green back, and it blinks red eyes as it studies me. Instead of the spiraled horns the fire dragon had, a stag's horns, black as midnight, shoot out from this dragon's head like twin branches that touch the forest canopy. I hear its laughter in my head and want to run. **You defeated Zhun? You?** it croons, its words quiet and tempered. I quiver and cling to my staff, and wonder what to do. From the corner of my eye, I see Golmarr draw his sword and dart out of the wagon circle, so it is just me facing the glass dragon.

My knees tremble, and my hands grow damp against the wood of my staff. "You will die by your own hand, Sorrowlynn," I whisper to myself. I find enough courage to call, "Leave me alone, and I will never breathe a word."

The dragon hisses and swings its tail, slamming it into a canary-yellow wagon. The side of the wagon is smashed to bits, and it tips over. A man and woman and three children climb out of the ruined wagon and run to another, but the dragon's eye doesn't even glance toward them.

The problem with humans is they never keep their promises. Pain and money are the great tools to make a fool talk. If I have learned one thing in my long life, it is to never trust a human, it says, and my mind is filled with so much hatred that I gag on the vile taste of it.

The glass dragon's muscles flex beneath its thick green scales, and it lashes its tail at me. I dive to the side and roll out of the way, and then spring back to my feet, brandishing my flimsy pine staff like it actually might be a formidable weapon against a dragon.

The creature laughs again, a sound so loud and grating that I throw my hands over my ears and whimper, but the laughter is coming from inside of my head. I cannot stop it no matter how I try. The laughter quiets, and I peer at the dragon just in time to see it pull its head backward and then thrust it at me, mouth open so wide I can see past its rows of fangs, deep into the blackness of its throat.

My body acts without a thought. I lift my arm over my

shoulder and throw my staff as hard as I can, right at the deepest part of the dragon's throat. As the weapon leaves my hand, I fall to the ground, swinging the cloak over me and pulling it tight around my head and shoulders.

The smell of winter engulfs me. Icy air whips at the cloak, blowing it from my ankles. Searing cold bites at my bare skin, and I scream. The cloak grows tighter, pressing on me, squeezing against my body until my bones want to crack, and I cannot move. The ground beneath my forehead turns frigid as a fine dusting of ice crawls over it like hair-thin veins, and then my hair freezes. I struggle to breathe against the pressure of the cloak but can barely inhale.

Someone yells something, and I recognize Golmarr's voice. "Help!" I gasp. The sound stays trapped in the cloak. I dig my fingers into the frosty ground and push against the cloak with all my strength, but I cannot move.

The cloak shudders around me, and then I feel it crack and split, allowing me to gasp a breath of air so cold I feel it stab into the deepest part of my lungs. The cloak cracks again and is tugged away from my head. Warm hands claw at my shoulders, and I stare into the frantic face of Edemond. "Hurry, lass!" he barks. He is holding a frost-tipped ax in his hand.

I try to move, but my feet are stuck. Edemond pulls harder against my shoulders, and I feel ice scrape my bare, numb ankles, feel the leather shoes torn from my feet, and then I can move. I crawl out of the frozen cloak and let Edemond drag me to the wagon I slept in. He shoves me inside and pulls the door shut behind us, slipping a wooden bar in place to lock it. "The young Antharian horse lord," Edemond says, his voice filled with excitement. He presses his face to the window and motions me over. "Look! The creature fears him!"

Trembling with cold, I stand beside Edemond at the small window. The clearing looks like something from a fairy tale. The foliage and wildflowers have been perfectly preserved beneath a thick layer of crystal-clear ice, and the trees look made of colored glass. I see my green cloak, frozen to the ground like the cracked shell of a turtle, and shudder.

At the farthest edge of the clearing, Golmarr is standing before the glass dragon, his curved sword held in both of his hands. The blade gleams a pale blue in the light of dawn. The beast's head is lowered so it is level with Golmarr, and it is circling him, its massive claws shattering the ice with every step. It pulls its head back to blast him with cold air, but Golmarr uses the motion to his advantage, leaping forward and slashing.

The dragon stumbles backward, crashing into two wagons and knocking them onto their sides. Golmarr dives toward the beast and rolls between its feet. When he tries to stand, he slips on the ice and slams down onto his back. Even through the window, I can hear the crunch of his head against the frozen ground.

"No!" I shriek, and turn from the window. With unsteady hands, I fumble with the lock, then throw the door wide and run back out into the clearing. The scene before me freezes my blood. Golmarr is flat on his back, his sword arm motionless on the ground, and the dragon is lifting its great, clawed foot over him.

"Golmarr!" I scream, and try to run, but the ice is too slick. My bare feet move, but they do not carry me forward. The dragon splays its claws, and as its foot comes down, Golmarr bursts into action, rolling to the side as the talons shatter the ice where he was a moment before. Golmarr holds his sword in both his hands and swings his blade at the back of the dragon's ankle.

The creature shrieks and stumbles to the side, and Golmarr climbs back to his feet. He swings his sword over his head and stabs forward, aiming for the dragon's chest. An intense hatred grips my head so strongly that I grab my hair in my hands and scream. Suddenly, I know what this dragon's treasure is. "Don't kill it!" I shriek. "Don't kill it, Golmarr!" Just as the tip of his sword pierces one of the scales on the creature's wide chest, the dragon opens its black wings and lifts its body into the air. Great drops of crimson blood rain down from its injured leg as it flies over the clearing and disappears behind a shield of leaves. Where the dragon's blood has landed on the ground, the ice is bright red and steam is rising up into the air.

Golmarr wobbles and collapses to his knees. I slip my way toward him and slide to a stop at his side. Dragon blood streaks his sword blade, and on the tip is a gleaming emerald dragon scale with a small patch of bloody skin still attached. Taking his head in my hands, I gently probe the back of his skull. A bump as big as a chicken egg has already formed beneath his scalp. Careful not to cause him more pain, I part his thick black hair over the wound to make sure it isn't bleeding, but yelp and lurch away, pulling my leg from his grasp. Pain is pulsing up my calf.

Golmarr reaches out and wraps his fingers around my ankle again, and the pain intensifies. His fingers are as hot as live coals. "Stop!" I hiss, and look down at his hand to see what is wrong with it. My skin is pale blue between his fingers.

"We need a fire as quickly as possible!" Golmarr yells. People are poking their heads out of their wagon doors, warily peering between us and the sky. "Please, someone help us! We need a fire as quickly as possible!" he calls again. No one leaves their wagons. "We just risked our lives to save you," Golmarr growls. "If you help her, I promise that we will leave your camp as soon as we are well enough to."

Edemond, still holding the ax he used to break me free from the ice, comes out of the pink wagon. "Alfenzo, Matteus, start breaking the ice so we can light a fire. Stefano, get kindling! I will get the wood." Still barefoot, he hurries outside of the wagon circle, and a moment later, I hear the rhythmic thumping of an ax.

"I need blankets!" Golmarr shouts. "Jayah needs to warm up!" His voice is panicked.

"I'm fine," I say. Golmarr lifts the skirt up to my knees. Blue veins are creeping up my legs beneath my skin. When I touch one, it is as cold as ice. And then I realize I cannot feel the ice beneath my bare feet. "My feet are numb," I whisper. Golmarr pales and lifts me off the ice.

Wagon doors open and women laden with piles of blankets in their arms come out. Not giving a care about the ice, they all make their unsteady way toward me and, one by one, place the blankets at Golmarr's feet. He grabs one and swings it around his shoulders and me, hugging me to him.

"I'm fine," I protest, and try to push the blanket away, but my fingers are numb with cold and too stiff to bend. My heart begins pounding with fear, and when it does, I can feel the ice start speeding through my body. "Golmarr?" I whisper. "I can feel it in my blood."

Frantically, Golmarr starts rubbing my arms with his hands, trying to force warmth into my skin as a group of Satari women circles us.

Mama puts her frail, wrinkled hand on Golmarr's bare fore-arm. "We have bed-warming pans in several of the wagons. Melisande is getting them. Can you get the girl indoors, young horse lord? We can warm her better inside."

He presses on the back of his head. "I'm too dizzy to walk with her." The words come out in a sob. "Is she dying?"

I shake my head vehemently, but the old woman nods. "Her flesh was touched by dragon breath. Your wife is going to slowly freeze to death."

Golmarr's arms start trembling. "How can we save her? There has to be a way!"

"Fire," I whisper, and yearn for the scorching heat of flames against my skin.

"We have to melt it out of her before it freezes her blood. It is going to hurt, but it has to be done," the woman explains, her dark eyes filled with sympathy. She pats Golmarr on the shoulder. "I'm sorry, lad." Turning from him she calls, "Enzio, come help this young man carry his wife to a wagon."

A gangly boy about my age, with narrow shoulders and curly, dark hair, steps forward and carefully walks across the ice to us. He holds his arms out for me, but Golmarr doesn't let me go. "Golmarr, I'll be all right," I whisper, running my stiff fingers through his hair. With a pained groan, he lets Enzio take me.

Despite his narrow frame, Enzio easily carries me to one of the biggest wagons. As the door shuts behind us, I can hear Mama giving orders to bring more blankets and hot broth to the wagon. Gently, Enzio lays me down on a bed and wraps the blanket securely around me, tucking it tightly beneath my feet. A woman enters the wagon with a brass bed-warming pan in her hands. She smiles at me and places the pan beside my feet. Another woman enters with a warming pan and puts it by my calves. More women come, each with a bed-warming pan, until I am surrounded on all sides. Next, they bring blankets and start layering them over me.

Enzio returns with Golmarr and helps him sit at a chair that has been moved beside the bed. Golmarr reaches beneath the covers and takes my hand in his.

"Your fingers are a little warmer," he says. "How are your feet?"

I wiggle my toes and whimper as a gush of hot blood circulates through them. "They're burning," I say. Tears fill my eyes and trickle out of the corners. Each tear feels like fire on my skin. The scorching heat in my feet starts slowly flowing upward, making my legs feel as if the skin is melting from them. More tears fill my eyes, and then I start quietly crying. "It hurts," I moan. "Get the covers off of me!" I start struggling against the blankets, but Golmarr stands and pins my shoulders down.

"You have to warm up," he says, his eyes severe. I fight against him, but my body is still stiff with cold, and I can barely move. I wail and moan, and more tears burn their way down my temples and into my hair.

"It burns!" I shriek, thrashing against the covers. "Let me go!"

"I'm sorry," Golmarr whispers, pressing more firmly against me. I arch my back and try to fling myself from the bed. "Enzio?" he yells. "Enzio! I need your help!"

Enzio steps inside and, without any instruction, pins my ankles to the bed. Kicking and shrieking, I try to break their hold until I am so drained I cannot find the energy to fight. Defeated, I close my eyes and sob while the heat pulses in time with my heart, and every pulse sends it higher up my body until it reaches my neck. When it gets to my face and scalp, the fire beneath my skin cools into comfortable warmth, and my eyes grow heavy. My body sags with relief, my eyes slip shut, and Golmarr cautiously lifts his hands from my shoulders.

"Here, have her drink this," a woman says. Her voice sounds far away, but a moment later, someone lifts my head and presses a hot clay cup to my lips.

"Drink, Sorrowlynn," Golmarr whispers. I part my lips and let a sip of hot, salty broth enter my mouth. When I swallow, I can feel the heat of it trickle all the way down to my stomach. I take another sip and turn my head from it. It is scorching my insides.

"We are warming water on the fire. When we have enough, we will put her into a hot bath." I recognize that voice as Edemond's. "Thank you for saving my people, Dragon Slayer. We are in your debt." I crack my eyes open and peer through my lashes. Edemond is patting Golmarr on the back.

"I didn't—" Golmarr says, but Edemond cuts him off.

"Of course you didn't, *Ornald*. But whatever you and your love need, we will get it for you." Edemond leaves the wagon, and it is just Golmarr and me inside. He leans forward and kisses my forehead, and I quietly sink into slumbering warmth.

Chapter 19

"Bath time!" I jump awake and stare into piercing pale blue eyes. Melisande, Edemond's wife, pulls my covers back, and I realize that for the first time in days, I am warm.

"I don't want to get up yet," I say, reaching for the covers. She yanks them away from me before I can pull them back on.

"We just spent an entire morning heating up enough water for you to soak in a hot tub. So get up." She has her hands on her hips, and one of her toes is impatiently tapping the wagon floor.

She makes me think of Nona, and a smile pulls against my mouth. "All right." I stand and stretch, and look for the tub. "Where am I to bathe?" I ask.

She grins. "Outside, of course. That way, when you are done, we don't have to haul the water back outside to dump it."

"Outside? But isn't that . . . improper?" I think of Golmarr watching me bathe, and heat floods my cheeks. "What if . . . someone . . . sees?"

The woman laughs. "We might be forest dwellers, but we aren't ill-mannered. I have already had the men tie up a barrier of blankets around the tub. Let's go."

I follow her out of the wagon, into the filtered green light of the forest. Only, not all of it is filtered. In the middle of the camp, where the dragon shattered the trees, golden sunlight is rippling through. Right in the middle of the sunlight is a circle of colorful blankets fluttering in a gentle breeze and hanging from ropes tied to tree trunks.

The ground is wet beneath my bare feet, and water seeps between the cracks of my toes every time I step. One spot I step on, the water gushes up pink, and I think of the dragon's blood splattering the ground. Here, the flowers are sagging, their leaves a rotting black pulp.

At the circle of blankets, Melisande holds one up, and I step inside. A big brass tub is centered in the circle, and steam is rising up out of it. Without a word, Melisande lifts the pale yellow dress off over my head. She helps me out of my lace bloomers and holds them up with a quiet chuckle. My cheeks flame. "Wedding undergarments," I explain.

Melisande steps in front of me, and one of her eyebrows is raised. She quickly lifts the camisole over my head. Holding her offered arm, I step over the side of the tub. As my leg sinks calf deep into the steaming water, I suck air through my teeth. "It hurts," I say, leaping back out.

She puts her hands on her hips and pulls her lips tight against her teeth, contemplating me. "If you don't get in and stay in," she says, voice low and menacing, "I am calling that young man of yours over here to help me *put* you in. What did you say his name was?"

I swallow and fold my arms over my naked chest. "Ornald."

She puts a finger over her mouth and shakes her head. "No, that is not the name you shrieked when he was fighting the dragon. You called him *Golmarr*. Do you know what *Golmarr* means?"

Shivering, I shake my head.

"*Gol* means dragon, and *Marr* means destroyer. Do you know what language that is?"

I shake my head again and wish I weren't naked. I want to run from this woman.

"That, my girl, is the ancient language of Anthar. In fact . . ." She takes a small step closer to me, and I back up until the backs of my legs are pressed against the side of the tub. "In fact, King Marrkul's youngest son, who disappeared with the reputedly beautiful Princess Sorrowlynn of Faodara not seven days ago, is named Golmarr. What do you think of that?"

"I think I'm ready to bathe," I say, and gingerly step over the side of the tub. The water sears my calves so intensely that I can't help but compare it to the whippings I got as a child. I whimper and grit my teeth. Slowly, millimeter by millimeter, I lower the rest of my body into the tub. The heat from the water scalds my skin, warms my blood, and finally seeps into my bones. I close my eyes and let the water lap at my chin.

"Something else noteworthy," Melisande says, and my eyes pop open, "is the way you stood there and let me, a perfect stranger, undress you. Most women would balk at having someone strip them down to their bare skin." She kneels beside the tub and dunks me under the water. When I come up, she starts talking again. "It is said that Faodarian royalty are waited on hand and foot, even when dressing and undressing." She wrinkles her nose and runs a cake of soap over my head. I blink at her. "I know you had a sponge bath before your wedding, yet still you stink like you've been rolling in coals and old blood," she explains. "But you don't stink quite as badly as the young horse lord Golmarr, son of King Marrkul of Anthar. He smells like melted hair, burned leather, and fire. That should be some consolation, *Princess Sorrowlynn.*"

My eyes grow guarded, and she smiles and nods her satisfaction. "How is his head?" I ask.

"He's been tended to, and he is soaking in a bath, just like you, only we call the place where the men bathe a cold stream. Tell me." She holds up the filthy lace bloomers. "Did he get to see you in these?" I shake my head and she dunks them in the bathwater and rubs them with soap. "In that case, I will wash them for you. You can still use them for your honeymoon."

I shake my head and sink down into the water until it is lapping against my earlobes. "I don't think he *truly* wants to marry me. Last night, that was just our way of trying not to get killed by . . . your people." I cringe.

"That kiss was *fake?*" she asks with a laugh. Her hands pause in their washing, and she looks at me. A smile softens her face. "*Would* you marry him? Do you love him?"

My heart starts to pound, and my stomach turns. "He has a woman waiting for him at home," I whisper. The words physically hurt.

"She might be waiting for him, but I don't think he is waiting for her. Maybe he was before he went to Faodara, but not anymore." She vigorously scrubs the bloomers and then rinses them and wrings them out. Without a thought for modesty, she hangs them up on top of one of the blankets forming the walls to my outdoor room, where the whole camp can see them. When she sees my stricken face, she laughs. "What, Princess? Every woman dreams of wearing lace bloomers on her honeymoon, and every man dreams of seeing his wife in a pair. Only, lace costs a fortune, so we don't have that pleasure. Let's give my people something to fantasize about!"

"Since you know who we are, are you going to try to kill us?" I say *try* because I won't go down without a fight, and neither will Golmarr.

She studies me for a moment. "Not today," she says, and then she dunks me under the water again and rinses the soap from my hair.

When my hair is clean, I run the bar of soap over my body and cringe as I scrub my ribs. They stick out like I am a half-starved peasant.

When I am done bathing, Melisande wraps me in a scratchy wool blanket and hurries me, dripping and embarrassed, through the bustling camp. Everyone stops what they are doing to stare wide-eyed at me. "I know you've never seen a princess before—especially a naked one," Melisande howls, "but for the sake of all that is virtuous in this world, will you at least wait until she is dressed to gawk at her?" No one stops staring, and Melisande throws her arms up. "Ignore me, then."

We enter the big wagon I was carried to earlier, and Melisande rifles through the drawers of a wooden chest until she finds a long purple skirt, a yellow shirt, a red camisole, and a pair of soft red leather shoes. Without asking, she dresses me, and I do not protest. I wouldn't know how to lace the skirt up the back without her help. She pulls the camisole over my head before the yellow shirt and then shows me how to weave the leather laces up the front to close it enough that the red camisole still shows.

When I am dressed, she holds a wide, worn leather belt out to me. I wrinkle my nose at it and do not take it from her. Aside from shoes, leather clothing is for peasants, barbarians, and warriors. "This is for your knife," she explains. "So you don't have to tuck it in your waistband." I still don't take it from her.

Melisande rolls her eyes and wraps it around my waist, cinching it tight just below my ribs. She thrusts the sheathed hunting knife into a loop on the side and glares at me.

With no gentleness whatsoever, she yanks a comb through my hair until it is smooth, and then braids it at the nape of my neck and ties the end with a red ribbon, like a commoner. She hands me a gold-framed mirror. "What do you think of yourself?"

I peer at my face and turn it from side to side. It is thinner than it was on my sixteenth birthday. My eyes are solemn and guarded, and through them I can see the weight of the dragon's treasure. Nothing about me looks like a princess, except for my long neck. I nod and force a smile to my lips. "Thank you."

Someone knocks at the wagon door, and I spin around, hoping to see Golmarr. "Enter," Melisande calls. The door swings wide, and Edemond strides in. My heart sinks. A moment later Golmarr steps inside. His hair is cut even shorter than before and is still wet from his bath. His face is clean-shaven, and he is wearing the brown garb of the Satari men—a loose light brown tunic that laces only halfway up his chest, leaving a bold V of naked skin exposed beneath his neck, with a pair of plain brown trousers. He stops in the doorway, and his gaze moves over every inch of my body, pausing on the leather belt. "You look more at home in Satari clothing than you did in Faodarian gowns," he says with a smile.

I blush and catch my bottom lip in my teeth, and the smile leaves Golmarr's face as he studies my mouth. He wets his lips with his tongue and looks away. "Would you mind feeding us once more, Edemond? We need to leave as soon as possible. Before the glass dragon comes back."

"Of course," Edemond says, running his thumb and finger

over his goatee. "It is a rare honor to bestow food on a prince and a princess, and we are in your debt. But I warn you, our food is simple."

"Thank you, Edemond. Simple food is a feast to a starving soul," Golmarr says humbly, and then he touches his forehead and crosses his fingers. Edemond chuckles and nods. He puts his hands on Melisande's shoulders, and they leave.

Golmarr pulls a chair out for me to sit at a small square table built into the side of the wagon. "May I look at your ankles?" he asks, his voice tentative.

I laugh. "I have nothing to hide from you, sir, since you stared at my bare legs for days." He grins and kneels at my feet, but when he lifts my skirt and drapes it over my knees, then takes my calf in his hand, running his fingers gingerly over my skin, all mirth is instantly drained from me. My cheeks flare at his touch, and my skin prickles with goose bumps. My mind and my heart start to battle. My heart desperately wants me to lean down and kiss the crease between Golmarr's brows, but my mind tells me I should throw my skirt back over my legs and tell him to stop touching me.

Golmarr takes my other leg in his hands and clears his throat. I stare at him while he is intent on my healthy skin and wonder how I could ever have thought that he was a wild, ferocious-looking barbarian. He is the handsomest man I have ever seen. My gaze moves to his mouth, to the tension tightening his lips, and all I can think about is how he kissed me last night. My cheeks warm further at the thought, so I close my eyes and try to push Golmarr out of my mind before I embarrass myself by yanking my legs away from him and accusing him of making me think indecent thoughts. Because they're *not* indecent. They're . . . *normal*.

After another moment, I feel my skirt dropped back around

my ankles and hear a chair scrape against the wooden floor. I open my eyes to find Golmarr sitting at the other side of the table. "Are you still cold?" he asks. "Your legs look good, but they're covered with goose bumps."

I take a deep breath of air and slowly blow it out. The goose bumps had nothing to do with being cold. "The chill from the glass dragon is gone," I say. "But not the chill from when I healed you. It is in my hands, mostly."

He reaches across the table and takes my hands, pressing my palms together. With his hands, he covers the outside of mine, encasing them in warmth. "Why did you scream at me not to kill the glass dragon?" he asks.

I shudder and try to pull away from him, but he holds me tight. "You would have inherited its treasure if you killed it," I whisper.

"What is its treasure?" Golmarr asks in a quiet voice, leaning closer to me. "Gold? Riches? Knowledge?"

I shake my head. "What use does a dragon have for gold and riches? Honestly, think about it. All the legends say dragons hoard their treasures, and as human beings we always assume a dragon would treasure the same things we do. But they don't. They are beasts. They kill when they are hungry. They sleep on rock. They do not buy and sell like we do, take no pleasure in *comfort* or *possessions*. They do not need gold. The glass dragon," I whisper, "treasures hatred of man above everything else, and of all the people living right now, *it hates me more than any other.* If you killed it, you would have inherited a hatred so intense, it would have driven you mad, or driven you to murder to satisfy your hatred. And I would have been the first person you killed."

All the warmth leaves Golmarr's hands and he lets go of

me. He leans back and folds his arms over his chest. Frowning, he asks, "What do we do when it comes back for you, Sorrowlynn, if we can't kill it?"

My throat seems to close at his question, because it *will* be back. I know this in my heart. I stand and start trying to suck air into my lungs, but can't. Turning to the front door, I throw it open and thrust my head out and let the damp forest air wash over my panic. A strong hand grips my shoulder and pulls me back inside of the wagon. "Are you sick?" Golmarr asks, gently turning me to face him. His eyes are tight with worry.

"No," I gasp. "I can't breathe."

One of his eyebrows arches. "I've heard that one before. Right about the time you decided to steal my father's horse." Despite everything, I laugh, and all of a sudden I can breathe again, as if Golmarr has broken my anxiety in two and taken half of it.

The wagon stairs creak, and Melisande steps inside carrying a tray of food. She places it on the table. "Porridge," she announces, her eyes defiant, as if daring us to refuse such a modest meal. "Porridge for the young lovers to celebrate their honeymoon morning." She winks at me and turns to leave, but stops. "Princess, I almost forgot." She pulls a brown-and-white bundle from her pocket and holds it up. My face starts to burn so brightly it hurts. I snatch my lace bloomers from her, and she and Golmarr instantaneously burst into laughter. I have no pockets on my skirt, so I wad up the bloomers and shove them down the front of my shirt. When their laughter increases, I bristle and square my shoulders and put my nose up in the air, forcing my face into an expression of regal indifference. "*Now* I see the princess," Melisande says, wiping tears of laughter from her cheeks. "Oh, I almost forgot one more thing."

I cringe with dread as she opens the wagon door, wondering what else she can do to embarrass me. She steps back inside with my staff, and I gasp. I take it from her hands and run my fingers over it. Instead of prickly pine bark coating it, it is covered with a slick, polished wood that has hair-thin veins of silver. I almost hand it back to the woman, thinking she is mistaken, until I recognize the narrow spot near the top where I hacked the rough bark away with my hunting knife.

Melisande leaves, and I lay the staff across the table and sit studying the wood. Taking the spoon from my bowl of porridge, I try to gouge the staff's surface but cannot. "What happened to it?"

"Don't you know?" Golmarr asks. I shake my head. "I saw you throw it at the dragon when it blew its breath on you. It went into the dragon's mouth and lodged in its throat until it coughed it out." The color drains from his face. "I thought it killed you with its breath."

"So did I." I shiver at the memory and lean my staff against the wall. Scooting my chair up to the table, I look at the lumpy, pale porridge—a peasant's meal—and frown. Leaning over the bowl, I sniff, and my mouth starts to water.

"Have you *never* eaten porridge?" Golmarr asks. I shake my head. "This is how you do it." He puts his spoon into his bowl and lifts a glob of the sticky food to his mouth and swallows without chewing. "It's good," he says, watching me with amusement.

I put my spoon into the bowl and lift a smidgen of porridge to my mouth. It is soft, and warm, and salty, and mixed with cream and cinnamon. I dig my spoon in again and lift a mountain of porridge to my mouth and proceed to devour it, savoring the feel of it sliding down my throat and into my hollow belly. When I have finished eating, I lean back and look into Golmarr's surprised face. "I know your education was sorely lacking in certain areas—like self-defense, and what is and is not proper—but were you not taught table manners?" Golmarr asks, laughing. His bowl is still half-full.

"Are you going to finish that, sir?" I ask. He puts one finger on the lip of the bowl and slides it across the table to me. I laugh. "I was just joking. I've had—"

From outside, a bell starts clanging, and then another, and another. Golmarr and I lock eyes for a heartbeat, and then we are both on our feet, I with my staff and him with his sword.

Chapter 20

We rush outside, and I look immediately to the stark blue sky, expecting to see the dragon appear above the broken trees. Golmarr slams into me and wraps his arm around my waist, and as we tip forward, I feel a gust of air swipe against my cheek as an arrow flies past. It lodges into the wagon behind us.

With a grunt, I land belly-down on the damp ground, and Golmarr lands on top of me. "Are you okay?" he asks. I nod. "We're being attacked by renegades. Get back inside of the wagon!" With those words, he leaps up and starts running toward a group of fighting men, his sword held high.

I lay on the ground and watch as armed men with red bands tied around their biceps pour into the clearing from between the wagons. Edemond's people are rushing to get children out of the fighting zone, or are running to wagons to arm themselves more fully. And while they do this, their unarmed people are not protected. I can see it all so clearly, how with the men running for their weapons, and the women trying to protect the children, the attackers have a moment to take or kill whatever they want.

To my left, a woman screams. Melisande is running with a

toddler in her arms, but a man has caught her by her braid. He kicks her in the small of her back, and she lets the child down with a command to get inside of a wagon. Whirling around, Melisande pulls a dagger from her belt and slashes at her attacker. Her weapon clangs against a sword and is knocked from her grasp. The man kicks her again, a boot to her stomach, and she crumples to the ground. He lifts his sword and grits his teeth, and I am already running, my staff gripped in my hands like a weapon. His sword swings downward, and Melisande screams, struggling to pull herself out of the way. Just as the weapon comes flush with her body, I thrust my staff in the way and knock it aside, and Melisande crawls away.

I do not wait for the man to recover from the shock of my attack. Using both of my hands, I swing the staff in a fast circle and slam it into the side of his chin, then thrust it forward into the soft space just below his ribs. He grunts and hunches forward, and I put all of my body weight into swinging the staff at the back of his knees and knock him off his feet.

As soon as he is down, another man with a red scarf tied to his arm takes his place. This man is younger and has thicker shoulders than the first man, and his biceps bulge against his sleeves. He's holding a short sword and wearing leather armor. Our eyes meet, and the man grins, motioning me forward with one hand. "Here, pretty girl, fight me and I will teach you how to deal with a real man."

I thrust my staff forward once and watch to see how this man fights. In spite of his large size, he is quick, his movements precise, and I know enough to realize that without strength to equal his, I am at a major disadvantage. A twinge of fear travels down my spine, but before I can run, the man lunges at me, but not with his sword. He reaches for my staff, and I can tell by the predatory way he is looking at me, he doesn't want to kill me. He wants to keep me.

Before he can wrap his fingers around my weapon, I swing hard and knock it against his knuckles. I pivot and thrust, aiming for his neck, but his sword is up and blocking me before I make contact. The metal clangs against my staff, and sparks fly. I attack again, our weapons meet, and he bears down on my staff with his sword. My arms tremble beneath the power of this man. Lower and lower he pushes me, his sweaty face mere inches from mine. When my knees are about to buckle, he grins, and I can see the lust in his eyes. I dive to the side and twist my staff so it catches his short sword, and the blade is yanked from his hand. As I try to spring to my feet to run, my red shoes tangle in my skirt. With a thud, I fall to the forest floor, landing on my back.

My opponent growls with fury and leaps at me, crushing my body to the ground with his. I stare into his dark eyes as cold steel presses against my throat. "Seems I caught myself a warrior woman," the man growls, pressing his dagger harder against my skin. "If I take you home with me, do you think your family will pay to get you back?"

I feel sick at the thought of this man taking me and holding me for ransom. What's worse, if this man discovered I was a Faodarian princess and held me for ransom, I do not know if my mother *would* pay anything to get me back. She might leave me to a life of slavery. But there is something about me that the brute overlooked. I quietly thank Melisande for buckling the belt around my waist earlier as I pull the hunting knife from it and quickly drive it into the man's side. "You are not taking me anywhere," I say, and yank it back out.

His eyes grow wide, and he lurches away from me. "You

wench!" He swings his dagger at my face, but I block it with my knife and quickly roll to my feet. He stands and swings the blade at me again, but wobbles. Pressing a hand to his side, he holds his bloody fingers before his astonished eyes. "You cut me good, and you're going to pay for that."

"No, I am not," I answer. I dealt him a death blow, and even if he doesn't know it, I do. It is only a matter of seconds before he bleeds out. He lifts his knife and runs at me.

"Sorrowlynn!" Golmarr screams from behind. I don't look at him because I know—thanks to the dragon's treasure—to never take my eyes from my opponent. Before the man's knife is close enough to cut me, I whip my staff against his hand, and his weapon goes flying through the air. He loses his footing and falls to the ground at my feet just as Golmarr reaches me.

With a gut-wrenching jolt, I feel the man die and grip my stomach as his knowledge and memories fill my brain. A horrifying realization hits me: not only did I absorb all of the knowledge that Zhun possessed, but I inherited his means of gathering what he considered treasure—when I kill, I steal my victim's knowledge. I fall to my knees and groan. Golmarr puts his sword tip between the man's shoulder blades and flexes his muscles to deal a death blow. "He's already dead," I blurt, loath at the thought of watching the man get stabbed again.

Golmarr looks from the thick set of shoulders beneath his sword to me. "You killed this renegade?" he asks.

I squeeze my eyes shut and nod. "I killed him, but he is no Trevonan renegade. He's a mercenary, born and bred here in the forest, and more are coming. All of the vilest men who hide in the forest are coming."

"Why?"

"The glass dragon. Somehow it is speaking to their minds and sending them to kill me." I look around the camp. The fighting has ceased, but there are a handful of dead bodies lying strewn on the ground. "We need to leave right now, Golmarr."

"Let's quickly help them bury the dead first."

I stand and grip the front of his light brown shirt in my fists. "If I stay, more people will die, and it will be because of *me*." My eyes fill with tears. "I am leaving with or without you, if it means saving these people, even if I die!" The tears spill down my cheeks.

He studies me with solemn eyes, and then he presses his hand to his chest and crosses his index fingers.

I sniffle and blink more tears from my eyes. "Does that mean you won't come with me? Does that mean goodbye?" I ask, and the thought hurts so much that I am tempted to knock him over the head and drag him away with me if he won't come of his own free will.

He shakes his head and frames my face in his hands, wiping the tears from my cheeks with his thumbs. "I will follow you to the end of the world, Sorrowlynn of Faodara." He leans down and puts his lips against my forehead, so soft and sweet and tender that more tears wet my eyes. The contact fills me with warmth, and hope, and joy—feelings so opposite from those still lingering in my mind from the mercenary I killed.

I wrap my arms around Golmarr and lean against his chest. His strong arms close about me and hold me. Silent, I stand there and simply exist in the shelter of his arms. After a long moment, I say, "Let's go." I step away from him, but he grabs my hands.

"Give me two minutes to ask Edemond for horses and a bow and arrows." He waits until I nod, and then strides off across the clearing. I kneel and wipe my hunting knife clean on the lush ground. Someone steps up to me. For a moment I stare at worn brown boots peeking out from beneath a red skirt. Peering up, my eyes meet Melisande's. Slowly, I stand and sheathe the knife.

Her bottom lip quivers, and she squeezes my shoulder in her hand. "You saved my life. Thank you."

I nod and think that if I weren't here in the first place, I wouldn't have had to save her, because the mercenaries wouldn't have come to her camp. But I don't say that. Instead I say, "You're welcome."

She looks me up and down and asks, "How did you learn to fight like that? The rumors we hear of your kingdom say your women are weaklings who don't know how to swing a weapon. And you, with nothing more than a walking stick, saved my life!"

A hint of a smile softens my mouth. "The noblewomen of Faodara are not taught to fight. I am the exception."

"Is that why you chose to face the dragon instead of marrying? Because you wanted to fight it?" She glances across the camp, at Golmarr. "Why *did* you choose the dragon over him? Look how handsome he is! You seem to like him well enough, and I saw him give the hand signal that he loves you just now."

My heart starts thumping. "Wait. This?" I press one hand to my chest, and then cross my two pointer fingers. "This means *I love you*?"

She crosses her fingers and says, "Friend." Pressing on her chest, she adds, "Of my heart. Or *heart friend*. That is how the horse clan says, *I love you*."

My body overflows with warmth. I look at Golmarr and find him staring at us with his head tilted slightly to the side, and I am wrapped in such a feeling of peace I can't help but smile despite the death surrounding me.

"Why *did* you choose the dragon?" Melisande asks again.

"Because being eaten alive seemed like a better choice than going home with my father or the horse clan," I say, staring at Golmarr's back and broad shoulders as he talks to Edemond. "I was a fool. If I could do it all over again, I would just outright ask to be betrothed to Golmarr."

"So you love him, too?" Melisande asks.

"I don't know what being in love feels like. The thought of not being with him hurts. And when I kissed him last night . . ." I swallow.

Melisande fans her face and clears her throat. "Yes, I think we all felt the attraction there." She looks over my shoulder. "That was some kiss you shared with your wife last night, young horse lord."

My skirts swish against my legs as I flip around and find Golmarr standing behind me holding the reins of a saddled horse in one hand and a saddlebag in the other. He has a bow and quiver strapped to his back, and a mischievous smile graces his face. "I can't keep her hands off me," he says, but then he frowns. "She's not truly my wife—you know that."

"I suppose not. But she should be!" she blurts.

Golmarr shrugs, and his clean-shaven cheeks turn bright pink beneath his tan skin. "Maybe one day she'll agree with you," he says, looking at me.

"Maybe she already does." Melisande winks at me, and I stiffen. She laughs and wraps her arms around my shoulders. "Goodbye, Princess Sorrowlynn. I will never forget that you saved my life today."

Edemond and Enzio, leading another horse, approach us. Edemond stands behind his wife and puts his arms around her shoulders, pressing a kiss to her temple. "I hear we owe you thanks for her life, Princess Sorrowlynn," he says. "To repay the debt, my son would like to travel with you."

Enzio, armed with a bow and a short sword strapped diagonally across his back, steps forward and goes down on one knee before me. "If you will have me, Princess Sorrowlynn, I will cross the forest with you and Prince Golmarr and see you safely to Anthar. I will fight at your side until I have saved your life, thereby repaying my family's debt to you."

The people moving about camp stop what they are doing and gather around us. "Please, Enzio, there is no need to kneel to me," I whisper. "No one has ever knelt at my feet before." Enzio makes no move to stand.

Golmarr steps to my side. Leaning close, he whispers, "You call yourself a princess? He is offering you his protection. Refusing him will dishonor his family. Thank him and accept his service!"

I firm my shoulders and try to soften my face to regal gratitude. "Yes, Enzio. Thank you. I accept." The glade erupts in quiet cheering as Enzio stands. He holds his head high and proud.

"Thank you, my son," Melisande says, kissing Enzio's cheek.

Golmarr claps Enzio on the shoulder. "Thank you. Your presence will be a great relief. I am happy to have you along." Golmarr mounts his horse, and Enzio mounts his. Taking my staff from me, Golmarr slides it into a strap attached to the saddle. I stare at the two mounted men and wonder where *my* horse is. Golmarr lowers a hand down to me. "You're riding behind me," he says. A young man kneels at my feet and cups his hands for me to step into. I put my red leather shoe into his hands and grasp Golmarr's wrist and they swing me up behind the saddle. My skirt crawls up to my knees, and as I move to yank it down, I pause. Every person in this camp has already seen my naked legs. Sighing with resignation, I lightly put my hands on Golmarr's waist and wonder what my mother would say if she could see me now.

With Enzio in the lead, we ride out of the clearing, and the children run alongside us, throwing flowers before our horses' hooves and blowing kisses at me. I smile at them and blow kisses in return. "She blew a kiss at me," some of them squeal. As the forest thickens around us, the children stop running and instead call goodbye.

We haven't been riding long when I realize my body is so heavy that I can barely sit straight. I reach my hand up to stifle a yawn, and it is trembling. Throwing propriety to the wind, I wrap my arms around Golmarr's waist and clasp my hands in front of him. Turning my head sideways, I lean it between his shoulder blades and close my eyes. Within seconds, the steady beat of his heart combines with the gentle motion of the horse and lulls me to sleep. As darkness claims my exhausted body, my hands slide apart and I start to tip, so I jolt awake. I clasp them once more, and this time Golmarr wraps his hand around them, holding them securely together.

He turns and looks at me over his shoulder. "You're battle weary. Sleep, Sorrowlynn. Sleep. I won't let you fall off."

Chapter 21

A spear flies at me, and I roll out of the way. When I get to my feet, I am standing on a hillside, and below me the ground is crawling with armed men. I know the men with the red griffin emblazoned on their shields. They are my men. I am their commander. I am the one who planned this attack. We will destroy the Antharian barbarians, and when we do, we will claim their land and their women and children for my king. My king will rule from the northern cliffs all the way to the southern sea.

With a single glance, I can see the perfection of this battle, with my men on higher ground and another force of my Faodarian soldiers coming up from the rear to surround the barbarians. With this battle, we may win the entire war. I thrust my sword in the air and prepare to fight, when I see a shadow speed over my men. I look up to the sky, and all of my hope to win this battle is vanquished. "Fire dragon!" I shout, and as the great beast flies over me, a ball of fire leaves its mouth and . . .

I wake to warmth. It takes me a moment to realize it is the warmth of Golmarr's back against the front of my chest and cheek—not dragon fire. His hand is still secured tightly around mine.

"Will we reach the border by nightfall?" Golmarr asks. His deep voice rumbles through his rib cage. "And are there any camps between us and Anthar that you know of?"

"Nightfall, if not earlier. The Black Blades have a claim to the southern region. Unless there are mercenaries squatting on our land, there should be no one between us and your border," Enzio says. "But we are not taking the normal trail to Anthar. I will not risk crossing paths with mercenaries or renegades. Not when we have a princess to protect." After a long pause, Enzio says, "I must have your word as an Antharian prince that you will not reveal the secrets of the forest. Not even to your father!"

"On my honor, I will keep your secrets," Golmarr says.

I pull my hands away from him and sit tall. My back is so stiff that I wince. Golmarr rests his hand on my bare knee and peers over his shoulder. I stare into his close eyes and wonder why I used to think they looked so fierce. "How are you feeling?" he asks.

Like there are so many emotions coursing through my body that I can scarcely draw breath, I think, glancing at his hand on my knee. His mere touch almost has the same result as his lips on mine. "My body hurts," I admit.

"That's from the fighting, a side effect of not conditioning regularly. When we stop for the night, we can spar. It will hurt at first, but it will loosen your tight muscles." He lifts his hand and turns back around. I close my eyes and smile. I like how Golmarr's touch makes me feel.

The forest looks the same as ever. It is reminiscent of being in the cave and seeing nothing but darkness, only we see nothing but green. We could be walking in circles for all I know, except I can see the path before us, and there are no fresh prints on it. And yet it is beautiful beyond my wildest dreams. Endless birdsong fills the air. When the wind stirs, it ruffles the roof of leaves overhead, opening it in places so pieces of golden sunlight shine through like stars. I close my eyes to breathe in the smell of the forest, and instead smell Golmarr, so I inhale more deeply. If I could make a moment last forever, this would be it.

Enzio stops his horse, and we stop behind him. Pressing a finger to his lips, he motions to the right and then turns his horse into a dense thicket of vines that hides him completely. Golmarr guides our horse into the vines, and I peer over his shoulder to see where we are going. On the other side, the foliage is much denser than the trail we were traveling. At first glance, it is just wild overgrowth, but then I can see the faint markings of old travel on the ground. Enzio dismounts, hands Golmarr his reins, and goes back to the trail we just left, walking a little farther down it. When he comes back, he rustles the vines and closes them so there is no evidence that we have come through this way.

He presses a finger to his lips again, and our horse follows his. We enter a tight tunnel of green that is so dense I cannot see any traces of sky. If I lift my hand, my fingers will trail over the lush tunnel ceiling. The ground begins to gradually slope downward. Our horses weave their way through the thick, clinging underbrush. Branches and vines scrape at my bare calves, and would hit my face if Golmarr didn't put his arm up to block them from the two of us. We go on this way for some time, while the ground slopes ever downward. The birds keep singing, and a breeze whispers through the forest, but the air grows darker.

Leaning against Golmarr's back, I rest my chin on his shoulder and whisper, "Is it already sunset?"

When he turns to answer, his face is so close to mine I can feel the warmth radiating from it. "It is early afternoon. I *think* we are in the shadow of the mountain." He turns back around, and I leave my chin on his shoulder.

We descend a steep patch of ground, and when the ground levels out again, the tunnel of green we have been traveling through opens up into forest once more. There is more birdsong, and a quiet rumble fills the air. The farther we go, the deeper and louder the rumble becomes. The air changes, too. I sit up tall and gasp. Reaching my upturned palm out, I watch as a snowflake drifts down and lands on it. I close my hand, expecting the flake to melt, but it is not cold. I look up. The dark green roof of the forest is speckled by floating white flakes. They fill the air, gently dancing on the wind. Some have settled in Golmarr's dark hair. Without a thought, I run my fingers through it, sifting the fluff out.

"What is this?" I ask, holding my hand out to his side. He runs his fingers over my palm.

"Cotton. From the trees."

I stretch my arms out to my sides and tip my chin up, letting the cotton swirl around me. Ahead, between a gap in the trees, a white veil of water is falling down the side of dark gray stone. Enzio stops his horse beside the falls and gets down. "I'm going to backtrack and make sure our tracks are hidden," he says, and ducks into the foliage. The moment he is behind the leaves, he seems to disappear.

Golmarr dismounts and holds his hands up to me, and I fall into them, throwing my arms around his neck. When my legs touch the ground, they are so stiff and awkward that I tighten my hold on Golmarr to keep from falling.

"Easy," he says. "Your body isn't used to riding. It's going to be stiff every time you dismount, so you need to expect it and be prepared."

"I'm fine," I insist, and let go of him. In some tucked-away part of the fire dragon's treasure, I remember the stiffness born of long riding. I can handle it. But my knees nearly buckle when I try to walk, and I stumble. A wave of frustration hits me. The memories I have, the human memories passed on to me, are from men and women who were much stronger than I am. I keep expecting my body to respond the way my memory says it should, but I am weak and soft.

When my muscles decide to react again, I look at the waterfall filling the air with its loud rumble, and all the frustration of a moment before is whisked away. The water spilling down the side of the cliff is white and no wider than my outstretched arms, but I have never seen something so simply beautiful. Mist is rising up from where the waterfall hits a wide, shallow pool. I step into the mist and close my eyes, slowly turning in a circle as the cool, damp air clings to my hands and neck.

"You've never seen a little waterfall like this before, have you?" Golmarr yells so his voice can be heard.

I shake my head and open my eyes and find him staring at me the same way I was staring at the waterfall. "I have never seen or done anything before," I call, stepping away from the roar so I can hear him better. "Everything is new for me. All of these things I am experiencing are firsts, and I am storing them away so I never forget any of it." I walk a little ways down the stream the waterfall has created and crouch. "I'm going to remember everything," I say, sticking my hands into the water and watching how it moves over them. "The cave, the fire dragon, the forest, the Satari. I will never forget any of it." I cup my hands, bringing water to my mouth.

"I'm sorry," Golmarr says.

I stand and shake the water from my hands. "Sorry for what?" His eyes are dark with guilt and something else that I can't identify, but it makes my heart start pounding. "Sorry for what?" I ask again.

"I'm sorry for last night. For that kiss." My cheeks flare with humiliation. He regrets the kiss. I duck my head and play with the laces of my shirt so I don't have to look at him, so he can't see my hurt and confusion. "That was your first kiss, wasn't it?"

I nod and roll the leather string back and forth between my thumb and middle finger and stare at it like it's the most fascinating thing I have ever seen. He grabs my hand and stills it. Startled, I look up and meet his eyes. "You deserve better than that for your first kiss. If I could redo it, I would," he whispers. He unbuckles my wide leather belt and pulls it from my waist.

"What are you doing?" I ask.

He grins and drops the belt and dagger to the ground, and his eyes turn fierce. "Making sure you don't stab me for what I'm about to do to you." I gasp. "Also, you won't feel my hands on you through that leather, and I won't be able to feel you," he adds, his voice a deep rumble. "A kiss isn't only about your lips on mine. It is about your hands touching me and my hands touching you, about my body against yours."

He cups the side of my face in his hand and runs his callused thumb over my bottom lip. My breath catches in my throat as I stare into his eyes. Taking my hand, he places it against his chest, in the space where his shirt hangs open, so my palm is flat against his warm skin. I can feel his heart beating slow and steady. "I want you to feel what you do to my heart when I kiss you, Sorrowlynn." With those words, my blood begins pumping so fast that my head starts to spin.

He puts both of his strong hands on my hips, and I can feel them there, warm and firm through the lightweight fabric of my skirt. Moving his face down to meet mine, he pauses and looks into my eyes, his lips hovering above my own. "You're going to want to hold on," he whispers.

I take my free hand and put it behind his neck. "I'm holding on," I say.

With a smile, he pulls my body flush against his. Everywhere our bodies touch, there's heat. I tip my head up, waiting for his kiss. "This . . ." He brushes his lips over mine. "Is how . . ." He brushes them over mine again, a feather-soft sensation. "You should have been kissed your first time." His hands tighten on my hips as he presses his lips firmly to mine, and where my hand is splayed against his chest, I feel his heart burst to life. Closing my eyes, I melt against him.

His mouth moves over mine, patiently coaxing my lips open, and I tighten my hold on the back of his neck as my knees wobble. He kisses me slowly, softly, like I am a new flavor and he has to take his time to taste all of me. I slide my hand up his chest and press it to the side of his face to feel his jaw working as he kisses me. One of his hands slowly traces my spine through my shirt and finds my neck. The other hand fiddles with my braid, tugging the ribbon from it, slowly undoing the weave until my hair falls long and loose all the way to my waist. Golmarr twists his fingers in my hair and kisses me harder. The sound of the waterfall is replaced with the roar of blood moving through my body. The forest seems to drop away and disappear, leaving Golmarr and me in a void where only the two of us exist. His lips slow against mine, then soften. His hands clamp down on my shoulders and he gently pushes me away so he can look into my eyes.

"If things at the binding ceremony had gone differently, you would be my wife right now, and I could kiss you all I want," he murmurs, making my cheeks warmer than they already are. I swallow and nod and reluctantly let my arms fall from his neck.

"If we would have been wed at the binding ceremony, I don't know that I would have wanted you kissing me," I say. "But now that I've spent every waking and sleeping moment with you for the past seven days . . ." I cannot find the words to finish.

He nods. "I know. I feel the same. Being *forced* into it would have been hard." He cups the side of my face and slowly kisses my forehead, then bends and picks up my belt. When he hands it to me, I can still see the energy of our kiss in his eyes. "In one week you've bewitched me with your magic, Princess Sorrowlynn."

I shake my head. "No, I haven't, I swear. I don't even know *how* to—"

Golmarr presses his fingertips to my lips to silence me. "Whether you realize it or not, whether you meant to or not, you most assuredly have. No one has ever made me feel the way you do." He kneels at the side of the stream and splashes water onto his face just as Enzio steps out of the bushes holding a black-bladed stone knife in his hand, muttering something under his breath. Golmarr stands and flicks the water from his hands. "What did you say, Enzio?" he asks.

Enzio looks from Golmarr to me, his eyes taking in my missing belt and loose, disheveled hair, and frowns. "I said I have been standing in the bushes cleaning my fingernails with my knife and waiting for you to finish kissing her for at least five minutes." He twirls the blade in his fingers and then tosses it into the air, catching it by the hilt before sliding it up his sleeve. "I didn't realize I was coming along to play chaperone."

I glare at him and pick up the ribbon from the ground, and then quickly rebraid my hair.

Golmarr throws his head back and laughs.

Chapter 22

With Enzio in the lead, we ride in the stream beneath the shadow of the cliff so our tracks are hidden. I am sitting in the saddle this time, with Golmarr behind me, his hands resting loosely on my leather belt, his legs dangling beside mine. When the air begins dimming and the crickets start to chirp, the undergrowth clogging the forest floor thins and the wind picks up, carrying with it warmer air. Golmarr takes a deep breath.

"Do you smell that?" he asks. I inhale. The damp forest air smells more like crisp, dry sunshine and less like mildew. It smells like my bedsheets right after they have been dried on the clothesline in the summer sun.

"What is it?" I sit a little taller in the saddle and try to get a glimpse through the trees.

"That is the smell of my home. Of Anthar." Golmarr laughs. "I can't believe we've made it this far. I didn't know if I would ever get to see my kingdom again." Like stepping from one room to another, the forest abruptly ends, replaced by yellow grass as tall as the horse's belly. The wind blows and the grass ripples like warm golden water in the last light of the evening. Above, the sky is a pale, unending blue. Goose bumps travel up my arms, and I wonder if I will ever see anything as stunning again in my life.

I turn to look back at the forest. To the east, it runs in a perfectly straight line as far as I can see. To the west, it runs in a perfectly straight line to the base of a mountain. North, a snowcapped peak juts up out of the forest. "Is that Gol Mountain?" I ask.

"Yes. That is the dragon's mountain. *Was*," Golmarr corrects.

Enzio slows his horse to walk beside us. "So is it true what my father believes?" he asks Golmarr.

Golmarr's hands hold a little tighter to my waist as he asks, "What does your father believe?"

Enzio looks up at the mountain. "My father believes that you killed the fire dragon."

Golmarr goes very still behind me. "The fire dragon is dead," he says quietly.

Enzio nods. Looking intently at Golmarr, he says, "It is an honor to travel with the Dragon Slayer." Enzio slips the black stone knife out of his shirtsleeve and presses the flat of the blade to his forehead. I can see the respect shining in his blue eyes.

"What are you doing, Enzio?" I ask, baffled.

"Giving the Antharian prince the Satari salute of honor," he explains.

"Did you make that knife? I have never seen anything like it."

He tosses the knife into the air. It arcs over his head, and he catches it behind his back with his other hand. "This weapon came out of Satar with my ancestors over one hundred years ago, when Grinndoar the dragon toppled our stone cities and forced us to flee or be killed." He holds the knife out to me, handle first, and I take it. The handle, cross guard, and blade are carved from a single piece of jet-black stone. It is perfectly balanced, with the weight of the handle in exact opposition to the blade.

"This would be a very precise throwing blade," I say, handing it back to him.

Enzio nods and grins like a rogue. "Why do you think my people are known throughout the forest as the Black Blades?" Faster than my eyes can follow, the blade disappears, and I know Enzio has hidden it in his sleeve again. "We should set up camp before full dark."

Golmarr peers back at the sheer, inky edge of the forest. "Let's get as far from the tree line as we can while we still have the light. The farther the better."

When the sun has set, and the sky has turned a brilliant, deep purple, we rein in the horses. Golmarr quickly dismounts, and without giving it a second thought, I swing my leg over the horse's hind end and gracefully hop down. My legs are like stone when they hit the ground, and I lean forward with my hands braced on my knees to keep from falling.

Golmarr laughs. "I warned you that you'd be stiff. Let's eat and then see if we can work some of that stiffness out. What do you say?"

"In the dark?" I ask, peering up the starry sky. "Are we going to light a fire?" I rub my hands over my arms. With the sun down, the breeze has a cool bite to it.

"No," Enzio says. "No fire this close to the border. It will be like a beacon for every cutthroat watching the grasslands." He holds something out to me, and when I hold my palm up, he puts a piece of stale flatbread into it.

Golmarr offers me a water skin. "Enzio," he says, "when are we most likely to be attacked?"

"In the dark," Enzio answers. "At night. That way the attacker has the advantage. He can sneak up on you and . . ." He pretends to throw a knife, and then gasps and presses a hand over his heart.

"I agree. Night is a good time to practice fighting because not all of your foes will be considerate enough to attack in broad daylight. Didn't you ever spar at night, in the dark, Princess Sorrowlynn, when you were being taught to fight at your fancy cliffside castle?" The sarcasm in his voice makes me bristle. I shove Golmarr's shoulder to quiet him, but he grabs my wrist and twists my arm behind my back, pinning it where it causes me nothing more than mild discomfort. He drops my arm, though, and leaps away from me like he's been burned. "One rule I need to mention." He leans forward and taps my hunting knife. "No blades allowed. I don't want a repeat of what happened when I did that to you in the cave." He rubs his chest in the very spot where my blade rested when he fake-attacked me before.

"Fair enough." I unbuckle my belt and hang it over the horse's saddle. The moment I set it down, Golmarr is behind me, pinning my arm against my back again, his other arm around my throat.

"Do you know how to get out of this?" he asks calmly, hugging me to him.

"If I had a weapon, I could just—"

"But you don't have a weapon. That's the point," he says, tightening his hold. "I've seen you fight with your staff and your knife, and you're going to be very good with them once you've gotten stronger. But do you know how to fight unarmed?"

I struggle for a moment, feeling the tension in his body, gauging the angle at which he is restraining my arm, and then I elbow him in the ribs with my free arm, duck under the arm holding my throat, and try to lunge out of his grasp. When my shoulder joint strains to the point of pain, I yelp and stop struggling. And then, without even thinking about it, my body knows exactly how to break free. A small, sly grin finds its way to my mouth.

"It looks like I've caught a princess," Golmarr murmurs, his mouth beside my temple. When he talks, I can feel the fresh scruff on his chin rub against my skin.

"I believe you are mistaken," I say, and thrust my elbow into his ribs again, then step to the right to relieve the tension in my shoulder, twist around, and break free. "There," I say, thinking the lesson is over, but Golmarr lunges for me. Without a thought, I swing my forearm against his reaching hands, knocking them away. He chuckles and tries again, but instead of grabbing for me, he ducks beneath my arm and tugs on the end of my braid.

"Hey, no hair pulling," I say.

"Sorry, Princess, that was not in our previously agreed-upon rules." He lunges behind me and tugs my braid again, and I stiffen with frustration. Enzio, watching us while he eats, laughs, which frustrates me even more.

When Golmarr tries for a third time to tweak my braid, I dive away and roll through the grass, swinging my foot toward his ankles before I come to a stop. He jumps out of the way a split second too late, and my heel catches the bottom of his boot, knocking him off balance. His arms flail, and he stumbles backward, and I hop to my feet and leap at him, knocking him onto his back. He lands with a thud and groans, and I land on top of him, pinning his wrists by his ears. My braid falls forward over my shoulder.

"My head," he gasps. It is at that moment I remember the wound he got fighting the dragon that morning.

"I'm sorry!" I say, letting his arms go. Before I have time

to climb off of him, he sticks his fingers through the loops of my braid and undoes it halfway. And then I am tipping to the side, and the ground is beneath my back, and Golmarr is straddling my waist and pinning my wrists by my ears.

Enzio claps. "Not bad, Sorrowlynn, but I think you need to work on your hand-to-hand combat."

I glare up at Golmarr and struggle to get my wrists from his hands, but his powerful grip doesn't loosen. "I thought you said your head was hurt," I grumble.

"It is, but that wasn't a good reason for you to stop fighting." Even in the dark I can see his wide smile and white teeth. "When you fight, you use every available weapon you have to win. I turned your own sympathy against you." He makes no move to get off me. I stare up into his shadowed eyes and contemplate his words. Gathering every bit of courage I possess, I lift my head and press my lips to his. For a moment his eyes widen and his hands tighten on my wrists, and then his body dips down and presses against mine. He releases his hold on me to lay his forearms flat on the ground on either side of my head. I smile against his mouth and flip him hard and fast, careful to cradle his head in my hand so it doesn't hit the ground again, and then hop to my feet.

"So, if you used my sympathy against me, what did I use against you?" I ask.

Golmarr sits up and wraps his arms around his knees. Grinning, he answers, "My lascivious, lustful nature, obviously."

I gasp, and Enzio starts laughing so loudly that the horses look up from their grazing. Golmarr's laughter joins Enzio's, and then I can't help but chuckle. Enzio walks to the horse lord and gives him a hand up. Stepping to me, Golmarr runs his hand through my hair until the braid has come completely undone and my hair is loose around my shoulders.

"You pulled my ribbon out the first time you tugged on my braid, didn't you? That is the second time you've done that today."

He studies me for a moment and simply says, "It is a shame to leave hair like yours bound all the time."

"You're not the one who has to brush it out every morning," I say.

"I wish I was." He runs his fingers through my hair again and takes a small step closer.

"Golmarr!" Enzio crouches low and I see the silhouette of the black knife in his hand. "Something has spooked the horses!"

Golmarr slides his sword from its sheath. I throw my hands up in the air and glare at him. "I am disarmed!" I whisper. Hiking my skirt up around my knees, I sprint toward the horses, who have wandered a little ways off.

"Sorrowlynn, wait," Golmarr whispers, but I ignore him.

The horses have stopped grazing and are both looking in the same direction, their ears facing forward. I grab the belt from my horse's saddle and swing it around my waist, fumbling with the buckle in the dark. Next, I slide my staff from the leather strap. When I turn back toward Golmarr, I freeze. He and Enzio are gone. It is just me and the horses standing in the tall grass . . . and whatever has spooked them.

Chapter 23

I grip my staff in my clammy hands and slowly start to spin in a circle, trying to get my bearings—trying to find Golmarr and Enzio. The moon has risen, painting the landscape silver, and the only sounds are chirping crickets and the gentle swish of the wind through the waist-high grass. When I have spun all the way around, a black mass is standing in front of me. I lift my staff to attack, but hesitate. For a moment my head fills with confusion as I stare at the outline of a tall, square-shouldered man with long black hair. In the dark he looks just like Golmarr . . . but Golmarr's hair is now short.

My staff swings into action and meets steel. I press forward hard, swinging so quickly, with so much adrenaline, that my opponent stumbles backward. I leap forward and thrust the end of my staff into his stomach. He doubles over, and I use that moment to swing my staff toward his head, but his free arm meets my weapon and blocks it.

An arm cinches around my neck, and I feel the prick of a knife against the side of my ribs and the body of a second man pressed firm against my back. I force myself to freeze and my hands begin to tremble on my staff. "A woman?" a deep, rough voice whispers against my hair. "Disarm her."

The man in front of me tears the staff from my hands and then slides the knife from my belt. Quickly, with featherlight fingers, he runs his hands over my arms and legs and then backs a step away. "This is all she has," he says, holding up the staff and knife.

The man holding me tightens his arm on my throat, and the knife that was at my ribs comes up to my neck, just below my ear. "Who are you?" he growls. When I do not answer, the blade presses harder. "I have no qualms about murdering mercenary women to protect my people," he says. "Who are you? Tell me or die."

"I am . . . ," I whisper. I remember dying, and no matter what anyone else believes, it does not hurt. "I am not afraid to die. A swift death is painless," I snap. The knife comes away from my neck, and he shoves me so hard that I fly forward and skid to a stop on my face in the coarse grass. I push myself up to sitting, swipe my long, loose hair out of my face, and glare up at my two captors even though my insides are quivering with fear.

"Who are you, and why are you in my kingdom with two armed men?" the man who held the knife at my throat asks. *My* kingdom? My fear melts in half, and I slowly climb to my feet.

"Keep your guard up, Jessen. She's a trained fighter," the man holding my weapons says. He sounds just like Golmarr—the tone of his deep voice, the slight accent. He lifts my dagger to the moonlight and studies it.

"This is your land?" I ask, studying Jessen.

He lifts his sword between us and answers, "Aye, lass. And what black deeds do you plan for my people?"

"You are Golmarr's brothers," I whisper.

His face hardens with fury at mention of his brother's name. "Who are you, and what—"

"Golmarr brought me!" I blurt, and turn from my captors to look for him.

"Our brother is dead," Jessen growls. "He followed a pretty face into a dragon's lair."

"He always was a fool for a pretty face, God rest his soul," the other brother says, shaking his head.

"We lived," I whisper, looking from one man to the other.

The man holding my knife looks at me. In the moonlight I can see that his eyes are narrowed, his mouth frowning. He looks at the knife again. "She is carrying Father's knife, Jessen. The one he gave to the northern princess before we lowered her down to the fire dragon's cave." He holds the knife out to his brother, who takes it from his hand and runs his finger over the hilt.

"Are you Princess Sorrowlynn?" Jessen asks. I nod, but even in the dim light I can see the skepticism in his narrowed eyes. "Northern princesses do not know how to fight."

"Not until now," I say, squaring my shoulders and lifting my chin in defiance.

"I am Yerengul of Anthar. If you are who you say you are, then *where* is my little brother?"

I turn in the direction I last saw him and point. "He was there a moment ago, but now—"

My words are cut short by Yerengul's laughter. "Jessen! We took down our own brother! I thought I recognized his voice before I cracked him over the head."

"We'll see," Jessen growls. He tucks my knife in his belt, grips my upper arm, and drags me forward. When we have gone ten paces, I see a dark mass hidden by the tall grass.

Jessen shoves me at it, and I trip on my skirt and crash down onto my hands and knees, landing beside an unconscious Enzio bound hand and foot by rope.

"Enzio?" I shake his shoulder and he groans. I move to Golmarr and lean over him, and my hair falls around his face. Gently, I lift his head and press my palm to his cheek. "Golmarr," I say. His skin is cold, and his neck is limp. "Golmarr?" I pat his cheek, and he doesn't stir. Carefully, I lay his head back onto the ground and glare up at his brothers. "What did you do to him?" I snap. "He already had a head wound!" I stand and ball my fists. "What did you do to him?" I shout, and shove Jessen as hard as I can. He stumbles back a step and grabs both my wrists.

"Yeren, check and see if it's really him before I knock this little fox on the head to shut her up," Jessen says, tightening his hold on me.

Yerengul kneels beside Golmarr and leans close to him. After a quick inspection, he gently shakes Golmarr's shoulders. He looks at Jessen and nods. "It is him, but his hair is short." Looking back at Golmarr he says, "Brother, wake up." He lifts Golmarr's hand and lets it go, and it flops back to the ground. "Evay is going to kill us if we've killed him."

Evay. Golmarr's sweetheart. The mere mention of her name makes me sick to my stomach.

Jessen curses and drops my wrists and kneels at Golmarr's side. He lifts something from his belt—a water skin—and pours water onto Golmarr's face. Golmarr flinches and swipes at his nose, and his eyes flicker open. Yerengul whoops with delight and throws his arms around his brother.

Golmarr groans. "Gently, Yeren," he croaks. "Did you really have to hit me so hard?"

"You're practically bald," Yerengul says with a laugh.

"I didn't recognize your ugly face without your hair hanging around it. And you're supposed to be dead! What happened?"

Golmarr pushes himself to sitting, and his eyes search the darkness until they find me. "You didn't hurt her, did you?" he asks his brothers.

"Not as bad as she hurt me," Yerengul says, rubbing his stomach.

Golmarr grips his brother's shirt. "You hurt her?"

"No, we didn't hurt her," Yerengul says. Golmarr's hand falls back to his side. "But speaking of hurting someone, Evay is going beat you to a pulp when she sees you're alive," Yerengul adds quietly. "When she found out you *willingly* pledged your troth to a Faodarian princess, and then followed her into the dragon's cave against Father's will, she flew into a grief-stricken rage. She's been taking her pain out on anyone who so much as looks at her."

Evay again. I drop my gaze and study my clasped hands.

"I never pledged myself to Evay. She has no claim on me," Golmarr says. "Why are you patrolling so close to the border, and where are your horses?"

Jessen stands and looks north toward the forest, and the wind blows his long, dark hair around his face. "Nayadi had one of her visions. She said something was going to be coming out of the forest."

"What?" Golmarr asks.

"She wasn't sure, but I am beginning to think she meant you. Rest for now. Yerengul and I will get our horses and stand watch."

Golmarr wobbles to his feet and clasps his brother's arm for balance. "I'll help keep watch," he says, but Jessen shakes his head.

"Rest, little brother. Yeren gave you quite a bonk. We will travel home at first light."

⊹—⊹—≡≎≍⊹—⊹—⊹

I do not sleep well, lying on the hard ground, wrapped in a cloak, between Golmarr and Enzio. The cool night air creeps into me, and no matter how I wrap the cloak around my body, I cannot keep the chill at bay.

My eyes pop open when I feel hands crushing my throat. Armed men lie dead in the smoldering grass beside me, and overhead a shimmering orange dragon circles through the cloudy sky—I can see it just beyond the face of the man trying desperately to suffocate me. I claw at his hands and squeeze my eyes shut. When I open them again, the sky is blue, no hands are on my throat, the golden grass is free of dead bodies, and I am looking up into Enzio's startled face.

"It is time to wake up," he says. I press my hands to my throat and swallow. Enzio takes an extra cloak off of me—Golmarr's—and helps me to my feet, studying me from the corner of his eye. "Nightmare?" he asks. I nod, and for a split second I see the charred grass again, feel the heat rising from it, and taste the smoke thick in the air. I close my eyes and rub them. "Sometimes, after the Black Blades have been attacked, I won't sleep because I know if I do, I will relive the battle through my nightmares. It is the price we warriors pay."

I nod. I *was* reliving a battle through my nightmare—just not my own battle.

"Golmarr has your breakfast," he says, nodding toward the rising sun.

Golmarr and his brothers are quietly talking beside our two horses, which have been joined by two more. The brothers are both a little bit taller and broader than Golmarr, they both have the same glossy, dark hair, but one has a bit of girth around his belly and his shoulders, like a man gets when he has long outgrown boyhood. I watch Golmarr slide the reforged sword from its sheath at his hip, and his brothers' eyes grow wide. The thinner one takes the sword and runs his hand reverently over the blade.

At my approach, Golmarr turns and looks at me, and a hint of a smile brightens his eyes. "Sorrowlynn." He strides over, his legs swishing against the grass, and wraps me in an embrace. His hand cradles the back of my head to his shoulder and tangles in my hair. I close my arms around his waist and breathe in the familiar smell of him.

"Good morning," he whispers, and kisses my forehead. His brothers are staring at us, both with shocked expressions on their faces.

"Evay is going to pummel you, Golmarr," the thinner brother says.

"I already told you that Evay has no claim on me, Yerengul. She has never said she loves me, and I have never said that I love her," Golmarr says, putting his arm around my waist and resting his hand on my hip.

"It's a good thing you know how to fight, Princess Sorrowlynn," Yerengul says, tossing my staff to me. I catch it with one hand.

"If Evay wants to pick a fight with someone, it is going to be me, not Princess Sorrowlynn," Golmarr snaps. He turns back to me, and I can see anger gathering in his eyes. "Princess Sorrowlynn, this is my brother Yerengul"—he motions to the thinner brother—"and my brother Jessen." He motions to the thicker, older brother.

"I am pleased to meet you, Prince Jessen, Prince Yeren-gul," I say, and grip the sides of my purple skirt and curtsy.

They both study me in silence, scowling, until Jessen clears his throat. "Welcome to Anthar, Princess," he says, and elbows Yerengul in the ribs.

"Yes, welcome," Yerengul repeats. His gaze moves slowly from my loose hair all the way down to my feet and back up. A gleam of mischief shines in his eyes, and he grins. "Nice going, little brother. You slayed the fire dragon *and* won the heart of the fair princess."

Golmarr shakes his head. "No, you've got that back-ward, Yeren." My heart starts hammering in my chest and I look at Golmarr, wondering if he's going to tell them that I slayed the fire dragon and not him. I shake my head the slightest bit, pleading with my eyes not to tell them the truth. He puts his hand beneath my chin. "I don't know if I won the heart of the fair princess, but she won mine." He stares into my eyes, searching them, looking for the answer to what he has said, looking to see if he has, in fact, won my heart.

Yerengul claps his shoulder. "Evay is going to kill you."

Golmarr grimaces. "Yes, she is."

"Do you know what Golmarr said the night of the feast, after he danced with you in your mother's hall?" Yerengul asks me, his eyes dancing with mischief.

Golmarr shakes his head. "Shut up, Yeren," he growls.

Yerengul laughs. "He said, 'If I was betrothed to her, I would have no problem taking her to my bed on our wed-ding night.'"

Golmarr flinches and looks at me.

I gasp. "You are a scoundrel!"

A slow smile spreads over his face. "What can I say? It's true. And if anything, it is even truer now." He quickly presses a kiss to my lips and then darts away before I can retaliate.

Chapter 24

I ride in front of Golmarr, with his hands loosely holding my waist. Enzio and Golmarr's brothers ride behind us so that I, at Golmarr's request, get an unobstructed view of the glorious Antharian grasslands. We ride in silence over rolling hills, and by the way he keeps fidgeting with my thick leather belt, I can tell something is bothering him. When the sun has crawled a quarter of the way across the sky, he clears his throat. "I need to ask you something, Sorrowlynn," he says quietly, so only I can hear.

"Then ask." I turn my head to the side so I can see him. He takes one hand from my hip and runs it through his short hair, and his eyes turn cautious. A touch of apprehension coils in my belly. "What's wrong?" I whisper, wishing I could reach back and smooth the crease from between his black eyebrows.

"I've never asked you . . . that is, I've only assumed, based on the way you kissed me, that you're not opposed to having me . . . how do they say it in your land? *Court* you?"

I turn away from him so he can't see the warmth that has risen to my cheeks, and a smile dances to my mouth. "No, I'm not opposed," I say. Releasing the reins with one hand, I lift his hand from my hip and wrap his arm around my waist, weaving my fingers over the top of his. "I'm not opposed at all."

"Sorrowlynn of Faodara. I am *courting* Princess Sorrowlynn of Faodara." He pulls my hair away from my neck and I feel his warm, moist lips against my skin. I shiver at the touch and tilt my head to the side, exposing more skin to be kissed.

"I see that, Golmarr!" Yerengul yells from behind.

Golmarr chuckles and drops my hair. "Maybe if you could find a woman who liked your ugly face, you wouldn't have to live vicariously through your younger brother," he yells back, and tightens his arm around my waist.

"How much older is Yerengul than you?" I ask.

"Two years," Golmarr says. "And Jessen is thirteen years older. Yerengul and I have the same mother—we were born by my father's second wife. She died giving birth to me."

"I'm sorry she died."

By the time the sun has reached the highest point in the sky and then moved a little way west, we are riding along a well-traveled dirt road lined with fenced pastures filled with cattle, sheep, and horses, or covered with row after row of corn or wheat. Men, women, and children are out in the fields, working and playing. They do not look like the fierce barbarians who are rumored to inhabit Anthar. I cannot make sense of it. "If your people are farmers, why do you all have such a reputation for fighting?"

"Three hundred years ago, when the fire dragon destroyed this land, he razed the ground with fire. Every living thing that could not find shelter was burned, almost all of our warriors were killed, and Anthar was populated by widows and their starving children," Golmarr explains. I blink and see the charred ground, how it looked three hundred years ago. "Out of necessity, our women learned to fight and taught their children how to fight. After the fire dragon was bound beneath the mountain, after my ancestors started to rebuild, we discovered that our soil was richer than it had ever been. Our crops grow larger and sweeter than any others. Our cattle grow bigger, our horses stronger and faster from grazing these fields. Because of the dragon fire, this is good, fertile land. We also discovered a woman who is fighting to protect her home and her children can be a fiercer warrior than a man. So ever since then, our women have trained to be warriors and fight alongside the men.

"The Trevonan to the west want our land, so they test us regularly to see how strong we are. The men hiding in the Glass Forest, too," he explains. "If my kingdom were not bound to your kingdom through the threat of a dragon and the possibility of arranged marriage, I would not be surprised if your father tried to take our land."

Lord Damar's face fills my mind—his cruel blue eyes, his cheeks flushed and beaded with sweat from whipping me so hard—and I stiffen. "Lord Damar is *not* my father," I whisper. "Queen Felicitia is my mother, but that man is not my father."

"Who is?" Golmarr asks, his voice gentle but not surprised.

"Ornald, the guard who found us out riding horses on the morning of the ceremony. When Lord Damar whipped me for riding astride, Ornald stopped him before he could draw more than one stripe of blood. At the time I didn't know why he intervened, but it is because he is my father." I think of him escorting me to greet the Antharian horse lords on the day of my sixteenth birthday, think of Lord Damar's shocked outrage, my mother's anger at the sight of my hand on Ornald's arm. Now I understand their reactions. My true father escorted me to my first official ceremony, and it enraged them.

"So you're the daughter of a Satari man," he says. "No wonder their clothes look so good on you."

I frown at him over my shoulder. "Satari man?" I shake my head. "Ornald is Faodarian. He used to be the captain of the guard."

"He's Satari, Sorrowlynn—at least he used to be. Have you never noticed the earring holes in his ears that never grew back? And the short sword he carries? And the slant to his eyes is very Satari. Look at Enzio." I study Enzio, riding directly behind us. His eyes are a striking blue, like his mother's, and at the corners they turn up. "Even the name *Ornald* is a Satari name."

I frown at Golmarr. "Surely you're wrong."

Golmarr turns and looks at Enzio. "Is Ornald a Satari name?" he asks.

Enzio nods. "It is a most respectable Satari name. My uncle was named Ornald."

"See?" Golmarr says, amused at my shocked expression. "Is that why you picked the name Ornald for me when we were taken by the Satari? Because it is . . . special to you?"

I nod. "I gave you the name of my father."

The amusement in his eyes is replaced with a more solemn emotion I cannot name. "You gave me a great honor, giving me your father's name. I thank you."

"You're welcome."

"Sorrowlynn, look. That is Kreeose, my city." Golmarr points forward. We crest a rolling hill, and at the top, the world opens up. Golmarr dismounts, and I do the same, groaning at the stiffness in my body. After a moment, I shield my eyes from the afternoon sun and look around. The farmers' green fields slowly taper off to the houses and streets and buildings of a large city. Beyond them, the horizon is a deep blue line before it touches the pale blue sky. "That is the ocean," Golmarr says, and I know he means the dark blue line, for I saw it on the maps I studied as a child, but to see it now, with my own eyes—my heart swells against my breast.

Jessen and Yerengul trot up to us. "We're going to ride ahead and tell Father we found you," Jessen says. "He's not been feeling well since we returned, and we don't want to give him too much of a shock."

"You nearly killed him with worry, Golmarr," Yerengul says. "He will be glad to see you . . . with your self-proclaimed betrothed at your side, no less," he adds with a wink. My stomach swirls at Yerengul's words. I *am* Golmarr's self-proclaimed betrothed. At the binding ceremony, he asked me to marry him—and I accepted. "Enzio, come on, man. We'll let these two take their time arriving, but you, my Satari friend, look like you could use a good, hearty meal and a bath." Jessen and Yerengul lean forward, and their mounts dig their hooves into the ground and gallop toward the city.

Instead of following, Enzio turns to me and says, "I am your sworn protector. Would you like me to stay with you?"

"No. Please go and have a bath and some food."

He grins and kicks his horse into a gallop, following Golmarr's brothers.

"Do you think we're still betrothed?" Golmarr asks. "I made a solemn promise to you at the binding ceremony." Speechless, I stare after his brothers. "I guess what I should be asking is . . . Sorrowlynn, if we are still betrothed, would you like me to ask my father to have it annulled?" He puts his hand under my chin and gently turns my face to his so I am looking at him.

"I have to ask you something first." The pit of my stomach swirls, and the air feels too heavy. "You said when you kissed me by the waterfall that I bewitched you with my magic."

He nods. "That's how it feels."

"What if that feeling is for the dragon part of me?"

His brow furrows, and he runs a hand through his hair. "I don't understand what you mean."

I start rolling the leather lace of my shirt between my fingers so I don't have to look at him. "It feels like you didn't start liking me until after I killed Zhun—after I changed. What if I somehow influenced you with the dragon's magic? Or maybe, because I healed you and a part of me went into you, I *have* bewitched you."

"You haven't bewitched me. I *love* you, Sorrowlynn. It started the moment I realized you were going to try to steal my father's horse and run." I look at him, and my eyes fill with tears. When I blink, they trickle down my cheeks. "And then, when you stood in front of your Faodarian nobles and screamed that you would rather be fed to the dragon than married against your will or sent home with your father, I loved you even more." He takes my face in his hands and rubs his thumbs over my cheeks, over the tears. "That first night in the cave, when you saved my life and got me to the lake, I woke up and your head was on my shoulder. Your teeth were chattering in your sleep, so I put my arms around you to warm you up, and we fit together perfectly. Holding you in my arms felt so right. I knew then that I wanted to hold you in my arms every night for the rest of my life. But when we were with the Satari and you told me you were going to leave with or without me because you wanted to protect them even if it meant you dying . . ." He stares down at me for a long time, his gaze moving over every inch of my face. "That was the moment I knew you had taken possession of my heart so fully, it would never be my own again. Those things have nothing to do with the dragon's treasure."

My heart seems to swell inside of me as familiar warmth fills my chest. I have faced death, learned unimaginable things, and seen part of the world, all at this man's side. In a mere eight days, I have lived a lifetime's worth of things with him. I have gained the knowledge of hundreds of men and a dragon. If there is one thing I know with certainty, with all of the dragon's victims' knowledge and experiences lending to my minute and inexperienced wisdom, it is that what I feel for this man is intense, profound love. But the most important piece of knowledge stored with the many thousands of things is that love is precious, priceless beyond all treasure, and not to be forsaken. Wars have been waged by men, laws broken, families torn apart, treasures squandered, all for love.

I put my frigid hands on Golmarr's warm cheeks and stare up into his uncertain eyes. "The dragons have it all wrong," I whisper. "I have the greatest treasure in the world at my fingertips."

"What is it?" he asks. His hands tentatively circle my waist.

"Love. Love is the greatest treasure of all, and I love you, Golmarr."

His eyes slip closed, and a gasp of air escapes his body, as if he were holding his breath. He falls to the ground, kneeling at my feet, and clasps my hands in his. For once, there is no mischief in his eyes; they are more serious than I have ever seen them. Looking up at me, he says, "Sorrowlynn of Faodara, I plight thee my troth."

I kneel in front of him so we are face to face, and blink

tears from my eyes. "And I promise to be true to you, Golmarr of Anthar."

"We need to kiss three times to make it binding," he says. We both lean toward each other and our lips touch. When Golmarr starts to lean away from me, I grab the back of his head and hold his mouth against mine a moment longer before releasing him.

Golmarr smiles and kisses me a second time, his lips more demanding, his hand twining in my hair. I sway backward with the power of the kiss and nearly lose my balance. Pulling away, he wraps his arm around my waist and slowly lowers me down into the grass so I am lying on my back, looking up at him, framed by the blue sky.

I trace my hand over his chin and slide it around the back of his neck. "I knew I never wanted to live without you when you walked away from me to fight the fire dragon, but I didn't realize what I was feeling was love until now," I whisper. He stares at me with intense, hungry eyes, and then he takes my mouth with his again, kissing me with such need that I pull his body down onto mine. I run my fingers over his back and feel the solid mass of his torso through his shirt, the strength there.

"I love it when you touch me," he breathes. He kisses the side of my jaw, my ear, and then trails kisses down my neck. The sun burns red against my closed eyes, and his lips find mine again. I am so lost in the physical sensation of Golmarr's mouth on my skin, on my mouth, of my hands against his body, that for a long time I think of nothing but him. The sun slowly moves farther across the sky, yet time seems to stand still. I almost forget everything but this moment. But not quite.

When his mouth leaves mine and trails kisses down my neck once more, I press my hand to his cheek and say,

"Golmarr, we're not married yet." The words hurt because I know they will put an end to this.

He presses a moist, lingering kiss to my throat and then rolls to the side, balancing on one elbow. He is breathing hard, and his cheeks are flushed. With a frown, he says, "I wasn't going to cross that line with you . . . yet."

His shirt is up around his ribs, exposing his firm, suntanned stomach. I place my hand on it, feeling the strong muscles beneath his skin. I slide my hand up over his ribs and press it against his heart. It is beating hard and so fast that the beats are all jumbled together.

"Sorrowlynn," he growls. I look up at him. His eyes are fiercer than I have ever seen them before. "You need to remove your hand from me right now."

I smile, and slowly, feeling every rippling muscle in his torso, trail my hand back down to his stomach and remove it. He pulls his lips tight against his teeth and cringes as if my touch has caused him physical pain.

"You northern princesses may play innocent, but you, Sorrowlynn, are going to drive me crazy. You have me asking to court you in the morning, begging you to marry me in the afternoon, and then you can't keep your hands off me!" He kisses me quickly on the nose and stands. "Come on. We need to hurry up and get around other people."

"Why?"

"I think we need a permanent chaperone if we don't want your mother's army coming after me for ruining your good name."

Chapter 25

We walk the rest of the way to town so I don't have to dismount on stiff, unbending legs in front of a group of people who prize horseback riding above every other sport. We cross a wide stone bridge that spans the Glacier River—the very river that flows down to the outskirts of Faodara—and when we step from the bridge, I pause and stare, for people are lining the city streets as far as I can see. They see us and start cheering, and a wave of panic makes it hard to breathe.

Golmarr puts his arm around my waist, with his hand resting on my hip, and looks at me. "It appears as if my brothers told more than my father that I was coming home. Are you nervous?"

I stare at the eager faces and nod. "I've rarely been around crowds," I whisper. Golmarr's arm tightens, and he kisses my forehead.

"I'll keep you safe, and I won't leave your side. My father's home—my home—is at the far end of town, close to the sea, so we still have a little way to walk. Will you be all right?"

I nod. Together, we walk forward, and the crowd starts calling Golmarr's name. Their beloved young horse lord has returned. As we walk down the cobbled street, with Golmarr holding the horse's reins in one hand, his other hand holding mine, people throw flowers at us. Children dart out of the crowd and hold chains of woven blossoms up to Golmarr. With a smile, he kneels so they can place them on his head or around his neck. When he has so many that there is room for no more, he takes them off and puts them around my neck, or on my head, or tucks them into my belt or the laces on the front of my shirt. By the time we reach the other end of town, he and I are both covered with flowers.

His people call a goodbye to us as we turn down a narrow dirt road. At the end of the road is a huge, two-story house, and behind it an open field with stables and grazing horses, and beyond that the blue-gray ocean. As we approach the house, people start pouring out of it: men, women, children of all ages. The children run to meet us, and the littlest ones throw their arms around Golmarr's legs. "Uncle Golmarr!" they cry, and pull him away from me.

Not far behind the children, Golmarr's tall, strapping brothers and their wives come striding toward him, clapping him on the back or hugging him, laughing at his short hair and Satari clothes. With each new person greeting him, I am shoved slightly farther away, until I am standing at the edge of the crowd, holding the reins of the horse, and no one seems to realize I am here.

Golmarr's father comes out, and even from where I am standing I can see the tears on his cheeks above his beard. "My son!" he bellows. He walks up to Golmarr, and they throw their arms around each other. The crowd circles them, so they are surrounded by family. "I thought I'd lost you, boy!"

"Not yet, Father," Golmarr says.

Suddenly, the people gathered around Golmarr and King

Marrkul become still and quiet. They have all turned toward the house, toward a young woman. She is wearing black pants that hug the curves of her legs, and a flowing red tunic that hangs below her hips. A black belt holding a sword on one side and a knife on the other is cinched over the red shirt. Her dark eyes are like a brewing storm. As she walks toward Golmarr, her straight black hair flows out behind her, and if she didn't look so furious, she would be beautiful.

The crowd parts for her, quickly stepping aside before she can knock someone over. "How dare you say you'll marry some weak northern princess just to save her from the dragon!" she growls, stopping right in front of Golmarr. She puts her hands on his chest and shoves him back a step. "No man deserves to be tied to a woman for the rest of his life because he feels it is his duty to *protect* her!"

Golmarr puts up his hands. "Evay, can we please speak in private?" She smacks his hands away, wraps her arms around his neck, and kisses him. He grabs her shoulders so hard that even from where I stand, I can see his knuckles have turned white. I grip the reins tighter and resist the urge to yell at her to stop kissing him. Golmarr turns his head to the side so Evay is kissing his cheek and pushes her back.

"I am still betrothed to that northern princess," he says, and I can hear the anger in his voice.

"Then have your father break it."

"No. I don't want him to," Golmarr patiently explains. "By my own free will and choice, I have given her my heart."

"You have given her your heart . . . just like that? But you've only know her a handful of days!" Evay snaps. "You have known me for years, yet you never fully gave your heart to me."

"You are right, but I don't think you truly love me, Evay,

and what I feel for you dims in comparison to what I feel for the Faodarian princess. You should be cherished and loved, and cherish and love in return. You deserve far more than we had." Golmarr looks at me, and everyone gathered around him turns to stare at the forgotten companion he returned with.

Evay's furious eyes lock on mine, and she shoves past Golmarr. The crowd parts for her, opening a pathway that leads directly to me, and she pulls the sword from her belt as she stomps forward.

"Evay, no!" Golmarr cries, but the crowd closes the pathway, sealing him away. "Move out of my way," he shouts, fighting against them, but they are so transfixed on me and Evay that they ignore him.

Without hesitating, I slide my staff from the strap on the horse's saddle and balance on my toes as my heart starts pounding so hard I feel like it is going to choke me. But then I look at her—really look. She is one person, closely matched to me in size and height. She is not a dragon. She is not a muscular mercenary. My heart steadies itself, and I step away from the horse as a quiet confidence settles over me.

Evay stops in front of me, and her eyes roam slowly over my body and fill with disgust. *Surely, she won't swing her sword,* I think. *Surely she is just trying to intimidate me.* And then her sword catches the afternoon light as she waves it in front of my face.

I recognize instantly that she does not mean to touch me with her blade, only scare me, but her actions fill me with anger, and I swing my staff up anyway. It shimmers in the sunlight as it clangs against Evay's sword. Pressing my weapon to hers, I step close to her and stare right into her dark eyes. "I am no fool, Evay. You did not intend to touch me with your sword—just frighten me," I say. "But I'm not scared of you. Not after the things I have fought."

For a moment the fury in her eyes is replaced with shock. Then her nostrils flare with anger and she swings her sword again, a blow that *will* injure me if I do not block it. So I slam her weapon aside and drive forward, attacking hard and fast. She stumbles back as she desperately tries to deflect my blows, but she is not as fast as I am, and not as strong as others I have fought in the last day. When I fight her, because of the dragon's treasure, I can almost see what she is going to do before she does it, and so I have the advantage. From the corner of my eye, I see Golmarr. He has broken through the crowd to come to my aid, but is standing aside and watching instead as Evay desperately tries to defend herself.

Within half a minute my arms start trembling, my heart feels like it is fluttering too fast, and sweat has beaded on my brow. I can feel the consequence of a week of near starvation, coupled with the strain of the fighting I have done in the same amount of time, not to mention my sedate life prior to going into the dragon's lair. My hunger, my fatigue, and my physical weakness are going to lose this battle for me. I am my own worst enemy.

Desperate to put an end to the fight, I swing my weapon behind Evay's knees and thrust my foot into her stomach, knocking her to the ground. She lands on her back with a noisy thud, and I pierce the shoulder of her voluminous red blouse to the dirt with the tip of my staff. "I do not want to fight anymore," I say.

The air explodes with clapping and whooping. Evay shoves my staff from her shirt and rolls to her feet, glaring at me over her shoulder as she storms away. Golmarr steps up to me and puts his hands on my shoulders. "I'm sorry," he says. "I didn't think she would actually—"

"She *wasn't* trying to hurt me at first. I provoked her," I admit.

He frowns and smiles at the same time. "You provoked her?" I nod and wipe the sweat from my brow with a trembling hand. He tips his head back and laughs, and wraps his arms around my shoulders. "I love you," he says, loud and clear, for everyone to hear. "Come and meet my family." I nod, but wrap my arm around his waist and lean into him because my body is so heavy with fatigue that I am about to fall down. "Are you all right?" he quietly asks.

I shake my head. "I am so tired I can hardly stand," I admit. "I need to lie down." A single tear trickles out of the corner of my eye.

Golmarr scoops me up into his arms and cradles me against him. I wrap my arms around his neck and lay my head on his chest. "It looks like I will be carrying you over another threshold," he says. We slowly walk through the gathered crowd. They peer at me curiously. Some of the children ask why their uncle is carrying me, but they are shushed by their mothers. Golmarr pauses beside his father, and the great man smiles at me as if it is totally normal for his son to carry princesses.

"It is a pleasure to see you alive, Princess Sorrowlynn," King Marrkul says. He looks to his son, and his forehead creases with worry. He puts his hand on Golmarr's shoulder and leans in close to him. "Is she all right? What does she need?" He speaks quietly, for only Golmarr and me to hear.

"Can you send Nayadi to my room?" Golmarr asks.

Marrkul looks at me and nods. "Of course, but son, you have got to be careful. If we do anything that so much as hints at impropriety concerning Princess Sorrowlynn, we risk starting a war between our two kingdoms. We need to treat this situation with as much formality as possible."

"I already know that, Father. I have been as careful as possible, under the circumstances."

"Now go get her settled. I will send Nayadi to you."

Chapter 26

King Marrkul's house is made all of golden wood—the floors, the walls, and even the ceiling. Bright, colorful rugs and wall tapestries add color to the wood, and it smells like beef, onions, and potatoes inside.

Golmarr strides through the house and carries me up a wooden staircase. With his toe, he pushes a door open and walks me to a bed, carefully laying me down on top of it. Taking my feet in his lap, he removes my red shoes and sets them down beside the bed. Next, he unstraps my belt and places it on the bedside table. He takes my staff from me and leans it in a corner of the room, and then pulls the bedcovers back and helps me under them. I press my face against the goose-down pillow and inhale. It smells like Golmarr.

The room is clean and organized, with a window to my left, framed by two bookshelves. One wooden bookshelf holds volume after volume of leather-bound books—all about either fighting or dragons. The other bookshelf holds row after row of weapons; knives, daggers, a short sword, arrow tips, throwing stars. "Is this your room?" I ask, turning on my side and pulling the covers up over my shoulder.

Mischief fills Golmarr's eyes and he nods. "Looks like I got you into my bed before we are married." Kneeling, he brushes the hair from the side of my face.

"What did your father mean about impropriety starting a war with Faodara?"

One of Golmarr's black eyebrows lifts ever so slightly. "Don't you know?"

My cheeks warm as I say, "I have my suspicions." I look at his lips, and my heart starts pounding.

Golmarr grins and puts his hand over my flushed cheek. "My father meant that if I bed the virgin princess of Faodara before we are wed, I will most likely start a war." He shrugs. "But I already knew that. Do you want me to bring up some dinner?" My stomach rumbles at the thought of food, and Golmarr laughs. "I take that as a yes. Do you need anything else?"

"I need to get warm." I burrow deeper under the covers and shiver. Worry tightens the corners of Golmarr's eyes. He climbs onto the bed, on top of the covers, and presses the front of his body against the back of mine, wrapping an arm around me. Pressing his nose against my neck, he exhales warm breath on my skin. "I'm worried about you," he whispers.

The bedroom door opens, and Nayadi, King Marrkul's witch, shuffles inside. I jump and wait for Golmarr to spring away from me so we are not caught in bed together, but all he does is tighten his hold around my waist. Nayadi walks to the side of the bed and peers down at me with her foggy eyes. A trickle of fear sends goose bumps up the back of my neck.

"It is about time you made it home," she says, her blind eyes surveying Golmarr. They shift to me, and she runs her hands through the air in front of me, like she is combing her fingers through hair. She pulls a handful of air toward her face and leans into it, breathing deeply. Her eyes slip shut for a moment, and the sides of her mouth slowly pull into a wide, toothless smile. With a growl, she opens her eyes and grasps my cheeks in her bony fingers, pinching them so hard that I yelp and pull away, but she doesn't let go. Golmarr's arm leaves my waist, and he grabs Nayadi's wrist, shoving her hand from my face.

"What are you doing?" he asks, climbing over the top of me without letting go of the old crone. Nayadi pulls her lips away from her gums, and for a moment it looks like she is snarling . . . but then she smiles, and I wonder if I imagined it.

"*She* killed the dragon," Nayadi says. "Not you."

Golmarr drops her wrist and steps between me and the witch. "Why would you say that?"

"She's marked with his magic for anyone with seeing eyes to behold. He left his golden aura around her." She runs her hand through the air in front of me again, but Golmarr grabs her wrist. And then her words register. She called the dragon *he*, not *it*.

"You knew him," I whisper and blink, and when I open my eyes again, the discoloration leaves Nayadi's eyes, and I see her how she once was: long, dark brown hair braided down her back, smooth pale skin, blue eyes, two curved swords held in either hand. Unbidden, a memory of this woman overtakes my thoughts, and I know I am witnessing something Melchior the wizard passed on to me.

When she walks into my tower, the first thing I notice is her face. She is barely older than a child. Her eyes are such a pale shade of blue that I cannot help but stare into them for a moment. They are framed by black lashes, and her dark, braided hair makes the pale color even more remarkable. At her waist she carries the black stone blade of her people. Her twin swords are strapped to her back, as I requested, and I can tell by the way she keeps tightening her shoulders, she is forcing herself not to draw them.

Piles of gold are behind me, the treasure I got from two desperate kings. The payment for binding the fire dragon beneath the mountain nearly two hundred years earlier. Not a single piece of the treasure has been spent or lost; it is as complete as the day it was delivered to me. She studies the treasure, and greed fills her eyes. It diminishes any beauty I first thought she had, for I have had hundreds of years to learn what true beauty is.

"I will divide this in half. You may pick either pile, Nayadi. You take half of the pile now, and when you have brought me the fire dragon's scale, you will get the other half," I say.

She forces her eyes away from the treasure to look at me. "What is the worth of a single dragon scale?" she asks.

I shrug. "They have no worth, for there are none except those attached to the beasts."

Her eyes narrow. "Then why are you paying me so much to bring you one, Melchior, son of Mordecai?" I frown at her words. "I know who you are, old man. And I know how old you are. That is what I want—eternal life, not your gold. Tell me how to get that, and I will bring you a dragon scale."

I take a deep, patient breath. "I have watched almost every person I have ever cared for die from old age or disease. Eternal life is not necessarily a treasure, though once I thought it was."

"Then tell me how to become like you, a wizard, so that I can bind the stone dragon that is destroying my kingdom beneath a mountain, the same way you bound the fire dragon. That is what I want in exchange for the fire dragon's scale."

I shake my head. "You don't know what you're saying, child. The price will be high. Everything comes at a price."

"I am no child! I am nineteen. And any price is worth saving my kingdom."

"Very well. If the ability to work magic is the payment you wish, then you have only to perform this feat and you will have it, but I make no promises regarding the stone dragon." She blinks at me and smiles. I stare into her striking blue eyes. Such a pity. Such a high price to pay. "Hold out your swords."

She reaches over her head and crosses her arms, sliding a short sword out from a sheath behind each shoulder. She lowers them before me, and I pull energy from the air and touch each blade. When I am done, the metal has turned from gray to a pale, silvery blue. "You have seven days before the magic leaves your blades. Seven days to face the fire dragon before your weapons are worthless against his scales."

"Why don't I just kill him?" she asks.

"Because you cannot." Her eyes burn with defiance at my words. "It is not in your destiny to kill him—at least not with your own hands. But your choices today will one day bring about his death, and set in motion the defeat of Grinndoar, the stone dragon."

"We'll see," she snaps. In one swift move, she crosses the swords behind her back and thrusts them into their sheaths. Without a backward glance, she strides from my room.

"Such a high price," I whisper.

I blink, and no time has passed. Golmarr still sits on the bed beside me with Nayadi's wrist in his hand, and she is still staring at me with her clouded eyes. "You tried to kill Zhun, didn't you?" I ask.

The old woman nods. "When I took his scale, I stabbed him." She touches her face. "His blood burned my eyes and gifted me with a tiny piece of his magic, but stole my sight."

I see her through Zhun's eyes, as she tears the scale free with one sword, and then thrusts the other deep into his chest. I see the blood rain down on her as the fire dragon takes flight in his columned, underground prison.

"Was it worth it?" I ask.

"It will be when the time is right," she says, studying me with hungry eyes.

"But you can still see."

She shakes her head. "Not in the way you do. I see energy, not flesh."

"Nayadi, what's wrong with Sorrowlynn?" Golmarr asks, releasing her wrist. "She healed me, and now she can't warm up."

"She needs to feed on what Zhun fed on," the crone says.

"Fire," I whisper. That has always been the answer.

"Yes, fire," she says. "But you don't know how to feed on fire, do you?"

I shake my head.

Nayadi smiles, and my skin crawls. "Then you might die."

Golmarr's hands close into tight fists, and his breathing accelerates. "There must be something you can do," he growls. "If she dies because she saved my life—"

"I can't," Nayadi snarls. "She has to do it herself." The crone leans toward me again and closes her eyes, as if basking in the golden aura she spoke of. Golmarr grabs her frail arm and drags her toward the door.

"Out. Go!" he orders, pushing her into the hall. He slams

the door shut and looks at me. "You stay there. I will have Enzio stand watch at your door while I get you some food."

I nod and curl my knees up against my chest. The sound of Golmarr's boots echoes on the wooden floor as he leaves the room and strides down the hall. Before he has gone down three stairs, I am drifting to sleep.

Chapter 27

It is the smell of bacon that wakes me, and I open my eyes to bright morning sunlight. I am still in Golmarr's bed, and the last thing I remember is him leaving the room to get me some food. On the bedside table is a bowl of cold stew and a piece of dry bread.

I pull the covers back, and my Satari clothes are creased with wrinkles. Standing, I try to smooth my blouse but give up when the wrinkles refuse to straighten out. My stomach growls, and I forget the wrinkled clothes as I quietly pad across Golmarr's bedroom on bare feet.

When I open the door, the smell of bacon and the sound of distant laughter swirl around me. The laughter dies down and is replaced with a deep, muffled voice. As I descend the wooden stairs, the voice becomes clearer. It is Golmarr's. He is telling the story of how the fire dragon burned his hair, and how he knelt at my feet and had me hack his hair off with the hunting knife his father gave me. And people are laughing.

"It is a good thing northern princesses prefer men with short hair," a woman says. "Otherwise, I don't think she would agree to marry you. You are a disgrace!"

Laughter spills out of a partially open door, along with the maddening scent of bacon. It is my overwhelming desire for food that gives me the courage to push the door open and step inside—barefoot, with rumpled and slept-in clothes, and unbrushed hair.

The kitchen is huge—more of a great hall, really—with a wide hearth, iron stove, and water pump for the food preparation, and a table big enough to seat Enzio, Golmarr, Golmarr's father, his eight brothers, and their wives. Those who don't have room at the table—mainly children—are sitting on benches pushed up against the wall, and everyone is eating.

Golmarr's eyes are on the door, like he's been watching for me, so the moment I step inside, he stops laughing and stands. "Speaking of knife-wielding, hair-chopping, skirt-hacking northern princesses," he says, "it is my pleasure to formally introduce you, once again, to Princess Sorrowlynn of Faodara."

My eyes grow round with horror, and I shake my head and point to my slept-in clothing. I am most definitely not attired properly to be presented to his entire family. But Golmarr simply smiles.

At my hesitation, King Marrkul hastily stands from the head of the table and motions to his chair, which is beside Golmarr's. "Please, have a seat and fill your belly, Princess Sorrowlynn," he says.

Holding my limp skirt in my hands, I curtsy to him and search for the proper response to give to the ruler of a neighboring kingdom. "Thank you, sir, but I cannot take *your* chair. You are the king!"

He waves his hand dismissively. "Nonsense. A king I might be, but shortly I will be your father as well. And I treasure my daughters-in-law."

A small smile cracks through my reserve. "Thank you,"

I say, and walk across the cool wood floor to the chair at the head of the table.

One of the women, dressed in brown leather pants and a green tunic, hurries over to the stove with a clean plate. A moment later she places it before me, and I recognize her. It is Jayah, the wife of Ingvar. She has loaded fried potatoes, bacon, and eggs so high, I cannot see the glazed plate beneath.

"Thank you," I say.

She nods. "There's more if you finish that."

A hand finds mine beneath the table—warm fingers against my cold ones. "Good morning," Golmarr says. He is clean and shaven. His clothes are fresh, and his hair is brushed. The mere sight of him makes my heart beat a little faster, and I tighten my fingers on his.

I start eating, with my free hand in Golmarr's, and listen as he tells of more of our adventures, embellishing them and making them funny in the retelling, like when he came running over to save me from the burly mercenary when we were fighting in the Satari wagon camp. Only, before he could impress me with his fighting skills and perform his knightly duty by killing the fiend, the vile man started to totter forward and back like a chopped tree, falling dead with his nose on the toes of my red leather shoes. "She had already saved herself," he adds, shrugging.

Golmarr's family burst into laughter, but I can barely muster up a weak smile. The memory is still too fresh for me to see the humor in it.

"Have you kissed her yet?" one of the older children asks—a boy with raven-black hair and the long, gangly legs and arms that are an indicator of an upcoming growth spurt.

Golmarr's eyebrows shoot up and he looks at me. "I didn't

have to. *She* kissed *me*," he says. "And in front of the entire camp of Satari forest dwellers, no less!"

I gasp and glare at Golmarr. "The only reason I kissed you in front of them is because you told me if I didn't, they might try to kill us." I turn and look at his amused brothers and sisters-in-law. "I figured if I could be sacrificed to a fire-breathing dragon and live, my chances at surviving the kiss of a horse lord were probably pretty good."

His family starts laughing so hard the table shakes. When they quiet down, Golmarr adds, "I am starting to think the stories we hear about the reserved and refined northern princesses of Faodara are tales made to hide their true colors."

Yerengul, sitting directly across the table from me, lifts his hand, and the room grows quiet. "Princess Sorrowlynn," he says, "you wouldn't happen to have any single sisters, would you? Because I am in need of a wife who can give the teasing as well as she takes it, and if she's beautiful and knows how to fight, all the better."

The laughter is back. Golmarr presses a quick kiss to my cheek, and I eat as he continues telling his family of our adventures.

<hr />

I spend the rest of the morning soaking in a tub and scrubbing my hair and body by myself for the first time in my life. When I am clean, I dress in a short-sleeve black tunic and light blue skirt embroidered with black vines—clothes left for me by Golmarr. The skirt is sewn with a hem so wide, I already know that if I sit astride a horse while wearing it, there will be enough fabric to span the horse's back while still covering my legs down to my ankles.

I fasten a narrow black belt around my waist and put on a pair of gray embossed-leather boots. Pulling my hair over my shoulder, I brush it and then braid it.

When I step from the bathing room into the hall, Golmarr is waiting for me. He looks me over and frowns. "Tell me this is real," he says, stepping in front of me.

I cannot stop my smile as I ask, "Tell you what is real?"

He steps closer and gestures to my clothes. "You. Here. Betrothed to me. Wearing the clothing of my people and looking at me in a way that makes my heart start pounding like I've just fought a battle." He leans close and takes a deep breath. "Tell me it is real," he whispers.

I grip the front of his dark blue tunic and pull his body flush against mine. Standing on my toes, I kiss him and am filled with a slew of emotions. I name each one as it fires through my body: joy, desire, pleasure, disbelief—followed immediately by belief, amazement, peace, and then an overwhelming sense of acceptance and belonging.

I pull my mouth from Golmarr's but keep holding him close to me. "It is real," I say.

"Yes," he agrees, and his eyes turn roguish a moment before he starts nuzzling my neck. "And you smell way too good for me to be expected to keep my hands off of you. Will you feed the horses with me?"

I laugh and gently push him away. "I smell good, and that makes you want to feed the horses?"

He shakes his head. "No, it makes me want to feed other things, namely my all-consuming desire for you, which is why we would be wise to go somewhere where there *aren't* twelve bedrooms with very comfortable beds in each."

"Your father's home has twelve bedrooms?" I ask.

He nods and twines his fingers with mine, pulling me

down the hall. "Twelve bedrooms, and we are the only two people in this house."

"Where are your father and Enzio?"

"They are with Ingvar, making preparations for a feast. Remember, I told you, when we were in the cave, that if we made it to Anthar, my brother would have a feast for me?"

I nod.

"Well, I was right."

We exit through a door at the back of the house and cross a wide yard with several goats cropping the lush green grass. "That is where I learned the basics of sword fighting before I was sent to our western fortress when I was eight to train with a weapons master," Golmarr says, pointing to a flat area of dirt. "That is where my brothers and I still spar and condition when we are here. Speaking of conditioning, we need to get you stronger. Starting tomorrow, you are going to train six days a week. You have the knowledge of how to move and fight, but your physical strength is . . . lacking."

I swat his arm. "Are you saying I am weak?"

He glances at the spot I swatted. "Did you touch me, or was that a gentle breeze ruffling my shirt?"

"You are lucky I left my staff in the house, because you are asking for a beating!"

We pass King Marrkul's stables; they are bigger than his house, and at least three times as large as the royal Faodarian stables. And then we stop at a fence separating the yard from a field of knee-high green grass. Dozens of horses are cropping the grass. Beyond them, the sun is glinting on the gray ocean, and I instantly know how the ocean sounds, feels, tastes, moves, and smells. It is as if *I* am the one remembering the briny water sliding through my fingertips, though

I have never seen the ocean up close. I shove the memory aside.

Golmarr hops over the fence in one swift, graceful move. I gather my skirt in my hands and follow. When we are on the other side, he puts his fingers to his lips and whistles, and the ground starts to vibrate beneath my feet as horses gallop toward us. Placing his hand on the small of my back, Golmarr pulls me close as dozens of horses press against us, nipping at him, whinnying, and pawing the ground.

"You missed me," Golmarr says, taking a moment to touch every single horse that is within his reach. "I missed you, too. I thought I might never see you again." He examines the horses and frowns. "Where is Dewdrop?" he calls. A pale gray horse with a white diamond on its forehead presses its way past the others and nuzzles Golmarr's shoulder. "There you are, Dewdrop."

"Dewdrop?" I ask. "You are an Antharian warrior, and you named your horse Dewdrop? Is it battle trained?"

Golmarr nods. "She is. She's the best horse I have ever trained—gentle, yet fierce and strong, smarter than most, and incredibly swift. But she is not mine."

"Whose horse is she?"

He puts his finger under my chin and tilts my face up. "She is yours. My betrothal gift to you."

I stare at him, and my heart feels so full that I cannot speak. Instead, I give him the Anthar hand signal for *I love you*.

He smiles and shakes his head in wonderment. "You're going to fit right in here with me and my family. Do you want to try riding Dewdrop?"

I nod, and he kneels at my feet and cups his hands. "I don't know how to ride bareback, Golmarr."

He peers up at me, squinting against the sun. "Surely there is at least one memory in your head of someone riding bareback."

I smile and put my foot into his hands and mount Dewdrop. The ample fabric of my skirt spreads over the horse's back and stays modestly around my ankles.

Golmarr mounts a black horse, and I know it is the same horse he rode to stop me from stealing his father's stallion back in Faodara. "This is Tanyani," he says. "That is the ancient Antharian word for the energy that vibrates the air when two armies collide on the battlefield." He pats Tanyani's neck. "Remember, Antharian horses are trained to respond to your movements. Lean forward to make Dewdrop run; lean back to slow down or stop. If you press against her with your right leg and lean to the right, she turns right. Same with the left. There are other things I will teach you about riding her, but not today." With that, Golmarr leans forward and Tanyani breaks into a gallop, the pound of his hooves sounding like the low rumble of thunder.

I wind my hands in Dewdrop's mane and lean forward. She doesn't start slow—simply goes from standing still to a full-out gallop, and the green field starts speeding past. The wind blows my hair from my face and presses my tunic against my chest. I feel like I am flying, and that is when the realization that I am blissfully, ridiculously happy settles over me.

The grass tapers off into sand, and Golmarr is waiting at the spot where sand and ocean meet, watching me. I lean back, and Dewdrop instantly slows, trotting up beside Golmarr.

"You are an incredibly graceful rider," he says. "Do you suppose it is because of the dragon's treasure, or are you naturally good at physical things?"

"Both, I think. I could learn a dance after seeing it done once, but my sisters always had to practice the steps over and over before they could remember them."

Golmarr dismounts and holds his hands up to me to help me down. When I am standing in front of him, he tightens his hold on my waist and says, "There is something I need to tell you." He frowns and fiddles with my belt, and I can feel tension oozing off of his taut body.

"What? Is it bad news?"

"No, nothing bad. At least, I don't think you will consider it bad news." He clears his throat. "Part of the Mountain Binding says that if the Antharian prince chooses to marry a Faodarian princess at the ceremony, he is instantly moved into the position of heir. But . . ." He studies my face, watching for a reaction. "Since the fire dragon was killed, we no longer have to follow the rules of the Mountain Binding. Tonight at the feast, I am going to formally request that I not be the Antharian heir. There are two reasons behind my choice. First, I would rather focus on protecting you from the dragons than be burdened with the duties of heir. Second, I believe some people will think that I chose to be wed to you simply to gain the throne. This is my way of proving to you and them that in no way was my choice influenced by any desire for power. How do you feel about that?"

Again, my heart does that expanding that makes it hard for me to talk. I tap my chin and try to put my thoughts into words. "If you are *not* the heir, does that alter our betrothal in any way?"

"No, of course not."

"Then I think what you just said makes me love you even more," I say. Relief washes over him, softening his entire body. "Did you think I agreed to marry you because you were going to be king one day?"

"No, it never occurred to me, but Ingvar brought it up last night while you were sleeping. I wanted to talk to you before I made my decision formal, in case you did care. And if you did, I would have rethought my decision."

"If I were not a princess, would you still want to marry me?" I ask.

He laughs. "I would marry you if you were a lowly Trevonan fishmonger's youngest daughter."

"Aren't you and the Trevonans enemies?"

"Yes, we are. That is the point." He turns and faces the ocean. "What do you think? This is the first time you have seen the ocean, right?"

I crouch and run my fingers through the damp yellow sand. "I feel like I have seen it hundreds of times before. I feel as if I have lived on its shores and fallen asleep to the constant lullaby of crashing waves." I stand and breathe in the damp, briny scent. "It is spectacular."

Golmarr abruptly turns his back to the ocean and shades his eyes with his left hand. His right hand is on his sword hilt. Two horses are approaching at a gallop. One rider has long, dark hair flowing out behind him. The other has short, dark hair.

"It is Enzio and Yerengul," I say, and Golmarr's hand falls away from his sword. Their horses' hooves throw sprays of sand behind them as they gallop to us and pull to a hard stop.

"What is wrong?" Golmarr asks.

"Nayadi is receiving a vision, but refuses to speak of it until we are all gathered," Yerengul says. "Father has called an urgent council meeting. You and Sorrowlynn are to attend.

He asks that you come with all haste and let Enzio accompany Sorrowlynn at her leisure."

"At my leisure?" I ask, looking between Yerengul and Enzio.

"They think that since you are a northern princess, you cannot ride as swiftly as a horse lord," Enzio says with a gleam in his eyes. "I told them I did not think my assistance would be needed, but I would come in case I was mistaken."

"She can keep up with us," Golmarr says.

Yerengul glances at Dewdrop. "Even riding bareback?"

"Believe me or not, Yerengul," I say, "but I know just about everything there is to know about riding."

Yerengul glares at Golmarr. "You are so lucky," he says, and then he turns and rides away.

I step through the door leading from the yard to the kitchen and pause. For the second time this day, Golmarr's family is gathered in the great kitchen, minus the children. This time, I am met by heavy silence and worried glances.

King Marrkul sits at the head of the table. On his right is Nayadi. Her eyes are closed, she is swaying from side to side, and her lips are moving. Evay is there as well, seated on one of the benches lining the wall with several other people I have never seen before. Yerengul sits beside her, but she hardly takes notice, instead watching as Golmarr and I cross the room to two empty chairs at the great wooden table.

Golmarr must notice who has caught my attention, because he whispers, "Evay leads our archers when we go to battle."

I look at him. "We are going to battle?"

He presses a finger to his lips. "We are about to find out." He speaks no louder than an exhaled breath. "When Nayadi is seeing visions, we have to remain silent unless she addresses us. Otherwise we might interfere with what she is seeing." He pulls a chair out for me.

The exact second I lower myself into the chair, Nayadi's milky eyes pop open and stare right at me. I press my spine against the chair back in an effort to get as far away from her as possible.

She points at me, and the sleeve of her tattered brown tunic conforms around an arm as thin as bare bones. "You are bringing darkness to us," Nayadi hisses. Every person in the room looks at me, and I can feel the weight of their eyes as if it were a physical burden.

"I don't know what you are talking about," I say.

"You lie. You know!" she says. "I can see his aura all over you! Because of you, they are all waking up again!"

The room suddenly feels too warm, and while my fingers continue to be plagued with cold, the rest of my body overheats. Sweat breaks out along my hairline and between my shoulder blades. I wait for Golmarr to say something, or for King Marrkul to explain why his witch is verbally attacking me, but everyone sits still and silent, watching, waiting. "Who is waking up again?" I finally ask.

Nayadi thumps her frail hands on the table, and I jump. "You already know." She leans closer and swings her hand in front of my chest, pulling my air toward her.

"Enough," Golmarr says, standing and glaring at the hag. There is a collective gasp.

"You are not to interrupt!" Nayadi growls. "You will stifle my sight if you do!"

Golmarr visibly bristles, but he balls his hands into fists and sits back down. "What vision have you seen?" he asks.

Nayadi grins, and her bald gums gleam with saliva. "They are coming for the northern princess." She swipes at the air around me again and sucks it in through her nostrils. The room remains tensely silent as everyone stares at the old hag, waiting for her to elaborate. People begin shifting in their chairs and looking at King Marrkul, but no one utters a word.

"They are coming, and they're going to get you," Nayadi says, and grins. She is binging on the emotional suspense filling the room. It is filling her up. She takes a deep breath of air and starts laughing.

There is a loud thunk, and Nayadi's laughter stops abruptly. A black stone knife is embedded in the headrest of her chair, pinning a lock of her greasy hair to the wood beside her ear. "Tell Princess Sorrowlynn who is coming, when, where, and why, you filthy old witch, or my next knife will find your heart," Enzio says. He is holding another black stone blade in his hand, and his gaze is riveted on Nayadi's chest.

Nayadi smacks her lips closed over her gums and slouches in her chair. "You Satari have always been prejudiced against the wielding of magic," she grumbles. "So now you spoil my fun?" She yanks the knife from her chair, and a tuft of severed yellow hair falls to her shoulder. Quick as the blink of an eye, Nayadi throws the knife at Enzio. It thunks into the headrest of his chair, right beside his ear. "An army comes. From the Glass Forest. Mercenaries and Trevonan renegades. The largest army that has ever come from that forest."

King Marrkul scratches his chin through his beard. "Why are they coming? How many men strong?"

Nayadi waves a dismissive hand at me. "Smaller than your army. They have been sent to kill *her*."

"Sent by whom?" Golmarr asks.

Nayadi huffs. "How should I know? You interrupted me while I was receiving my vision. But they will reach Kreeose shortly before sunset tomorrow." Nayadi stands, and Ingvar hops to his feet, pulling the crone's chair out. "Hopefully I have seen enough to spare this people from slaughter." She steps from the table and shuffles away, leaving the kitchen without a backward glance.

King Marrkul rests his elbows on the table and frowns. "So we are going to battle." The wrinkles around his eyes seem deeper than I remember, and he looks exhausted. "We will postpone the feast until after the fighting. For now, we need to prepare to defend our land and our people." He looks at me. "And my son's betrothed."

Battle. The single word opens so many memories inside of my brain that my head begins to hurt. It hurts all day, so by the time the sun sets, I take my leave and retire to Golmarr's room, alone, in hopes that sleep will ease the pain.

Chapter 28

I open my eyes to a battle on the side of a sun-drenched hill—men slaughtering men. With perfect clarity, I can see the strategy of the battle. I know who is winning, and why. Blinking, I open my eyes to another battle being fought in the courtyard of my mother's castle and again know the inner workings of battle strategy. I blink and see another battle, with rain-sodden soldiers and the ground awash with blood. I blink again and open my eyes to more fighting. Again, fighting. Again, fighting. Again, fighting, until I have witnessed every single battle of every single person whose memories live in my head, and all I want to do is close my eyes forever!

And then I blink and see the great green dragon, the dragon of the Glass Forest, sitting in its cave made of tree boughs, vines, and dirt. Thoughts are flowing out of the beast, rippling through the misty forest air, and settling in the dreams of sleeping men. I reach my mind out to the thoughts, and when I touch one, I hear what the dragon is communicating: Attack the horse clan. Kill any who oppose you. Take their land for your own. Accompanying the thoughts is the fierce, yearning desire to obey them.

The dragon's thoughts shift as it grows aware of me, and I realize this dragon is female. With that knowledge comes a name: Corritha.

Something sharp clamps down on my mind and wraps around it, stifling it, smothering my ability to think. Everything is stripped from my brain until all that is left is a dull gray void, and then something darker than the gray is forced into my head. Corritha's treasure. The thing she craves above everything else. The weapon she has hoarded for a more than a millennium—hatred: the weapon that gives her the ability to kill and hate and terrorize without remorse. Her hatred is so intense, I want to take my own life—because her abhorrence feels like my own self-loathing. Her treasure of hatred once focused on a jewel prized above all others: the fire dragon. And since I killed him, all of that hatred has been transferred onto me. I am the new jewel.

I lash out at the glass dragon's blackness with thoughts of my own, thoughts in opposition to the creature's all-consuming hatred: I summon up every good memory I have, every single kindness I can recall, every type of love that exists in my hundreds of memories, and shove it at the black space devouring my conscience.

The glass dragon recoils, and I can feel the blackness dissipating from my brain like hissing steam. But my victory is only temporary.

Corritha spreads her wings, and I feel her wicked anticipation, for tomorrow she will eat me.

I sit up, throw the covers from me, and press my fingertips against my eyes, trying to remove the horrible things I have seen. I force my eyes open and stare at a square of light on the bedroom floor, from the moon shining in through the window, and then I get up. More than mercenaries and renegades are coming tomorrow, and King Marrkul needs to know. I glance at my nightgown and consider changing clothes, but what I have to say is too important to delay.

The hallway outside is dark, the wood floor cold on my

bare feet. Beside my door is a black lump. I crouch and put my hands on it and discover something warm and firm and snoring, so I give it a gentle shake.

"Sorrowlynn?" I recognize Enzio's voice. "Is everything all right?" He sits up, and I can barely make out his face.

"Why are you sleeping on the floor? Do you not know that there are twelve bedrooms in this house?" I ask.

"I could not sleep, knowing that witch was in the same house as you," he says, his voice cold. "I was afraid, after the way she looked at you like she was going to eat you . . ."

Warmth fills my breast despite the chill left from the battles I witnessed in my dreams. "You are protecting me."

"I was thinking tonight might be the night I repay the debt I owe you."

"Thank you, Enzio," I whisper. I reach out and clasp his hand, wrapping my frigid fingers around it. "If you want, sleep in the bed I was in. I won't be sleeping anymore tonight. And Nayadi won't be able to sneak up on me now that I'm awake."

"Do you know how to throw a knife?"

When he asks, I can feel in my fingers and wrist the precise muscles and technique used to throw a knife. "Yes."

Enzio stands. "If she comes anywhere near you, aim for her heart. Do not let her get close enough to touch you."

"All right. Do you know where Golmarr is sleeping?"

He scratches his head. "His father insisted he sleep somewhere you were not, to protect your honor, but I do not know where," he explains, and stumbles into Golmarr's room.

The low rumble of deep voices penetrates the quiet house. I press my hand to the wall and wander down the dark hall, toward the stairs and the voices. The stairwell flickers and glimmers with orange light.

At the bottom of the stairs is a big room with a giant hearth at one end, surrounded by three sofas, which make three sides of a square. A small fire is burning in the hearth, giving off just enough light to illuminate King Marrkul, Jessen, Ingvar, and a horse lord I do not know sitting on two of the sofas, their stocking feet propped up on a table, their backs to me.

"So you think we should wait and let them come to us, Olenn?" Marrkul asks, his voice so deep it almost sounds more like a growl.

"Yes," his son—Olenn—replies. "Let them wear themselves out with travel before they fight us. It will give us the advantage. What do you think, Ingvar?"

Ingvar nods. "We can arm ourselves and wait just north of the city. Golmarr will lead the foot soldiers, and I will lead the mounted troops. They won't know we're there until our archers have taken down a third of their soldiers." His strategy is sound, but . . . "And then we will pounce on them and give them the choice to continue the fight or turn back." All four men nod and make deep grunts of approval. Olenn yawns and scratches the back of his head, his fingers tangling in his long black hair.

King Marrkul leans forward and rests his elbows on his knees. "All right. At first light, we will finalize the preparations to draw the mercenaries to us and end this battle before sundown."

"No, you can't," I blurt. All four men whip around and look at me.

"Good evening, Princess Sorrowlynn." King Marrkul stands and walks over to me. His shirt is wrinkled and untucked, his eyes weary. Smiling, he takes my hand in his and brings it to his lips. His bushy beard tickles my skin.

"Good evening, sir." I dip a respectful curtsy even though I am wearing a nightgown.

"Don't worry yourself over us, young lady. We are merely talking battle strategy," Marrkul says. He studies me for a long moment, and I wish I *had* changed back into my skirt and tunic before coming downstairs. I firm my shoulders and lift my chin. "Do you want for anything, Princess? A glass of warm cinnamon milk, or some buttered bread?"

I take a deep breath and look up into his eyes. "I need nothing. I know that you are discussing battle plans, sir. You can't fight here!" My voice rings with authority.

Golmarr's brothers quietly chuckle. Marrkul schools his face to concerned sympathy. "And what would a young northern princess like yourself know about battles fought in Anthar, hey?"

The hundreds of battles flash before my eyes again. "More than you can imagine," I whisper. "Your strategy is good— *very* good, if all you are going to be fighting tomorrow is men. But a dragon is coming."

Marrkul frowns and looks at his sons. Looking back to me, he says, "But the fire dragon is dead."

"Not him—not the fire dragon. The dragon of the Glass Forest is coming for me."

"The glass dragon has never left the forest," Ingvar says, glaring at me like I am an idiot.

For a heartbeat I see the grasslands covered with a thick layer of sheer ice. "Yes, she does, and she will freeze your city and your people if I am here, until she finds me." I look out a window to the moonlit field behind the house, to the horses. They are the best horses in the world—the fastest, strongest. I could saddle Dewdrop this very moment and gallop away, and the glass dragon threat would be removed from the horse clan. "If I am gone . . ." The thought of leaving hurts so badly, it robs me of the ability to speak.

A warm hand closes over mine. "Jessen, wake Golmarr," the king commands. He gently pulls me over to the empty sofa, and I sit. Lifting a wool blanket, he wraps it around me, tucking it behind my shoulders and beneath my bare feet. "Your hands are like ice, Princess."

A moment later Golmarr, his hair mussed from sleep, wearing only a pair of wrinkled pants, strides into the room stretching his long arms over his head. He sees me sitting on the sofa and sits down beside me, lifting half of my blanket and covering himself so my arm is against his bare chest. Even through the fabric of my nightgown I can feel his warm skin, and I can't help but wonder what his father thinks of his son walking around in front of me with no shirt. Golmarr fumbles under the blanket until he finds my hand and twines his fingers with mine and then he looks at me. "Jessen says you're raving about dragons attacking us tomorrow and trying to tell them how to fight their battle?" he asks, a curious grin spreading over his sleepy face.

I nod. "The glass dragon is coming for me." I feel Golmarr's heart speed up beneath my shoulder, and his hand turns as cold as mine as the grin is replaced with a frown. "If I run tonight—"

"No," Golmarr blurts. He looks to his brothers and father.

"No," King Marrkul echoes. His brothers nod in agreement.

"But—"

Marrkul leans forward and cuts me off. "You are my son's betrothed, Princess Sorrowlynn. That makes you part of our clan. We will fight this dragon with you, so you don't have to run and fight it alone."

My battle with the mercenary in the forest comes to mind, when he told me he would capture me and ask my family for ransom, and the gut-wrenching realization that I didn't know if my own mother would pay to get me back. I look into King Marrkul's sincere eyes and a lump rises in my throat. "I . . . ," I whisper, and then sniffle as tears fill my eyes. Golmarr drops my hand and wraps his arms around my shoulders, hugging me tightly to him so my cheek is pressed to his neck.

"You belong here with us, Sorrowlynn," he whispers against my hair.

"That's settled, then. You will stay," Marrkul says. He turns to his sons. "Ingvar? Olenn? Jessen? Should we redo our battle strategy to incorporate the threat of a possible dragon attack?"

"Yes," I say, sitting forward and clenching my skirt in my fists. They all turn their eyes to me, and Ingvar and Jessen hide their smiles behind their hands. It takes every bit of self-control I possess not to glare at them.

"What would you suggest?" King Marrkul asks, and I know he is merely humoring me—a weak northern princess.

I clear my throat. "There is a hill about halfway between your city and the forest, right at the edge of your farmland—"

"Crow Hill," Golmarr says.

"Hide the foot soldiers at the base of Crow Hill, and hide the archers on top. The hill is big enough for a large mounted army to wait behind it without the mercenaries spotting them. If you have your archers attack first, you will drastically cut the mercenaries' numbers before any of your people risk their lives. When the enemy engages in battle with your foot soldiers, bring out the cavalry from behind the hill and surround them." Now four pairs of shocked dark eyes are staring at me. I uncurl my fists and smooth the wrinkles from my skirt.

"What about the glass dragon?" Jessen asks. "It will freeze our soldiers hiding in the grass."

"Not if they are covered by cloaks. The beauty of the grasslands is you can see for miles in every direction, especially on a hilltop," I say. "Assign several people to watch the sky, and we will see the beast coming long before it can breathe its ice on us. If we lure it to the hill, the people here in Kreeose will be safe. Your crops and women and children will be spared."

"I think that sounds like a well-thought-out plan," Golmarr says, laying his hand flat against my back. "That way, if the glass dragon comes, we risk it freezing our warriors only if they are too slow to shelter beneath a cloak."

"And you wield the sword that can kill the dragon," Ingvar says to Golmarr. "For the first time in the history of our people, we stand a chance at beating a dragon."

I peer back at Golmarr. His lips are pulled tight against his teeth, and his brow is furrowed. After a moment he nods. "I wield the sword," he whispers.

King Marrkul stands. "Then we are finished here. Go to your wives, boys. Keep them warm for the rest of the night. Tomorrow we will travel to Crow Hill." He turns to Golmarr and me. "After the battle, we shall have the feast. What say we marry you then, as part of the celebration?"

Golmarr's hand, still pressed flat against my back, slowly closes on the fabric of my shirt. "What say you, Sorrowlynn?" he asks, and I can hear the mischief in his voice. "If we marry tomorrow, I won't make you think improper thoughts anymore—at least, they won't be improper because they will be about your husband."

My heart starts pounding. "Yes," I say.

"All right. If all goes well tomorrow, we will get married at the feast," Golmarr says, and I can hear the smile in his voice.

Marrkul looks between the two of us. "Very well. Now, I trust you will behave yourselves if I leave you alone out here and go to bed?"

"I don't know," Golmarr says, tugging on my shirt so I lean back against him. "Sorrowlynn can't keep her hands off me, Father."

I glare at him and smack his shoulder, and Marrkul laughs. "Soon enough you will be married and you can have your hands on him all you want, Princess, though I suspect it is the other way around—him not keeping his hands off you." He gives his son a meaningful glance. "I will see you before first light." Marrkul yawns and leaves.

"I can't believe you said that to your father," I say.

He shrugs. "I am his youngest son. I don't think anything can shock him anymore." He clears his throat. "I've come up with a plan to *not* kill the glass dragon tomorrow."

"What is the plan? How can I help?"

"The dragon is coming for you, so no matter what I do, you will have to be there with me. Otherwise I would fight it alone."

I lean in closer to him. "I will be there with you."

He trails his hand up my arm. "First of all, you have to wear a cloak. You are going to try to distract it any way you can, without getting close enough for it to use its claws or teeth on you. If it breathes ice at you, fine. You shelter under the cloak. You'll survive that. Meanwhile, I will use the reforged sword to immobilize and injure it to the point that it cannot come after you for a long time. And then, while it is healing from its wounds, we learn how to kill a dragon without being forced to inherit its treasure." He looks at me. "What do you think?"

I nod. "I think that is our only option."

"Then we are ready for tomorrow's battle." He lies down and pulls me so my head is on his chest and my back is against the back of the sofa. Turning his body to face me, he lifts the blanket up over us.

"What are you doing?" I whisper, smiling. He wraps both his arms around me and tangles his legs with mine, just like he did when we slept in the cave by the lake. He is right. I fit perfectly against him.

"I am savoring every moment we have together and keeping you warm until morning." He slowly trails his hand up the length of my spine, and I shiver. "It is a family tradition," he whispers. "On the night before a battle, we keep our women warm just in case . . ." His voice trails off.

I press my hands against his chest and feel the deep, steady beat of his heart. "In case it is our last night together," I finish.

He kisses my forehead and leaves his lips there, and with the feel of his heart beating against my hands and the quiet noise of the fire, I sleep.

Chapter 29

Wearing tan leather pants and a metal-lined leather vest over a simple cream shirt, I sit astride Dewdrop and breathe the cool dawn air. The wind blows, tugging on my braided hair, swishing Dewdrop's mane, and whispering through the tall grass, creating ripples that spread as far as the eye can see. At my waist, I wear the belt from Melisande and king Marrkul's hunting knife, and my staff is tucked into a leather loop on the side of my saddle. For all the rigid things I wear, purple and yellow flower garlands are draped over me and my horse, thanks to the tearful goodbye given us by those not fighting. Every single soldier is wearing flowers of some sort, such a sharp contrast to their armor and weapons.

Each soldier has one extra weapon today—or piece of armor, rather—that is not made of metal, wood, or leather: a heavy wool cloak. Protection of a sort against a dragon's breath of glass. Axes are also tucked into saddlebags for cracking ice, should the need arise.

We ride hard, and every once in a while I glance behind me and meet the scowling dark eyes of Evay. I can feel her stare like fire against my back.

I look at Golmarr, sitting astride Tanyani and riding beside me. His eyes have a familiar fierceness burning in them, his mouth is pulled down in a frown, and the first hint of dark scruff shadows his chin. His body moves with his horse's steps like they are one single, lethal entity. And yet I can't help but smile. He is wearing a crown of pale pink baby's breath flowers on his head.

We arrive at Crow Hill before midday. The archers, dressed in leather tanned to match the gold grass, take their places at the top of the hill and disappear into their surroundings when they crouch. The soldiers who fight on horseback, including Golmarr's eight brothers and his father, stay on the far side of Crow Hill, waiting. The footmen take their places below the hill and hunker down in the grass. That is where I will be fighting.

I stand at the top of the hill, the tall golden grass swaying against my waist, and stare at the bright blue sky. I feel like I have done this before, hundreds of times—this waiting for the possibility of my death, the knowledge that I might be taking life, the surety that I will see men die today, and I feel so tiny in the grand existence of humanity.

Arms wrap around my shoulders and pull my back close against a warm body. "What are you thinking?" Golmarr asks, his mouth beside my ear.

"That one life is so small. My existence is so trivial." I put my hand on his wrist, right below my chin.

"Not to me," he says. He has been quiet all morning, his hand gripping and releasing the pommel of his sword over and over.

"What are you thinking, Golmarr?" I turn in his arms to look at him, and his hands loop behind the small of my back.

His eyes sweep the sky behind my shoulder, study the collar of my cream shirt—look anywhere but at my eyes.

"When I am leading the foot soldiers, hold back. I don't want you on the front line with me. Enzio says he will stay with you." He still hasn't looked at me.

"What else are you thinking?" I coax.

He sighs. "I'm thinking that life is unpredictable. When a person finally gets what he wants, even though he didn't know he wanted it in the first place, the thought of willfully losing it, of making a choice to destroy it, is almost too hard to bear." He looks at me now. The sorrow in his eyes makes my breath catch in my throat. I throw my arms around his neck and hold him as tight as I can. "Sometimes our lives turn out in ways we never imagined they would," he whispers, and tightens his arms around me until I am nearly being crushed against him. He presses his face to my neck, and I feel moisture against my skin. I pull back to look at Golmarr just as a bird calls.

Golmarr ducks down to the ground, taking me with him. "That's the signal. One of our scouts has seen movement on the horizon," he whispers, quickly wiping the back of his hand over his eyes. Within seconds, every visible person is gone, hiding in the waving grass. I follow Golmarr to the warriors who will fight on foot and crouch beside them. The women nod at me. Some touch a single finger to their foreheads. "Our female warriors are honoring your presence among them," Golmarr whispers. "Everyone knows you beat Evay with your staff. They know you can fight."

Enzio crawls over to me. "I will not leave your side," he says. His gaze flickers to Golmarr, and from the corner of my eye I see Golmarr nod.

"Thank you, Enzio." I try to smile but can't. Not in the moments before battle.

When the approaching army becomes visible—a gray stripe on the horizon dividing the golden grass and blue sky—the hiss of steel fills the air. Everyone has drawn a weapon. They crouch in the grass, silent and intent as the gray stripe approaches. I study these Antharian people, with their aggressive eyes and strong bodies—violent barbarians, my mother would say, and yet, what they are doing is necessary. No, not necessary. Fighting to protect the greater good is *more* than simply necessary. It is noble, honorable, and self-sacrificing. I am among good people.

Golmarr grabs my chin and turns my face to his. "Whatever happens out there, I will always love you," he whispers, pulling my face to his and kissing me. He is wearing chain mail and holding a sword, and his eyes are fierce from thoughts of the approaching fight, but the gentleness of his lips makes my heart ache.

I cup his jaw with my hand and run my thumb over his bristly cheek. "I know. And I will always love you." As the last word leaves my lips, the twang of a hundred bowstrings echoes through the air. I look up as a burst of arrows zoom overhead, darkening the bright sky for a fraction of a second. "So it begins," I whisper.

"Hold until I give the word," Golmarr quietly calls. Through the tall grass, we can just make out the approaching mercenaries. The archers shoot again, and men fall. We watch as those still standing run toward us. My blood curdles at the sight of them. They have smeared their faces with blood, and wear armor covered with spikes and human bones. My heart starts pounding in my chest.

Again, the archers let loose their arrows, and then Golmarr leaps to his feet and thrusts his sword into the air. "Forward!" he screams. From behind us, a horn blares, and then I am on my feet, running, my staff gripped in my hands. For a split second I wonder what I am doing here on this battlefield, on the front line. I am a princess. I am soft and regal. I am quiet, forgotten Sorrowlynn, who never leaves her rooms. And yet I am so much more. I have the capacity to be anything. To be everything! This girl running to fight for the greater good *is* me. For the first time ever, I feel like I am living the life I was meant to be living all along.

As the foot soldiers spread out on the field, the mounted soldiers come galloping out from behind the hill and surround the mercenary army. They have half the numbers that the Antharian army has. I can already see we have won this battle, and no one besides the archers has raised a weapon to fight.

When the foot soldiers meet the mercenaries, there is a giant clang that rattles against my eardrums as energy bursts between the two armies. Tanyani: the energy that vibrates the air when two armies collide on the battlefield. A mercenary leaps for me. He snarls, and the bones hanging around his neck clang together. He swings a flail in a circle above his head once and then uses all the momentum to crash it into my skull.

There is a sudden physical shifting inside of me, as if I have lived my whole life half-blind, and now, for the first time, I can truly see. My body, my muscles, my bones, and my head blend into one perfect, highly functioning entity. I know how to do this—this *fighting*. My physical weakness is my only flaw. I growl and thrust my staff up. The flail hits my weapon and clangs against it; then the chain attached to the metal loops once around the staff. I yank on my staff and thrust my foot into my opponent's stomach. The flail is stripped from his hand. He falls to his back, and I press my staff to his throat. Glaring up at me, he waits to die, but I freeze. I cannot kill him. I do not want his knowledge contaminating my brain. Enzio springs to my side and drives his short sword into the mercenary's chest.

Before I can thank him, a blood-painted mercenary swings a sword at my neck. My body responds before I have time to think, thrusting my staff between me and the sword. Enzio rams his shoulder into the mercenary's ribs, slamming him to the ground, and quickly kills him.

A third man charges me, slicing at the air with two short, curved swords in either of his hands. I duck and parry just as one of his swords touches the side of my cheek. I thrust my staff into the man's stomach, and as he stumbles back, an arrow pierces his chest. Turning, I see Evay behind me. She nocks another arrow to her bowstring and fires again, killing the man with the two swords. I nod my thanks, but she turns away without acknowledging it.

A horn blares, the very same as started the battle. Far ahead, I see Golmarr raise his sword into the afternoon sunshine. A man and woman on horseback approach Golmarr and stop at his side. It is Ingvar and Jayah, his wife. "Where is your leader?" Ingvar bellows.

The fighting slows and then stops. A long moment passes before a massive man steps up to Ingvar. "We answer to no leader," the man says. "We fight for ourselves."

Ingvar studies the man. "We are ready to end this battle!" he yells, loud enough that his words carry to every person on the battlefield. "Already we have killed well over half of your leaderless men. If you surrender your weapons to us and go back to the Glass Forest, we will spare your lives. If you do not, every single one of you will be dead within the hour. Go now and live, or choose death. I do not care either way."

The mercenary roars and swings his blade at Ingvar's torso, but Golmarr blocks it and throws the man to the ground, killing him swiftly.

Another mercenary charges at Golmarr. Golmarr turns around to fight, but Jayah guides her horse between the enemy and her brother-in-law and strikes the mercenary down with her sword.

"We are always looking for ways to hone our battle skills," Jayah bellows. "Slaughtering every single one of you would hone not only our battle skills, but also our reputation for being brutal, bloodthirsty barbarians. Who else wants to fight us? Who else wants to die to hone the Antharian reputation?" she bellows, and swings her sword in a figure eight over her head.

The mercenaries look around. One man throws his sword to the ground and starts running north. Another starts to run, keeping his club and shield with him. An arrow hits him between the shoulder blades before he has taken ten steps, and he falls to the ground.

"Leave your weapons or die!" Ingvar bellows, lowering his bow.

One by one, the mercenaries drop their weapons to the ground, turn north, and start running. The few who cling to their weapons are shot down. I stare after them as the people around me cheer and thrust their swords high into the air. We have won, and the dragon has not come. It seems too easy. An arm comes around me, squeezing my shoulders, and I look into the smiling face of Enzio.

Before me, the crowd parts. Golmarr is striding through

the tall grass, his skin shiny with sweat, his eyes locked on mine. When he reaches me, he grabs my face with both hands and stares into my eyes. His thumb gently wipes the blood from the wound on my cheek, and then he leans in and kisses me with the fierceness of battle. The world seems to spin, and I grab his chain mail to keep from falling. He pulls away. "We won." He smiles. "We won, and the glass dragon never came, and tonight you will be my wife!"

I laugh and throw my arms around his neck, and he swings me off the ground.

"But first, we need to burn the dead mercenaries and gather our own fallen to take home." Golmarr puts me back on the ground. Already, men and women are piling up wood from a wagon that followed us into battle. Other men are flattening the grass around the wood so the fire won't spread. Some of the horses are being used to drag dead mercenaries over to the fire. The horse clan's dead and injured are lifted into the wagon that once carried the wood. There are three dead, and five too injured to ride home.

Ingvar guides his horse over to us. "Well fought, brother," he says, holding his hand down to Golmarr. They clasp wrists and Ingvar smiles. When he smiles, he doesn't look nearly as intimidating as I first thought, even wearing full armor. Turning his attention to me, he holds his hand out and I clasp his wrist, like Golmarr did. "Well fought, Suicide Sorrow; well fought, indeed."

"Thank you, sir."

I stand in the field and watch Golmarr help carry mercenary bodies to the edge of the fire. When it is blazing, the dead are thrown onto it. The smoke blackens and makes a dark, inky trail against the turquoise sky. I watch it rise, and when my head is tilted back and my gaze is straight up, I see it: a tiny, dark speck. My knees knock together and tears fill my eyes as all of the energy of victory is stripped from me. I shake my head and squeeze my eyes shut, hoping that when I open them, the dark speck will be gone. But it is not. "Dragon!" I try to shout the word, but it comes out as a choked whisper.

Chapter 30

I reach out and grab the nearest person and point straight up. Enzio shades his eyes and looks to where I am pointing. "What is that?"

"The dragon has come for me," I whisper.

"The glass dragon!" Enzio bellows. "Get your cloaks and move out!" Horns bellow and everyone runs. I do not run. I stand still and wait because I already know that no matter where I go, there the dragon will be.

In three heartbeats the field is clear of every living person but me, Enzio, and Golmarr. Golmarr's sword is out, gleaming in the sunlight, and he is sprinting toward me. "Do you have it?" he asks Enzio.

"Yes." Enzio presses on his chest and I hear paper crinkle.

"Then clear out with the rest so you don't die!" Golmarr orders.

A horse and rider come galloping up to Golmarr and me, and from the saddle, Jessen hands us each a cloak. "Are you sure you don't want us to fight with you, brother?" he asks Golmarr.

"Your weapons will make no difference, and you know it.

You will die if you try to fight it. But . . ." He grabs Jessen's arm. "If I die, take up my sword and protect her."

"You know I will," Jessen says, his eyes smoldering as he glances at me. Looking back to his brother, he gives the hand signal for *honored warrior.*

I put a deep blue cloak on, clasp it at my neck, and pull the hood up over my head. Golmarr swings a bright saffron cloak over his shoulders but does not put the hood up. We stand side by side in the battle-flattened, blood-splattered grass and stare up at the sky, at the circling black speck that is slowly getting closer and closer, bigger and bigger. When it is so close that I can see its deep green scales, a shower of arrows streaks across the sky. They hit the great beast and bounce off her gleaming scales, raining down on Golmarr and me. One hits my arm and slices my skin just below the elbow before bouncing on the grass at my feet.

"Hold your fire," Golmarr bellows. Turning to me, he says, "You remember our plan?"

"Of course I do. I am ready to distract the beast," I say, when in reality, I am ready to do no such thing. I grip my staff as tightly as I can. "Just don't kill her."

Golmarr's nostrils flare and his jaw muscles tighten. "I will do my best to protect you, Sorrowlynn. This I swear."

The beast completes one last, lazy circle through the air and then dives at us, her massive black claws tearing through the ground and digging deep fissures in the dirt and grass. Before she settles to a stop, Golmarr lifts his sword and starts sprinting toward her. As the dragon opens her massive jaws to catch the horse lord up in her yellow teeth, Golmarr dives under the great beast's chin, stopping between her feet. He swings his blade with the skill and perfection of a practiced dragon slayer. The reforged blade carves through the scales on the back of the dragon's ankle. The beast shrieks as great drops of blood splatter the ground beneath her foot. I blink and stare at the limping beast. Golmarr has severed her hamstring, making it impossible for the creature to run. And then I realize something I should have known the first time I watched him fight. Because of Golmarr's birth prediction, that he would be the first dragon slayer in his family, he has been training for and thinking about killing dragons his entire life. He has been practicing for this moment since the day he was born. I am witnessing his destiny.

Golmarr leaps to his feet and grabs a dragon scale, pulling himself up onto the creature's wounded leg. Grabbing another scale higher up the beast's side, he swings onto her wide back. He falls to his knees and stabs his sword into the base of one of the leathery black wings just as the dragon lifts her spiked tail and swings. Golmarr tries to duck, but the blunt side of the tail hits his shoulder, flinging him through the air. He thumps onto the ground and rolls to a stop. Slowly, he climbs to his hands and knees and shakes his head.

"Golmarr?" I call. He doesn't move.

The dragon looks at the horse lord and takes a step toward him. Fear turns my stomach and fills me with adrenaline. If I don't do something, the beast will eat Golmarr. "Your quarrel is with me, Corritha! If you don't kill me now, I will shout your secret for all to hear," I shriek, and for the first time I look at the gently sloping hill behind me. It is dark with spectators; the horse clan warriors are silently watching.

The dragon steps away from Golmarr, opens her good wing, and tries to fly, but the injured wing whips around erratically, splattering the ground with blood, and the creature flails and wobbles. Pulling back her head, she opens her mouth and hisses pale, misty breath at me. I fall to the ground and pull my cloak tight over my body as her breath presses against the blue wool. Frigid air seeps through the fabric, but it doesn't stiffen into a sheet of ice like it did in the forest. When the chill has passed, I sit up. A thin layer of white frost has dusted my cloak; nothing more. "The mist," I whisper, thinking of the dense fog that hides the forest floor. It is dragon-made. Without it, the dragon has freezing breath only—not the ability to encase things in ice. And that is when I see the first tendrils of white seep between the grass and curl around my knees. I stand and back away from it, but it is growing, rising up from the ground and swirling around my legs.

Golmarr, still on his hands and knees, is almost entirely surrounded by mist. Only his head rises above it. I grip my staff in my hands and run toward him, making the mist dance and swirl away from me. When I reach him, he looks up. His skin is ashen and beaded with sweat. "My head," he mumbles. "It's been hit one too many times." Slowly, he gets to his feet.

"The mist turns into glass," I blurt. "Without the mist, nothing will freeze. We have to stop the mist!"

"How?" Golmarr asks.

The answer comes to me, just like it did before: fire. I look across the field, to the smoldering and smoking bodies, and I want that fire. I want it to warm me, to feed me, to take the icy chill out of my hands that has been there for days. I need that fire. A single spark bounces out of the smoldering pile and lands on the grass, rising up to a small flame. And then, like a narrow stream of water, the fire trickles its way toward me through the grass—a perfectly straight line of orange. Everywhere the fire touches, the mist turns to steam and evaporates.

"Sorrowlynn?" Golmarr says, backing away as the fire starts licking the hem of my pants. I bend down and thrust my hands into the bright orange flames. The fire flares around them and wraps itself over my entire body. I stand and the fire clings to me, so everything I see has turned orange, for I am seeing it through flames. My clothes fill with warmth and heat seeps into my skin. Energy enters my flesh and soaks into my blood. With every beat of my heart, warmth pulses through my body, feeding me more perfectly than any food I have ever eaten.

A dense weight slams into my back, and I am thrown to the ground. Golmarr is atop me, smothering the flames with his cloak, but when he pulls away, my clothes and flesh are unmarked. "That didn't burn you," he whispers.

I open and close my warm hands and look at him in wonder. "It fed me."

Golmarr helps me to my feet and readies himself to fight the dragon again.

Fire might protect you, but ice will still kill him. I assure you, his death will be more painful to you than anything else I could do, the dragon says, her voice soft and lilting in my head. I look at Golmarr and the mist swirling around his feet in the exact moment the glass dragon blasts her breath at him. Without thinking, without understanding how, I thrust up a tall wall of flames between Golmarr and the dragon. When Corritha's breath hits it, the fire billows and scatters like gold stars and then re-forms into a wall. The white breath turns to pale wisps of steam that disappear against the sky. The dragon blows another blast of freezing air and tries to scatter the fire, but it holds. On one side of the fire wall, the golden grass is encased in solid, immovable ice. On the other side, the grass ripples in the wind; there isn't so much as a speck of frost on it.

A wave of hatred shudders through my body. **You think you have won this battle simply because you have used Zhun's magic to shield my breath, but you are no match for my strength, little girl,** the dragon says. Her great, spiked tail sails through the air, and for a moment the memory of the fire dragon's tail crushing my ribs makes my knees tremble. Clutching my staff to my chest, I dive forward and roll onto slick, frigid ice just as the tail soars over my head. The dragon swings her tail again, and I dig my staff into the ice, trying to move out of the way. Her tail collides with my hip, and I slide across the frozen ground. Before I can get up, a massive foot lowers over my body, its claws shattering the ice I am lying on, but stops before it crushes me. Slowly, one tiny bit at a time, the pressure increases. I swing my staff at the creature's hind leg—at the bloody gash made by Golmarr—but it merely bounces off the green scales.

Every knight in shining armor feels it is his duty to save a helpless maiden, Corritha says. **You are my bait. I know the hearts of men well enough to know that the noble ones will risk their lives to do what they think is right. If he is noble, he will come and try to save you, and then I will have the pleasure of freezing him and eating him before your very eyes. If he is not noble, I will slowly crush you.** A forked tongue darts out of the dragon's mouth and touches my face. **And then I will eat you, and he will be eaten up with guilt until the day he dies.** The pressure on my body increases until I feel my ribs start to bend inward, and I cannot breathe.

From the corner of my eye, I see Golmarr in his bright

cloak start sprinting toward the dragon. As the dragon draws in a massive breath of air, the mist hovering on the ground is sucked toward her mouth.

"Stop," I try to shriek to Golmarr, but I cannot get enough breath into my lungs. Golmarr runs faster, and the dragon's mouth is opening. Reaching toward the fire still hovering in a straight line along the grass, I pull it to me and throw it in the dragon's gaping mouth just as a blur of blinding vermilion streaks over my head and onto the dragon's leg. Golmarr lifts the reforged sword and plunges it into the dragon's side, all the way to the hilt. The moment the sword pierces through the scales, the pressure pinning me to the ground eases. Golmarr pulls his sword out and thrusts it into the great beast again. The reforged metal cuts through the dragon's inky green scales like they are great drops of water. The talon lifts off my body and the dragon hisses as she tries to snap Golmarr from her back, but he ducks and thrusts again, plunging his sword into the space where the dragon's neck meets her body, and then yanks it free. Slowly, the dragon tips to her side and lands beside me with shattering force. Shards of ice explode around the creature's body, creating a cloud that shimmers like diamonds in the sunlight and pierces my skin.

Golmarr pulls me to my feet and wraps his left arm around my waist, dragging me away from the dragon, his sword still poised to strike. But the great beast merely watches us while her huge chest slowly rises up and down. Blood is pouring out of the three sword wounds, making a growing pool of red around the dragon's body.

My eyes meet Golmarr's. They are tight with pain, and my heart starts to pound with fear. Something is horribly wrong. Tears spill from his eyes and stream down his face, mixing with blood on his left cheek. "How badly are you hurt?" I ask, cupping his cheek in my hand and running my thumb over the cut. It is merely a shallow scrape. "Where are you hurt? Where is this pain coming from?"

"I'm sorry," he gasps, and leans his forehead against mine. "I am so sorry, Sorrowlynn." He grabs my face with his left hand and looks into my eyes. The agony I see there makes me sick, and I wonder if he is about to die.

I shake my head. "Please don't die," I whisper. "Please."

"Listen to me," he says. "No matter what happens, I want you to know that I would have fought by your side until I died. I would have protected you with my own life." I press my fingers to his mouth to silence him, for every word he speaks tears at my heart and makes it hard to breathe. He clasps my fingers and moves my hand away. "I have to leave." He steps from me and slowly lets his fingers slide over mine.

I look from him to the dragon and understanding dawns on me. If the dragon dies from her wounds, her treasure is going to be transferred to Golmarr. He is leaving to protect me. Tears fill my eyes and a sob tears at my chest. "I love you," I say. He cringes and holds his heart. Turning, he starts striding away, and I stand frozen in place as I watch him go.

Before he has taken five steps, he gasps and falls to his knees. Gripping his head in his hands, he moans. I reach a hand toward him just as the glass dragon bursts into flame. Flinching, I throw my arms in front of my face. Icy blue fire shoots up from the dragon's body, reaching halfway to the sky like a pillar of light, as all of the power and magic she once possessed exits her body and then dwindles to nothing, leaving the dragon's massive figure as dull and lifeless as stone. My arms slowly drop to my sides. I stare at the dead beast framed by ice and crimson blood, and stifle a sob. She is dead. It is done.

Golmarr moans again and slowly climbs to his feet, still holding his head. He looks at me over his shoulder, and the anguish in his eyes slowly fades until he looks like he is half-asleep. His tears stop, and he blinks as if the sun is hurting his eyes.

He takes four tentative steps toward me and then his hand darts out and cinches around my throat. For a moment he looks confused, but slowly his mouth turns down into a frown. I claw at his hand and look into his eyes, and even though I know these eyes, there is nothing familiar in them. They narrow with a hatred so intense that every bit of mischief, every bit of youth, even every bit of love leaves them. Golmarr tightens his hold on my neck and drags me to him so only the tips of my toes slide across the ice.

Glaring down at me, his lips pull back in a growl. "You!" he snarls, and throws me down to the ground hard. My back slams into ice, and all the air is knocked from my lungs. He swings his sword, and I struggle to lift my staff and block it before it pierces my heart. His weapon hits mine with so much force that my shoulders and elbows shudder with pain. He swings again, both hands gripping the sword hilt, and slams his weapon into my staff with every ounce of strength and hatred he possesses. My staff shatters, and his sword continues its downward strike. It cuts through my leather vest and lodges deep in my left shoulder. I cry out, and the broken pieces of my staff fall from my hands.

"Please, Golmarr," I beg, and my eyes fill with tears. "Please don't kill me. This isn't you—this is the dragon's treasure!"

He smirks and raises his weapon again, and as he plunges

it downward, I roll to the side and shield my face with my arms. The sword slices through the back of my vest, shatters the ice where I had been lying, and sinks deep into the ground. Scrambling to my feet, I turn to run, but he dives for me, gripping the hair at the nape of my neck. I tip forward and he slams my face into the frozen ground. I feel a crack in my forehead and the world seems to tilt. Numbness seeps into my body, and I feel nothing as a hazy fog spreads from my head, into the rest of my body. I am rolled onto my back, a boot is pressed firmly to my chest, and I watch Golmarr raise his sword with both his hands cinched around the hilt, his knuckles white. As I stare up at him through my tears I can't help but wonder—when he kills me, will he feel any type of remorse?

The sword starts to drive toward my heart just as the twang of a bowstring reverberates through the air. Golmarr's body lurches to the side, and his sword plunges into the ground beside my arm. Not five steps away stands Evay, her bow still aimed at Golmarr, the string still quivering. Her dark eyes are round with horror, yet she pulls another arrow from her quiver and takes aim at Golmarr, waiting.

He presses on his chest, in the space where his shoulder meets his body, the space where his armor has a hair-thin gap. His fingers come away red, and I can see the black fletching sticking out of the back of his shoulder. Golmarr squeezes his eyes shut and shakes his head. When he opens them again, he looks down at me lying beside his sword, and his face drains of color.

"No!" He shakes his head and slowly draws his sword out of the ground. He stares at the weapon like he has never seen it before. Thrusting it into its sheath, he backs away from me.

I can feel his pain and it is tearing my heart in two, stripping me of everything I am made of but despair. "No!" He turns his face to the sky and shrieks. Looking at me, he presses a hand to his heart, then crosses his fingers. Without a backward glance, he runs.

I close my eyes as the pain from all of my wounds slowly starts to grow, merging with the horror of Golmarr trying to kill me. Tears trickle over my temples and into my hair as the thump of galloping hooves echoes against the ground. Without looking, I know that Golmarr is gone. And now, despite the people milling around me, I am alone.

I lie on the ice with my eyes closed until Enzio comes and carefully lifts me into his arms. He carries me to the wagon of dead and injured soldiers and presses a piece of cloth to my wounded shoulder to slow the bleeding. "I'm sorry," he whispers. "I should never have left you. I thought, since you were with Golmarr . . ." I curl on my side and put my head in his lap. As the tears start pouring from my eyes, he puts his hand on my head. "I'm so sorry."

Chapter 31

When we arrive at King Marrkul's house, Yerengul and Enzio help me out of the wagon. Without a word, Yerengul lifts me into his arms and carries me to the kitchen. He lays me on the long, rectangular wooden table and cuts the blood-soaked clothing away from my left shoulder.

"What are you doing?" I ask.

"I have been trained as a healer. I am tending to your wounds." For the first time since I met him, there is no mischief in his eyes. I stare silently up at the ceiling as he pokes and prods my wound. While he examines me, Enzio wads up a blanket and puts it beneath my head.

"There's water heating on the fire," Yerengul says to Enzio. "Can you add a few more logs?" Without a word, Enzio goes to the hearth.

King Marrkul strides into the kitchen and studies me with worried eyes. "How bad is it?" he asks Yerengul.

His son looks up. "Bad. He would have hit her heart if she hadn't blocked his attack."

Marrkul presses his hands over his eyes and slowly slides them down his battle-weary face. "Do you know why he tried to . . ." He grunts, and I realize he cannot say the words *kill her.*

Yerengul shakes his head and his eyes meet mine. "Do you know why he tried to kill you?"

I nod and close my eyes. "It's not what you think," I whisper, and fresh tears spill over my temples. "The glass dragon . . . Her treasure was hatred. Especially hatred for me."

King Marrkul runs his hand through his tangled black hair. "I'm sorry, lass."

"Do you know where he went?" Yerengul asks. I shake my head the tiniest bit.

When the water is hot, Yerengul washes my face and frowns. "Her forehead is split, too," he says. "Enzio, will you hold her down while I mend her shoulder?"

Enzio nods and his warm hands press on my arms. Hot water is poured over my wound. I gasp and whimper at the pain and try not to writhe. A minute later, I moan as a needle is stuck through my skin and pulled beneath the cut and out the other side. Every time the needle stabs, I moan, and Enzio flinches and pushes me down a little harder, holding me immobile.

"I'm sorry I wasn't there for you, Princess," Enzio whispers.

Through a fog of pain, I hear Marrkul ask, "What think you of the fire, son?"

For a moment Yerengul stops stitching my shoulder. "You mean the one that didn't burn her, or the one that consumed the dragon?"

"I mean the one the she used to save Golmarr from the dragon. The one that burned her without burning her. Every-one saw it! It is all our soldiers whispered of on the ride home."

"I will tell you what I think," someone calls as booted feet thud on the wooden floor. Seven dark and strapping horse lords stride into the kitchen. They gather around the table and stare down at me—some with pale hazel eyes, some with dark. They are still dirty from battle and dressed in bloodstained armor. Silently, they study me, laid out on the table, and my heart starts to pound—a weak, tired flutter befitting my ravaged body.

After a drawn-out moment, Ingvar breaks the silence. "She is a witch. That is what I think," he states, eyeing me.

"And as such, she will be sought after by every king and queen in the world," Jessen says, folding his arms over his broad chest.

"Wars will be waged over her," another brother says, narrowing his deep brown eyes and studying me further.

"Men will die to own her," Yerengul adds.

"Or they will try to buy her," Olenn says.

"Or steal her," King Marrkul muses.

"And dragons will seek to destroy her," Nayadi's aged, grating voice rings out. Two brothers step aside, letting the hunched, withered hag join the circle. She stands beside my wounded shoulder. Reaching out a bent, gnarled finger, she touches the half-stitched gash. Before I can open my mouth to protest her closeness, all the pain is whisked away from the wound, and muscles I didn't realize I was clenching relax as I sigh and sink against the hard table. "Stitch the rest quickly," Nayadi instructs Yerengul. "I, unlike some, do not have the power to bring one back from the brink of death, let alone heal a small wound. The pain will be back before long." Her unseeing eyes meet mine, and she licks her pink gums.

Yerengul bites the side of his cheek and leans over my shoulder, deep in concentration as he finishes stitching. I feel nothing but a light tugging on my skin.

"So, what shall we do with this Faodarian princess, who is pledged to your youngest brother?" King Marrkul asks. His troubled eyes meet mine.

Yerengul, still intent on my shoulder, says, "We fight for her." When no one answers, he looks up at his brothers' solemn faces.

Ingvar draws his sword and holds it forward, blade centered above my heart and pointed toward the ceiling. "Agreed," he says. Yerengul firms his shoulders and stands. With a hand stained red by my blood, he draws his sword and holds it beside his brother's. Steel hisses all around me as every man, even Enzio, draws his sword and holds it above my prostrate body. Last of all, King Marrkul adds his well-worn sword to the others and smiles a grim smile.

"It is agreed upon, then," King Marrkul says. "Princess Sorrowlynn of Faodara, we pledge to thee our lives, our protection, and our kinship. We will fight for you. We will keep you safe until Golmarr finds his way back to you."

Despite the horrors of the day, a tiny smile tugs at my mouth, and my throat constricts with the desire to cry.

All of the men gathered around me repeat the words three times: "We pledge to thee our lives, our protection, and our kinship." As the room grows silent, I can feel their pledges bind to me, and my eyes fill with tears yet again. King Marrkul leans forward and presses his lips to my forehead. Ingvar does the same. And then Jessen and Olenn. One by one, all of Golmarr's brothers kiss my forehead before leaving the kitchen. When they have gone and only the king, Yerengul, and Enzio remain, I peer at my stitched, swollen shoulder and cringe.

"You know, Princess, in Anthar, scars are a badge of honor," Yerengul says as he wraps my shoulder with clean, dry rags. He sounds just like Golmarr. "They are proof that you've experienced pain and overcome it." His words, so like his brother's, hurt so much that I start to sob. He puts his hand on my hair. "You'll overcome this, too."

I press my hands to my eyes as I gasp giant breaths of air and shake with the power of emotions wracking my body. Warm, gentle hands lift me off the table and I am cradled against a massive chest.

"There now, child," King Marrkul whispers as he carries me up a flight of stairs. "Things will turn out all right. They always do. Have faith. Have hope. One day you will look back at this moment and see that you have grown far more than you did when things were easy. And then, when you get so many of these hard and trying days, these days that test you to your core, they will refine you, beat out your weaknesses, and turn you into the best version of yourself that there is." He lowers me onto Golmarr's bed and pulls the blanket up to my chin. "Sleep now, and when you wake, things will be easier to face."

He walks out of the room and shuts the door, so I am alone in the dark, and all I can hear are the sound of his receding steps and the sound of my breathing. After a moment, the darkness recedes as my door is opened again. Enzio, carrying a candle, steps inside and shuts the door. He reaches under his leather vest and pulls out a folded piece of paper. "This is from Golmarr," he says. "He told me to give it to you if things turned out this way. I will be sleeping in the hall outside your door, so if you need anything, just call." He places the candle and the paper on the bedside table.

"Thank you," I whisper as he leaves the room. Taking the paper, I open it and stare at Golmarr's handwriting. It is polished and precise, just like everything else about him. By the light of the flickering candle, I read his words and fresh tears fill my eyes.

Dear Sorrowlynn,

If Enzio gave you this letter, it means I have killed the glass dragon and we both survived. It means that our plan didn't work and I was unable to simply wound the beast. Thus, I made the choice to save your life in spite of the consequences that have obviously followed. Please believe me, if I could have defeated the dragon without killing it, I would have. Now my only consolation is that you are alive, and I am alive. That is the least I could hope for.

You need to know that I have been thinking about this day since the time we were sitting in Edemond's wagon eating porridge, and you told me what the dragon's treasure was. Every single time I looked at you from that moment on, I drank in the sight of you. Every time I touched you, I savored it like it might be the last. Every word you spoke, I memorized for when we would be apart.

I chose hating you over watching you die. That was the less painful of the two outcomes. If you'd died, it would have been the end of us. At least now there is hope that one day I will learn how to overcome the dragon's treasure and we will be together again. There are myths about an Infinite Vessel that holds all the history of the dragons. As surely as you are reading these words, know that I am, at this very moment, on a quest to discover the Infinite Vessel. I will find out how to beat this. Until that day, know that I will always love you. Even while I hate you, I will still love you.

Golmarr

Epilogue

I have the grain of the lacquered wood ceiling memorized by the fifth day. It is the only thing I see from Golmarr's bed, lying on my back, trying to deal with the pain, hardly eating. Some of the pain is from my stitched and healing shoulder, but most of it comes from missing Golmarr and not being able to do anything about it.

I hate it. The ceiling, not the pain.

So, on the sixth day, I decide to stop wasting my life studying the cursed wooden ceiling and do something about missing him. I roll out of bed before the sun rises and walk barefoot, hair a mass of tangles, cradling my left arm, through King Marrkul's giant wooden house and out back to the stables. All I need is a horse, and then I will find Golmarr.

I open the stall housing Dewdrop and walk up to the magnificent animal. A brand-new saddle is hanging by a hook on the wall. I grip the edges of the saddle in my hands and lift. My arms tremble, and then sharp agony steals all the strength from my left shoulder. I groan and hug my left arm to my chest. Fresh blood seeps through my nightgown a hand span above my heart, and tears form in my eyes.

Slowly, I lift my hands before my face and turn them back and forth, palms, backs, palms. They look like the hands of a princess who never dresses herself, never brushes her own hair, never cooks her own food or even pulls her bedding back at night before she slips under her covers. They look like hands that never hold anything but the sides of a fancy skirt for a curtsy.

They are my hands. And I do not like them. They are my hands, and I need to make them into something formidable. I spin around and stomp out of the stable.

A light glows in the kitchen window of King Marrkul's house, so I hurry across the yard to it. I crash into the house like a wave of fury, slamming the door open so hard it bangs against the wall. King Marrkul, Yerengul, and Enzio are sitting at the massive table, bowls of food in front of them. They all three stop chewing their breakfast and stare at me.

Marrkul wipes his mouth with a napkin and stands. "Princess Sorrowlynn. You've finally decided to get out of bed." Walking over to me, he gently moves me farther inside the house and shuts the door. His gaze lowers to the blood on my nightgown, and worry tightens his eyes. "Yerengul." He nods toward my injury.

Yerengul and Enzio get to their feet and stop in front of me. Yerengul gently loosens the laces that hold the neck of my nightgown closed. He slides the fabric aside so my wound is exposed and wipes away the blood with his napkin. "She tore one of the stitches, that's all," he tells his father. "How did you do that?" he asks me suspiciously. When I stay silent, he looks at my feet, covered with straw from the stable and wet with dew, and understanding lightens his eyes. "You were going to run, weren't you? Take one of the horses? Ride off with nothing but your nightgown? You were going to find my brother."

I close my eyes and nod. "But I'm not strong enough to lift a measly *saddle*." I open my eyes and look between Enzio and Yerengul. "I want to be strong. Make me strong." It is not a request.

A slow smile spreads across Enzio's face, and Yerengul laughs.

"I will make you strong, but only if . . ." Yerengul trails off and leaves the end of his sentence hanging like a piece of bait. I grab it.

"If what? I will do anything."

"You have been in bed for five days. That is not okay. You have to get out of bed every day, when I say. No more lying around feeling sorry for yourself. And you can't go chasing after my brother in nothing but a nightgown. You wait to leave until you're strong enough to defend yourself, and then you leave with money, food, shoes, and weapons."

Strong enough to defend myself. How long will that take? I wonder. The thought of staying here when all I want to do is find Golmarr makes me feel like I am locked in my skin and cannot move. But I nod. Yerengul is right. I need to be strong enough to survive.

"I will do it," I say.

"I have a request," Enzio adds.

"Yes?"

"You do not leave without me. I have yet to repay my mother's debt to you, and my own debt now." He glances at the blood on my shoulder. "I should not have left your side, even when you were fighting the dragon." He pulls a black stone blade from each of his sleeves and presses the flat of one blade to his forehead, and then holds it out to me. "Take it," he urges.

I take the blade and look at him askance.

"That is yours until I have repaid my debts to you. Twin blades, yours and mine, to bind us until we have both achieved our goals."

I press the flat of the blade to my forehead. "Thank you, Enzio."

"All right," Yerengul says. A wicked grin lights up his face, and he leads me to the table and pulls out a chair. "Just so you know, Sorrowlynn, you will be training with the fiercest, toughest, most disciplined people known in the history of the world. It isn't going to be easy. It isn't going to be fun. But I promise you, if you do everything I say, you and Enzio will be off looking for my brother before the first snow starts to fall."

King Marrkul puts a bowl of steaming porridge in front of me. "Eat up," he says with a grin, clapping me on the back. "First rule of being a warrior is you have to feed your weapon. Your body is your weapon. Everything else—sword, bow and arrows, staff, knife—is just an extension of your weapon. To be the strongest you can be, you have to eat."

I dip the spoon into the porridge. When the bowl is empty, I say, "I am ready. Let's get started."

Acknowledgments

First and foremost, I have to thank *you*. Yes, I am writing this to you—the person who is at this very moment absorbing these words into his/her brain. Thank you. You read my book. You are the reason I write. You are the reason I didn't give up after a rocky start as a writer, when nearly three hundred people told me I wasn't good enough to succeed. But you are proof that I have succeeded. I love you, dear reader, even though the only way we know each other is through the bond of my words between our minds.

And then there is my family. Thank you, Jaime, my husband, for working all these years so I could stay home with the kids and write in my spare time. (Is there such a thing as spare time if you have five kids? I will let you know if I ever have time to find out.) Speaking of those five kids, thanks for listening to this story and loving Sorrowlynn and Golmarr.

Bonny Anderson, thanks for being my critiquing go-to girl, and thanks for loving this story. Speaking of go-to girls, Kristin Wester, I wish you were still here. I finally switched back to fantasy. This book would have been your favorite of all of my books—I miss you!

I must mention my literary agent, the incredibly smart, professional, stalwart, knowledgeable Marlene Stringer. Remember those nearly three hundred rejections mentioned earlier? She was the yes that changed everything. I am here because of that one simple, yet not-so-simple yes. Thank you, Marlene, for giving me that tiny three-letter word that changed my life.

Emily Easton, it is a pleasure and an honor to be working with you again. I write the best story I can, and you open it up and show me how much better it can be. I wish I could reach across the United States and throw my arms around you and give you a great big hug.

That goes for everyone at Crown who has put thought and energy and creativity and time into this book: Samantha Gentry, Phoebe Yeh, and the entire team at Random House Children's Books. Thank you!

Last of all, with deepest humility, I thank God, my Heavenly Father. Everything I have, he has given to me.

About the Author

BETHANY WIGGINS is the author of *Stung, Cured,* and *Shifting. The Dragon's Price* came to life one night at dinner, while the Wiggins family was having their customary mythical beast conversation and Bethany's son asked about the worth of a dragon's scale. Bethany lives in the desert with her husband, five quirky kids, and four black cats. You can follow her on Instagram, and on Twitter at @wiggb, and visit her at bethanywiggins.com.